Right-wing Women

Also by Andrea Dworkin

Woman Hating
Our Blood: Prophecies and Discourses on Sexual Politics
The New Womans Broken Heart
Pornography: Men Possessing Women

Right-wing Women

ANDREA DWORKIN

A Perigee Book

Perigee Books
are published by
G. P. Putnam's Sons
200 Madison Avenue
New York, New York 10016

The author gratefully acknowledges permission from the following sources to reprint material in this book:

The University of California Press for the excerpt from "The Coming Gynocide," in *Sappho: A New Translation*, Mary Barnard, translator (1973), © copyright 1957 by The Regents of the University of California.

New Directions Publishing Corporation for six lines from "Canto 91" from *The Cantos of Ezra Pound* by Ezra Pound. Copyright © 1956 by Ezra Pound.

Portions of this book have been published in slightly different form in *Ms.* and *Maenad.*

Library of Congress Cataloging in Publication Data

Dworkin, Andrea.
Right-wing women.

Includes index.
1. Women's rights—United States. 2. Conservatism—United States. 3. Right and left (Political science). I. Title.
[HQ1426.D898 1982b] 305.4′2′0973 82-9784
ISBN 0-399-50671-3 AACR2

First Perigee printing, 1983
Printed in the United States of America

Acknowledgments

Many people went out of their way to help me in different ways in the course of my writing this book. I owe sincere thanks to Geri Thoma, Anne Simon, Robin Morgan, Catharine A. MacKinnon, Karen Hornick, Emily Jane Goodman, Rachel Gold, Sandra Elkin, Laura Cottingham, Gena Corea, and Raymond Bongiovanni.

I am very grateful to Sam Mitnick for supporting this project and to all the people at Perigee involved in publishing it.

This book owes its existence to Gloria Steinem, whose idea it was that I expand an earlier essay, "Safety, Shelter, Rules, Form, Love: The Promise of the Ultra-Right" *(Ms.*, June 1979), into a book. I thank Gloria not only for the idea but also for her insistence on its importance.

And I thank, once again, both John Stoltenberg and Elaine Markson, who sustain me.

Andrea Dworkin
New York City
March 1982

For Gloria Steinem

In Memory of Muriel Rukeyser

Contents

Nothing strengthens the judgment and quickens the conscience like individual responsibility. Nothing adds such dignity to character as the recognition of one's self-sovereignty; the right to an equal place, everywhere conceded—a place earned by personal merit, not an artificial attainment by inheritance, wealth, family and position. Conceding, then, that the responsibilities of life rest equally on man and woman, that their destiny is the same, they need the same preparation for time and eternity. The talk of sheltering woman from the fierce storms of life is the sheerest mockery, for they beat on her from every point of the compass, just as they do on man, and with more fatal results, for he has been trained to protect himself, to resist, and to conquer. Such are the facts in human experience, the responsibilities of individual sovereignty.

Elizabeth Cady Stanton, 1892

1

The Promise of the Ultra-Right

There is a rumor, circulated for centuries by scientists, artists, and philosophers both secular and religious, a piece of gossip as it were, to the effect that women are "biologically conservative." While gossip among women is universally ridiculed as low and trivial, gossip among men, especially if it is about women, is called theory, or idea, or fact. This particular rumor became dignified as high thought because it was Whispered-Down-The-Lane in formidable academies, libraries, and meeting halls from which women, until very recently, have been formally and forcibly excluded.

The whispers, however multisyllabic and footnoted they sometimes are, reduced to a simple enough set of assertions. Women have children because women by definition have children. This "fact of life," which is not subject to qualification, carries with it the instinctual obligation to nurture and protect those children. Therefore, women can be expected to be socially, politically, economically, and sexually conservative because the status quo, whatever it is, is safer than change, whatever the change. Noxious male philosophers from all disciplines have, for centuries, maintained that women follow a biological imperative derived directly from their reproductive capacities that translates necessarily into narrow lives, small minds, and a rather meanspirited puritanism.

This theory, or slander, is both specious and cruel in that, in fact, women are forced to bear children and have been throughout history in all economic systems, with but teeny-weeny time-outs while the men were momentarily disoriented, as, for instance, in the immediate postcoital aftermath of certain revolutions. It is entirely irrational in that, in fact, women of all ideological persuasions, with the single exception of absolute pacifists, of whom there have not been very many, have throughout history supported wars in which the very children they are biologically ordained to protect are maimed, raped, tortured, and killed. Clearly, the biological explanation of the so-called conservative nature of women obscures the realities of women's lives, buries them in dark shadows of distortion and dismissal.

The disinterested or hostile male observer can categorize women as "conservative" in some metaphysical sense because it is true that women as a class adhere rather strictly to the traditions and values of their social context, whatever the character of that context. In societies of whatever description, however narrowly or broadly defined, women as a class are the dulled conformists, the orthodox believers, the obedient followers, the disciples of unwavering faith. To waver, whatever the creed of the men around them, is tantamount to rebellion; it is dangerous. Most women, holding on for dear life, do not dare abandon blind faith. From father's house to husband's house to a grave that still might not be her own, a woman acquiesces to male authority in order to gain some protection from male violence. She conforms, in order to be as safe as she can be. Sometimes it is a lethargic conformity, in which case male demands slowly close in on her, as if she were a character buried alive in an Edgar Allan Poe story. Sometimes it is a militant conformity. She will save herself by proving that she is loyal, obedient, useful, even fanatic in the service of the men around her. She is the happy hooker, the happy homemaker, the exemplary Christian, the pure academic, the perfect comrade, the terrorist par excellence. Whatever the values, she will embody them with a perfect fidelity. The males rarely keep their part of the bargain as she understands it: protection from male violence against her person. But the militant conformist has given so much of herself—her labor, heart, soul, often her body, often children—that this betrayal is akin to nailing the coffin shut; the corpse is beyond caring.

Women know, but must not acknowledge, that resisting male control or confronting male betrayal will lead to rape, battery, destitution, ostracization or exile, confinement in a mental institution or jail, or death. As Phyllis Chesler and Emily Jane Goodman make clear in *Women, Money, and Power*, women struggle, in the manner of Sisyphus, to avoid the "something worse" that can and will always happen to them if they transgress the rigid boundaries of appropriate female behavior. Most women cannot afford, either materially or psychologically, to recognize that whatever burnt offerings of obedience they bring to beg protection will not appease the angry little gods around them.

It is not surprising, then, that most girls do not want to become like their mothers, those tired, preoccupied domestic sergeants beset by incomprehensible troubles. Mothers raise daughters to conform to the strictures of the conventional female life as defined by men, whatever the ideological values of the men. Mothers are the immediate enforcers of male will, the guards at the cell door, the flunkies who administer the electric shocks to punish rebellion.

Most girls, however much they resent their mothers, do become very much like them. Rebellion can rarely survive the aversion therapy that passes for being brought up female. Male violence acts directly on the girl through her father or brother or uncle or any number of male professionals or strangers, as it did and does on her mother, and she too is forced to learn to conform in order to survive. A girl may, as she enters adulthood, repudiate the particular set of males with whom her mother is allied, run with a different pack as it were, but she will replicate her mother's patterns in acquiescing to male authority within her own chosen set. Using both force and threat, men in all camps demand that women accept abuse in silence and shame, tie themselves to hearth and home with rope made of self-blame, unspoken rage, grief, and resentment.

It is the fashion among men to despise the smallness of women's lives. The so-called bourgeois woman with her shallow vanity, for instance, is a joke to the brave intellectuals, truck drivers, and revolutionaries who have wider horizons on which to project and indulge deeper vanities that women dare not mock and to which women dare not aspire. The fishwife is a vicious caricature of the small-mindedness and material greed of the working-class wife who harasses her humble, hardworking, ever patient husband with petty tirades of insult that no gentle rebuke can mellow. The Lady, the Aristocrat, is a polished, empty shell, good only for spitting at, because spit shows up on her clean exterior, which gives immediate gratification to the spitter, whatever his technique. The Jewish mother is a monster who wants to cut the phallus of her precious son into a million pieces and put it in the chicken soup. The black woman, also a castrator, is a grotesque matriarch whose sheer endurance desolates men. The lesbian is half monster, half moron: having no man to nag, she imagines herself Napoleon.

And the derision of female lives does not stop with these toxic, ugly, insidious slanders because there is always, in every circumstance, the derision in its skeletal form, all bone, the meat stripped clean: she is pussy, cunt. Every other part of the body is cut away, severed, and there is left a thing, not human, an it, which is the funniest joke of all, an unending source of raucous humor to those who have done the cutting. The very butchers who cut up the meat and throw away the useless parts are the comedians. The paring down of a whole person to vagina and womb and then to a dismembered obscenity is their best and favorite joke.

Every woman, no matter what her social, economic, or sexual situation, fights this paring down with every resource at her command. Because her resources are so astonishingly meager and because she has been deprived of the means to organize and expand them, these attempts are simultaneously heroic and pathetic. The whore, in defending the pimp, finds her own worth in the light reflected from his gaudy baubles. The wife, in defending the husband, screams or stammers that her life is not a wasteland of murdered possibilities. The woman, in defending the ideologies of men who rise by climbing over her prone body in military formation, will not publicly mourn the loss of what those men have taken from her: she will not scream out as their heels dig into her flesh because to do so would mean the end of meaning itself; all the ideals that motivated her to deny herself would be indelibly stained with blood that she would have to acknowledge, at last, as her own.

So the woman hangs on, not with the delicacy of a clinging vine, but with a tenacity incredible in its intensity, to the very persons, institutions, and values that demean her, degrade her, glorify her powerlessness, insist upon constraining and paralyzing the most honest expressions of her will and being. She becomes a lackey, serving those who ruthlessly and effectively aggress against her and her kind. This singularly self-hating loyalty to those committed to her own destruction is the very essence of womanhood as men of all ideological persuasions define it.

Marilyn Monroe, shortly before she died, wrote in her notebook on the set of *Let's Make Love:* "What am I afraid of? Why am I so afraid? Do I think I can't act? I know I can act but I am afraid. I am afraid and I should not be and I must not be."[1]

The actress is the only female culturally empowered to act. When she acts well, that is, when she convinces the male controllers of images and wealth that she is reducible to current sexual fashion, available to the male on his own terms, she is paid and honored. Her acting must be imitative, not creative; rigidly conforming, not self-generated and self-renewing. The actress is the puppet of flesh, blood, and paint who acts as if she is the female acting. Monroe, the consummate sexual doll, is empowered to act but afraid to act, perhaps because no amount of acting, however inspired, can convince the actor herself that her ideal female life is not a dreadful form of dying. She grinned, she posed, she pretended, she had affairs with famous and powerful men. A friend of hers claimed that she had so many illegal abortions wrongly performed that her reproductive organs were severely injured. She died alone, possibly acting on her own behalf for the first time. Death, one imagines, numbs pain that barbiturates and alcohol cannot touch.

Monroe's premature death raised one haunting question for the men who were, in their own fantasy, her lovers, for the men who had masturbated over those pictures of exquisite female compliance: was it possible, could it be, that she hadn't liked It all along—It—the It they had been doing to her, how many millions of times? Had those smiles been masks covering despair or rage? If so, how endangered they had been to be deceived, so fragile and exposed in their masturbatory delight, as if she could leap out from those photos of what was now a corpse and take the revenge they knew she deserved. There arose the male imperative that Monroe must not be a suicide. Norman Mailer, savior of masculine privilege and pride on many fronts, took up the challenge by theorizing that Monroe may have been killed by the FBI, or CIA, or whoever killed the Kennedys, because she had been mistress to one or both. Conspiracy was a cheerful and comforting thought to those who had wanted to slam into her until she expired, female death and female ecstasy being synonymous in the world of male metaphor. But they did not want her dead yet, not really dead, not while the illusion of her open invitation was so absolutely compelling. In fact, her lovers in both flesh and fantasy had fucked her to death, and her apparent suicide stood at once as accusation and answer: no, Marilyn Monroe, the ideal sexual female, had not liked it.

People—as we are always reminded by counterfeit egalitarians—have always died too young, too soon, too isolated, too full of insupportable anguish. But only women die one by one, whether famous or obscure, rich or poor, isolated, choked to death by the lies tangled in their throats. Only women die one by one, attempting until the last minute to embody an ideal imposed upon them by men who want to use them up. Only women die one by one, smiling up to the last minute, smile of the siren, smile of the coy girl, smile of the madwoman. Only women die one by one, polished to perfection or unkempt behind locked doors too desperately ashamed to cry out. Only women die one by one, still believing that if only they had been perfect—perfect wife, mother, or whore—they would not have come to hate life so much, to find it so strangely difficult and empty, themselves so hopelessly confused and despairing. Women die, mourning not the loss of their own lives, but their own inexcusable inability to achieve perfection as men define it for them. Women desperately try to embody a male-defined feminine ideal because survival depends on it. The ideal, by definition, turns a woman into a function, deprives her of any individuality that is self-serving or self-created, not useful to the male in his scheme of things. This monstrous female quest for male-defined perfection, so intrinsically hostile to freedom and integrity, leads inevitably to bitterness, paralysis, or death, but like the mirage in the desert, the life-giving oasis that is not there, survival is promised in this conformity and nowhere else.

Like the chameleon, the woman must blend into her environment, never calling attention to the qualities that distinguish her, because to do so would be to attract the predator's deadly attention. She is, in fact, hunted meat—all the male *auteurs*, scientists, and homespun philosophers on street corners will say so proudly. Attempting to strike a bargain, the woman says: I come to you on your own terms. Her hope is that his murderous attention will focus on a female who conforms less artfully, less willingly. In effect, she ransoms the remains of a life—what is left over after she has renounced willful individuality—by promising indifference to the fate of other women. This sexual, sociological, and spiritual adaptation, which is, in fact, the maiming of all moral capacity, is the primary imperative of survival for women who live under male-supremacist rule.

*

> . . . I gradually came to see that I would have to stay within the survivor's own perspective. This will perhaps bother the historian, with his distrust of personal evidence; but radical suffering transcends relativity, and when one survivor's account of an event or circumstance is repeated in exactly the same way by dozens of other survivors, men and women in different camps, from different nations and cultures, then one comes to trust the validity of such reports and even to question rare departures from the general view.[2]
>
> Terrence Des Pres, *The Survivor: An Anatomy of Life in the Death Camps*

The accounts of rape, wife beating, forced childbearing, medical butchering, sex-motivated murder, forced prostitution, physical mutilation, sadistic psychological abuse, and the other commonplaces of female experience that are excavated from the past or given by contemporary survivors should leave the heart seared, the mind in anguish, the conscience in upheaval. But they do not. No matter how often these stories are told, with whatever clarity or eloquence, bitterness or sorrow, they might as well have been whispered in wind or written in sand: they disappear, as if they were nothing. The tellers and the stories are ignored or ridiculed, threatened back into silence or destroyed, and the experience of female suffering is buried in cultural invisibility and contempt. Because women's testimony is not and cannot be validated by the witness of men who have experienced the same events and given them the same value, the very reality of abuse sustained by women, despite its overwhelming pervasiveness and constancy, is negated. It is negated in the transactions of everyday life, and it is negated in the history books, left out, and it is negated by those who claim to care about suffering but are blind to this suffering.

The problem, simply stated, is that one must believe in the existence of the person in order to recognize the authenticity of her suffering. Neither men nor women believe in the existence of women as significant beings. It is impossible to remember as real the suffering of someone who by definition has no legitimate claim to dignity or freedom, someone who is in fact viewed as some thing, an object or an absence. And if a woman, an individual woman multiplied by billions, does not believe in her own discrete existence and therefore cannot credit the authenticity of her own suffering, she is erased, canceled out, and the meaning of her life, whatever it is, whatever it might have been, is lost. This loss cannot be calculated or comprehended. It is vast and awful, and nothing will ever make up for it.

No one can bear to live a meaningless life. Women fight for meaning just as women fight for survival: by attaching themselves to men and the values honored by men. By committing themselves to male values, women seek to acquire value. By advocating male meaning, women seek to acquire meaning. Subservient to male will, women believe that subservience itself is the meaning of a female life. In this way, women, whatever they suffer, do not suffer the anguish of a conscious recognition that, because they are women, they have been robbed of volition and choice, without which no life can have meaning.

The political Right in the United States today makes certain metaphysical and material promises to women that both exploit and quiet some of women's deepest fears. These fears originate in the perception that male violence against women is uncontrollable and unpredictable. Dependent on and subservient to men, women are always subject to this violence. The Right promises to put enforceable restraints on male aggression, thus simplifying survival for women—to make the world slightly more habitable, in other words—by offering the following:

Form. Women experience the world as mystery. Kept ignorant of technology, economics, most of the practical skills required to function autonomously, kept ignorant of the real social and sexual demands made on women, deprived of physical strength, excluded from forums for the development of intellectual acuity and public self-confidence, women are lost and mystified by the savage momentum of an ordinary life. Sounds, signs, promises, threats, wildly crisscross, but what do they mean? The Right offers women a simple, fixed, predetermined social, biological, and sexual order. Form conquers chaos. Form banishes confusion. Form gives ignorance a shape, makes it look like something instead of nothing.

Shelter. Women are brought up to maintain a husband's home and to believe that women without men are homeless. Women have a deep fear of being homeless—at the mercy of the elements and of strange men. The Right claims to protect the home and the woman's place in it.

Safety. For women, the world is a very dangerous place. One wrong move, even an unintentional smile, can bring disaster—assault, shame, disgrace. The Right acknowledges the reality of danger, the validity of fear. The Right then manipulates the fear. The promise is that if a woman is obedient, harm will not befall her.

Rules. Living in a world she has not made and does not understand, a woman needs rules to know what to do next. If she knows what she is supposed to do, she can find a way to do it. If she learns the rules by rote, she can perform with apparent effortlessness, which will considerably enhance her chances for survival. The Right, very considerately, tells women the rules of the game on which their lives depend. The Right also promises that, despite their absolute sovereignty, men too will follow specified rules.

Love. Love is always crucial in effecting the allegiance of women. The Right offers women a concept of love based on order and stability, with formal areas of mutual accountability. A woman is loved for fulfilling her female functions: obedience is an expression of love and so are sexual submission and childbearing. In return, the man is supposed to be responsible for the material and emotional well-being of the woman. And, increasingly, to redeem the cruel inadequacies of mortal men, the Right offers women the love of Jesus, beautiful brother, tender lover, compassionate friend, perfect healer of sorrow and resentment, the one male to whom one can submit absolutely—be Woman as it were—without being sexually violated or psychologically abused.

It is important and fascinating, of course, to note that women never, no matter how deluded or needy or desperate, worship Jesus as the perfect son. No faith is that blind. There is no religious or cultural palliative to deaden the raw pain of the son's betrayal of the mother: only her own obedience to the same father, the sacrifice of her own life on the same cross, her own body nailed and bleeding, can enable her to accept that her son, like Jesus, has come to do his Father's work. Feminist Leah Fritz, in *Thinking Like a Woman*, described the excruciating predicament of women who try to find worth in Christian submission: "Unloved, unrespected, unnoticed by the Heavenly Father, condescended to by the Son, and fucked by the Holy Ghost, western woman spends her entire life trying to please."[3]

But no matter how hard she tries to please, it is harder still for her to be pleased. In *Bless This House*, Anita Bryant describes how each day she must ask Jesus to "help me love my husband and children."[4] In *The Total Woman*, Marabel Morgan explains that it is only through God's power that "we can love and accept others, including our husbands."[5] In *The Gift of Inner Healing*, Ruth Carter Stapleton counsels a young woman who is in a desperately unhappy marriage: "Try to spend a little time each day visualizing Jesus coming in the door from work. Then see yourself walking up to him, embracing him. Say to Jesus, 'It's good to have you home Nick.'"[6]

Ruth Carter Stapleton married at nineteen. Describing the early years of her marriage, she wrote:

> After moving four hundred fifty miles from my first family in order to save my marriage, I found myself in a cold, threatening, unprotected world, or so it seemed to my confused heart. In an effort to avoid total destruction, I indulged in escapes of every kind . . .
>
> A major crisis arose when I discovered I was pregnant with my first child. I knew that this was supposed to be one of the crowning moments of womanhood, but not for me. . . . When my baby was born, I wanted to be a good mother, but I felt even more trapped. . . . Then three more babies were born in rapid succession, and each one, so beautiful, terrified me. I did love them, but by the fourth child I was at the point of total desperation.[7]

Apparently the birth of her fourth child occasioned her surrender to Jesus. For a time, life seemed worthwhile. Then, a rupture in a cherished friendship plummeted her into an intolerable depression. During this period, she jumped out of a moving car in what she regards as a suicide attempt.

A male religious mentor picked up the pieces. Stapleton took her own experience of breakdown and recovery and from it shaped a kind of faith psychotherapy. Nick's transformation into Jesus has already been mentioned. A male homosexual, traumatized by an absent father who never played with him as a child, played baseball with Jesus under Stapleton's tutelage—a whole nine innings. In finding Jesus as father and chum, he was healed of the hurt of an absent father and "cured" of his homosexuality. A woman who was forcibly raped by her father as a child was encouraged to remember the event, only this time Jesus had his hand on the father's shoulder and was forgiving him. This enabled the woman to forgive her father too and to be reconciled with men. A woman who as a child was rejected by her father on the occasion of her first date—the father did not notice her pretty dress—was encouraged to imagine the presence of Jesus on that fateful night. Jesus loved her dress and found her very desirable. Stapleton claims that this devotional therapy, through the power of the Holy Spirit, enables Jesus to erase damaging memories.

A secular analysis of Stapleton's own newfound well-being seems, by contrast, pedestrian. A brilliant woman has found a socially acceptable way to use her intellect and compassion in the public domain—the dream of many women. Though fundamentalist male ministers have called her a witch, in typical female fashion Stapleton disclaims responsibility for her own inventiveness and credits the Holy Spirit, clearly male, thus soothing the savage misogyny of those who cannot bear for any woman to be both seen and heard. Also, having founded an evangelical ministry that demands constant travel, Stapleton is rarely at home. She has not given birth again.

Marabel Morgan's description of her own miserable marriage in the years preceding her discovery of God's will is best summarized in this one sentence: "I was helpless and unhappy."[8] She describes years of tension, conflict, boredom, and gloom. She took her fate into her own hands by asking the not-yet-classic question, What do men want? Her answer is stunningly accurate: "It is only when a woman surrenders her life to her husband, reveres and worships him, and is willing to serve him, that she becomes really beautiful to him."[9] Or, more aphoristically, "A Total Woman caters to her man's special quirks, whether it be in salads, sex, or sports."[10] Citing God as the authority and submission to Jesus as the model, Morgan defines love as "unconditional acceptance of [a man] and his feelings."[11]

Morgan's achievement in *The Total Woman* was to isolate the basic sexual scenarios of male dominance and female submission and to formulate a simple set of lessons, a pedagogy, that teaches women how to act out those scenarios within the context of a Christian value system: in other words, how to cater to male pornographic fantasies in the name of Jesus Christ. As Morgan explains in her own extraordinary prose style: "That great source book, the Bible, states, 'Marriage is honourable in all, and the bed undefiled . . .' In other words, sex is for the marriage relationship only, but within those bounds, anything goes. Sex is as clean and pure as eating cottage cheese."[12] Morgan's detailed instructions on how to eat cottage cheese, the most famous of which involves Saran Wrap, make clear that female submission is a delicately balanced commingling of resourcefulness and lack of self-respect. Too little resourcefulness or too much self-respect will doom a woman to failure as a Total Woman. A submissive nature is the miracle for which religious women pray.

No one has prayed harder, longer, and with less apparent success than Anita Bryant. She has spent a good part of her life on her knees begging Jesus to forgive her for the sin of existing. In *Mine Eyes Have Seen the Glory*, an autobiography first published in 1970, Bryant described herself as an aggressive, stubborn, bad-tempered child. Her early childhood was spent in brutal poverty. Through singing she began earning money when still a child. When she was very young, her parents divorced, then later remarried. When she was thirteen, her father abandoned her mother, younger sister, and herself, her parents were again divorced, and shortly thereafter her father remarried. At thirteen, "[w]hat stands out most of all in my memory are my feelings of intense ambition and a relentless drive to succeed at doing well the thing I loved [singing]."[13] She blamed herself, especially her driving ambition, for the loss of her father.

She did not want to marry. In particular, she did not want to marry Bob Green. He "won" her through a war of attrition. Every "No" on her part was taken as a "Yes" by him. When, on several occasions, she told him that she did not want to see him again, he simply ignored what she said. Once, when she was making a trip to see a close male friend whom she described to Green as her fiancé, he booked passage on the same plane and went along. He hounded her.

Having got his hooks into her, especially knowing how to hit on her rawest nerve—guilt over the abnormality of her ambition, by definition unwomanly and potentially satanic—Green manipulated Bryant with a cruelty nearly unmatched in modern love stories. From both of Bryant's early books, a picture emerges. One sees a woman hemmed in, desperately trying to please a husband who manipulates and harasses her and whose control of her life on every level is virtually absolute. Bryant described the degree of Green's control in *Mine Eyes:* "That's how good a manager my husband is. He willingly handles all the business in my life—even to including the Lord's business. Despite our sometimes violent scraps, I love him for it."[14] Bryant never specifies how violent the violent scraps were, though Green insists they were not violent. Green himself, in *Bless This House*, is very proud of spanking the children, especially the oldest son, who is adopted: "I'm a father to my children, not a pal. I assert my authority. I spank them at times, and they respect me for it. Sometimes I take Bobby into the music room, and it's not so I can play him a piece on the piano. We play a piece on the seat of his pants!"[15] Some degree of physical violence, then, was admittedly an accepted part of domestic life. Bryant's unselfconscious narrative makes clear that over a period of years, long before her antihomosexual crusade was a glint in Bob Green's eye, she was badgered into giving public religious testimonies that deeply distressed her:

> Bob has a way of getting my dander up and backing me up against a wall. He gets me so terrifically mad at him that I hate him for pushing me into a corner. He did that now.
>
> "You're a hypocrite," Bob said. "You profess to have Christ in your life, but you won't profess Him in public, which Christ tells you to do."
>
> Because I know he's right, and hate him for making me feel so bad about it, I end up doing what I'm so scared to do.[16]

Conforming to the will of her husband was clearly a difficult struggle for Bryant. She writes candidly of her near constant rebellion. Green's demands—from increasing her public presence as religious witness to doing all the child care for four children without help while pursuing the career she genuinely loves—were endurable only because Bryant, like Stapleton and Morgan, took Jesus as her real husband:

> Only as I practice yielding to Jesus can I learn to submit, as the Bible instructs me, to the loving leadership of my husband. Only the power of Christ can enable a woman like me to become submissive in the Lord.[17]

In Bryant's case, the "loving leadership" of her husband, this time in league with her pastor, enshrined her as the token spokeswoman of antihomosexual bigotry. Once again Bryant was reluctant to testify, this time before Dade County's Metropolitan Commission in hearings on a homosexual-rights ordinance. Bryant spent several nights in tears and prayer, presumably because, as she told *Newsweek*, "I was scared and I didn't want to do it."[18] Once again, a desire to do Christ's will brought her into conformity with the expressed will of her husband. One could speculate that some of the compensation in this conformity came from having the burdens of domestic work and child care lessened in the interest of serving the greater cause. Conformity to the will of Christ and Green, synonymous in this instance as so often before, also offered an answer to the haunting question of her life: how to be a public leader of significance—in her terminology, a "star"—and at the same time an obedient wife acting to protect her children. A singing career, especially a secular one, could never resolve this raging conflict.

Bryant, like all the rest of us, is trying to be a "good" woman. Bryant, like all the rest of us, is desperate and dangerous, to herself and to others, because "good" women live and die in silent selflessness and real women cannot. Bryant, like all the rest of us, is having one hell of a hard time.*

Phyllis Schlafly, the Right's not-born-again philosopher of the absurd, is apparently not having a hard time. She seems possessed by Machiavelli, not Jesus. It appears that she wants to be The Prince. She might be viewed as that rare woman of any ideological persuasion who really does see herself as one of the boys, even as she claims to be one of the girls. Unlike most other right-wing women, Schlafly, in her written and spoken work, does not acknowledge experiencing any of the difficulties that tear women apart. In the opinion of many, her ruthlessness as an organizer is best demonstrated by her demagogic propaganda against the Equal Rights Amendment, though she also waxes eloquent against reproductive freedom, the women's movement, big government, and

---

*This analysis of Bryant's situation was written in 1978 and published in *Ms.* in June 1979. In May 1980, Bryant filed for divorce. In a statement issued separately from the divorce petition, she contended that Green had "violated my most precious asset—my conscience" *(The New York Times,* May 24, 1980). Within three weeks after the divorce decree (August 1980), the state citrus agency of Florida, which Bryant had represented for eleven years, decided she was no longer a suitable representative because of her divorce: "The contract had to expire, because of the divorce and so forth," one agency executive said *(The New York Times,* September 2, 1980). Feminist lawyer and former National Organization for Women president Karen DeCrow urged Bryant to bring suit under the 1977 Florida Human Rights Act, which prohibits job discrimination on the basis of marital status. Even before DeCrow's sisterly act, however, Bryant had reevaluated her position on the women's movement, to which, under Green's tutelage, she had been bitterly opposed. "What has happened to me," Bryant told the *National Enquirer* in June 1980, "makes me understand why there are angry women who want to pass ERA [Equal Rights Amendment]. That still is not the answer. But the church doesn't deal with the problems of women as it should. There's been some really bad teachings, and I think that's why I'm really concerned for my own children—particularly the girls. You have to recognize that there has been discrimination against women, that women have not had the teaching of the fullness and uniqueness of their abilities." *Pace,* sister.

the Panama Canal Treaty. Her roots, and perhaps her heart such as it is, are in the Old Right, but she remained unknown to any significant public until she mounted her crusade against the Equal Rights Amendment. It is likely that her ambition is to use women as a constituency to effect entry into the upper echelon of right-wing male leadership. She may yet discover that she is a woman (as feminists understand the meaning of the word) as her male colleagues refuse to let her escape the ghetto of female issues and enter the big time.* At any rate, she seems to be able to manipulate the fears of women without experiencing them. If this is indeed the case, this talent would give her an invaluable, cold-blooded detachment as a strategist determined to convert women into antifeminist activists. It is precisely because women have been trained to respect and follow those who use them that Schlafly inspires awe and

---

*According to many newspaper reports, Phyllis Schlafly wanted Reagan to appoint her to a position in the Pentagon. This he did not do. In a debate with Schlafly (Stanford University, January 26, 1982) lawyer Catharine A. MacKinnon tried to make Schlafly understand that she had been discriminated against as a woman: "Mrs. Schlafly tells us that being a woman has not gotten in her way. I propose that any man who had a law degree and graduate work in political science; had given testimony on a wide range of important subjects for decades; had done effective and brilliant political, policy and organizational work within the party [the Republican Party]; had published widely, including nine books; and stopped a major social initiative to amend the constitution just short of victory dead in its tracks [the Equal Rights Amendment]; and had a beautiful accomplished family—any man like that would have a place in the current administration. . . . I would accept correction if this is wrong; and she may yet be appointed. She was widely reported to have wanted such a post, but I don't believe everything I read, especially about women. I do think she should have wanted one and they should have found her a place she wanted. She certainly deserved a place in the Defense Department. Phyllis Schlafly is a qualified woman." Answered Schlafly: "This has been an interesting debate. More interesting than I thought it was going to be. . . . I think my opponent did have one good point—[audience laughter] Well, she had a couple of good points. . . . She did have a good point about the Reagan administration, but it is the Reagan administration's loss that they didn't ask me to [drowned out by audience applause] but it isn't my loss."

devotion in women who are afraid that they will be deprived of the form, shelter, safety, rules, and love that the Right promises and on which they believe survival depends.

*

At the National Women's Conference (Houston, Texas, November 1977), I spoke with many women on the Right. The conversations were ludicrous, terrifying, bizarre, instructive, and, as other feminists have reported, sometimes strangely moving.

Right-wing women fear lesbians. A liberal black delegate from Texas told me that local white women had tried to convince her that lesbians at the conference would assault her, call her dirty names, and were personally filthy. She told me that she would vote against the sexual-preference resolution* because otherwise she would not be able to return home. But she also said that she would tell the white women that the lesbians had been polite and clean. She said that she knew it was wrong to deprive anyone of a job and had had no idea before coming to Houston that lesbian mothers lost their children. This, she felt, was genuinely terrible. I asked her if she thought a time would come when she would have to stand up for lesbian rights in her hometown. She nodded yes gravely, then explained with careful, evocative emphasis that the next-closest town to where she lived was 160 miles away. The history of blacks in the South was palpable.

---

*"Congress, State, and local legislatures should enact legislation to eliminate discrimination on the basis of sexual and affectional preference in areas including, but not limited to, employment, housing, public accommodations, credit, public facilities, government funding, and the military.

"State legislatures should reform their penal codes or repeal State laws that restrict private sexual behavior between consenting adults.

"State legislatures should enact legislation that would prohibit consideration of sexual or affectional orientation as a factor in any judicial determination of child custody or visitation rights. Rather, child custody cases should be evaluated solely on the merits of which party is the better parent, without regard to that person's sexual and affectional orientation."

Right-wing women consistently spoke to me about lesbians as if lesbians were rapists, certified committers of sexual assault against women and girls. No facts could intrude on this psychosexual fantasy. No facts or figures on male sexual violence against women and children could change the focus of their fear. They admitted that they knew of many cases of male assault against females, including within families, and did not know of any assaults by lesbians against females. The men, they acknowledged when pressed, were sinners, and they hated sin, but there was clearly something comforting in the normalcy of heterosexual rape. To them, the lesbian was inherently monstrous, experienced almost as a demonic sexual force hovering closer and closer. She was the dangerous intruder, encroaching, threatening by her very presence a sexual order that cannot bear scrutiny or withstand challenge.

Right-wing women regard abortion as the callous murder of infants. Female selflessness expresses itself in the conviction that a fertilized egg surpasses an adult female in the authenticity of its existence. The grief of these women for fetuses is real, and their contempt for women who become pregnant out of wedlock is awesome to behold. The fact that most illegal abortions in the bad old days were performed on married women with children, and that thousands of those women died each year, is utterly meaningless to them. They see abortion as a criminal act committed by godless whores, women absolutely unlike themselves.

Right-wing women argue that passage of the Equal Rights Amendment will legalize abortion irrevocably. No matter how often I heard this argument (and I heard it constantly), I simply could not understand it. Fool that I was, I had thought that the Equal Rights Amendment was abhorrent because of toilets. Since toilets figured prominently in the resistance to civil rights legislation that would protect blacks, the argument that centered on toilets—while irrational—was as Amerikan as apple pie. No one mentioned toilets. I brought them up, but no one cared to discuss them. The passionate, repeated cause-and-effect arguments linking the Equal Rights Amendment and abortion presented a new mystery. I resigned myself to hopeless confusion. Happily, after the conference, I read *The Power of the Positive Woman*, in which Schlafly explains: "Since the mandate of ERA is for sex equality, abortion is essential to relieve women of their unequal burden of being forced to bear an unwanted baby."[19] Forcing women to bear unwanted babies is crucial to the social program of women who have been forced to bear unwanted babies and who cannot bear the grief and bitterness of such a recognition. The Equal Rights Amendment has now become the symbol of this devastating recognition. This largely accounts for the new wave of intransigent opposition to it.

Right-wing women, as represented in Houston, especially from the South, white and black, also do not like Jews. They live in a Christian country. A fragile but growing coalition between white and black women in the New South is based on a shared Christian fundamentalism, which translates into a shared anti-Semitism. The stubborn refusal of Jews to embrace Christ and the barely masked fundamentalist perception of Jews as Christ killers, communists and usurers both, queers, and, worst of all, urban intellectuals, mark Jews as foreign, sinister, and an obvious source of the many satanic conspiracies sweeping the nation.

The most insidious expression of this rife anti-Semitism was conveyed by a fixed stare, a self-conscious smile and the delightful words "Ah just love tha Jewish people." The slime variety of anti-Semite, very much in evidence, was typified by a Right to Life leader who called doctors who perform abortions "Jewish baby killers." I was asked a hundred times: "Am Ah speakin with a Jewish girl?" Despite my clear presence as a lesbian-feminist with press credentials plastered all over me from the notorious *Ms.* magazine, it was as a Jew that I was consistently challenged and, on several occasions, implicitly threatened. Conversation after conversation stopped abruptly when I answered that yes, I was a Jew.

*

The Right in the United States today is a social and political movement controlled almost totally by men but built largely on the fear and ignorance of women. The quality of this fear and the pervasiveness of this ignorance are consequences of male sexual domination over women. Every accommodation that women make to this domination, however apparently stupid, self-defeating, or dangerous, is rooted in the urgent need to survive somehow on male terms. Inevitably this causes women to take the rage and contempt they feel for the men who actually abuse them, those close to them, and project it onto others, those far away, foreign, or different. Some women do this by becoming right-wing patriots, nationalists determined to triumph over populations thousands of miles removed. Some women become ardent racists, anti-Semites, or homophobes. Some women develop a hatred of loose or destitute women, pregnant teenage girls, all persons unemployed or on welfare. Some hate individuals who violate social conventions, no matter how superficial the violations. Some become antagonistic to ethnic groups other than their own or to religious groups other than their own, or they develop a hatred of those political convictions that contradict their own. Women cling to irrational hatreds, focused particularly on the unfamiliar, so that they will not murder their fathers, husbands, sons, brothers, lovers, the men with whom they are intimate, those who do hurt them and cause them grief. Fear of a greater evil and a need to be protected from it intensify the loyalty of women to men who are, even when dangerous, at least known quantities. Because women so displace their rage, they are easily controlled and manipulated haters. Having good reason to hate, but not the courage to rebel, women require symbols of danger that justify their fear. The Right provides these symbols of danger by designating clearly defined groups of outsiders as sources of danger. The identities of the dangerous outsiders can change over time to meet changing social circumstances—for example, racism can be encouraged or contained; anti-Semitism can be provoked or kept dormant; homophobia can be aggravated or kept under the surface—but the existence of the dangerous outsider always functions for women simultaneously as deception, diversion, pain-killer, and threat.

The tragedy is that women so committed to survival cannot recognize that they are committing suicide. The danger is that self-sacrificing women are perfect foot soldiers who obey orders, no matter how criminal those orders are. The hope is that these women, upset by internal conflicts that cannot be stilled by manipulation, challenged by the clarifying drama of public confrontation and dialogue, will be forced to articulate the realities of their own experiences as women subject to the will of men. In doing so, the anger that necessarily arises from a true perception of how they have been debased may move them beyond the fear that transfixes them to a meaningful rebellion against the men who in fact diminish, despise, and terrorize them. This is the common struggle of all women, whatever their male-defined ideological origins; and this struggle alone has the power to transform women who are enemies against one another into allies fighting for individual and collective survival that is not based on self-loathing, fear, and humiliation, but instead on self-determination, dignity, and authentic integrity.

2

The Politics of Intelligence

> Why is life so tragic; so like a little strip of pavement over an abyss. I look down; I feel giddy; I wonder how I am ever to walk to the end. . . . It's a feeling of impotence: of cutting no ice.
>
> Virginia Woolf, her diary,
> October 25, 1920

Men hate intelligence in women. It cannot flame; it cannot burn; it cannot burn out and end up in ashes, having been consumed in adventure. It cannot be cold, rational, ice; no warm womb would tolerate a cold, icy, splendid mind. It cannot be ebullient and it cannot be morbid; it cannot be anything that does not end in reproduction or whoring. It cannot be what intelligence is: a vitality of mind that acts directly in and on the world, without mediation. "Indeed," wrote Norman Mailer, "I doubt if there will be a really exciting woman writer until the first whore becomes a call girl and tells her tale."[1] And Mailer was being generous, because he endowed the whore with a capacity to know, if not to tell: she knows something firsthand, something worth knowing. "Genius," wrote Edith Wharton more realistically, "is of small use to a woman who does not know how to do her hair."[2]

Intelligence is a form of energy, a force that pushes out into the world. It makes its mark, not once but continuously. It is curious, penetrating. Without the light of public life, discourse, and action, it dies. It must have a field of action beyond embroidery or scrubbing toilets or wearing fine clothes. It needs response, challenge, consequences that matter. Intelligence cannot be passive and private through a lifetime. Kept secret, kept inside, it withers and dies. The outside can be brought to it; it can live on bread and water locked up in a cell—but barely. Florence Nightingale, in her feminist tract *Cassandra*, said that intellect died last in women; desire, dreams, activity, and love all died before it. Intelligence does hang on, because it can live on almost nothing: fragments of the world brought to it by husbands or sons or strangers or, in our time, television or the occasional film. Imprisoned, intelligence turns into self-haunting and dread. Isolated, intelligence becomes a burden and a curse. Undernourished, intelligence becomes like the bloated belly of a starving child: swollen, filled with nothing the body can use. It swells, like the starved stomach, as the skeleton shrivels and the bones collapse; it will pick up anything to fill the hunger, stick anything in, chew anything, swallow anything. "José Carlos came home with a bag of crackers he found in the garbage," wrote Carolina Maria de Jesus, a woman of the Brazilian underclass, in her diary. "When I saw him eating things out of the trash I thought: and if it's been poisoned? Children can't stand hunger. The crackers were delicious. I ate them thinking of that proverb: He who enters the dance must dance. And as I also was hungry, I ate."[3] The intelligence of women is traditionally starved, isolated, imprisoned.

Traditionally and practically, the world is brought to women by men; they are the outside on which female intelligence must feed. The food is poor, orphan's gruel. This is because men bring home half-truths, ego-laden lies, and use them to demand solace or sex or housekeeping. The intelligence of women is not out in the world, acting on its own behalf; it is kept small, inside the home, acting on behalf of another. This is true even when the woman works outside the home, because she is segregated into women's work, and her intelligence does not have the same importance as the lay of her ass.

Men are the world and women use intelligence to survive men: their tricks, desires, demands, moods, hatreds, disappointments, rages, greed, lust, authority, power, weaknesses. The ideas that come to women come through men, in a field of cultural values controlled by men, in a political and social system controlled by men, in a sexual system in which women are used as things. (As Catharine A. MacKinnon wrote in the one sentence that every woman should risk her life to understand: "Man fucks woman; subject verb object."[4]) Men are the field of action in which female intelligence moves. But the world, the real world, is more than men, certainly more than what men show of themselves and the world to women; and women are deprived of that real world. The male always intervenes between her and it.

Some will grant that women might have a particular kind of intelligence—essentially small, picky, good with details, bad with ideas. Some will grant—in fact, insist—that women know more of "the Good," that women are more cognizant of decency or kindness: this keeps intelligence small and tamed. Some will grant that there have been women of genius: after the woman of genius is dead. The greatest writers in the English language have been women: George Eliot, Jane Austen, Virginia Woolf. They were sublime; and they were, all of them, shadows of what they might have been. But the fact that they existed does not change the categorical perception that women are basically stupid: not capable of intelligence without the exercise of which the world as a whole is impoverished. Women are stupid and men are smart; men have a right to the world and women do not. A lost man is a lost intelligence; a lost woman is a lost (name the function) mother, housekeeper, sexual thing. Classes of men have been lost, have been thrown away; there have always been mourners and fighters who refused to accept the loss. There is no mourning for the lost intelligence of women because there is no conviction that such intelligence was real and was destroyed. Intelligence is, in fact, seen as a function of masculinity, and women are despised when they refuse to be lost.

Women have stupid ideas that do not deserve to be called ideas. Marabel Morgan writes an awful, silly, terrible book in which she claims that women must exist for their husbands, do sex and be sex for their husbands.* D. H. Lawrence writes vile and stupid essays in which he says the same thing basically with many references to the divine phallus;† but D. H. Lawrence is smart. Anita Bryant

---

*See *The Total Woman* or the quotations from it in chapter 1 of this book. Or: "In the beginning, sex started in the garden. The first man was all alone. The days were long, the nights were longer. He had no cook, no nurse, no lover. God saw that man was lonely and in need of a partner, so He gave him a woman, the best present any man could receive" *(The Total Woman,* [New York: Pocket Books, 1975], p. 129). "Spiritually, for sexual intercourse to be the ultimate satisfaction, both partners need a personal relationship with their God. When this is so their union is sacred and beautiful, and mysteriously the two blend perfectly into one" *(Total Woman,* p. 128).

†For instance: "Christianity brought marriage into the world: marriage as we know it. . . . Man and wife, a king and queen with one or two subjects, and a few square yards of territory of their own: this, really, is marriage. It is true freedom because it is a true fulfillment for man, woman, and children" *(Sex, Literature, and Censorship* [New York: The Viking Press, 1959], p. 98). "It is the tragedy of modern woman. . . . She is cocksure, but she is a hen all the time. Frightened of her own henny self, she rushes to mad lengths about votes, or welfare, or sports, or business: she is marvellous, out-manning the man. . . . Suddenly it all falls out of relation to her basic henny self, and she realises she has lost her life. The lovely henny surety, the hensureness which is the real bliss of every female, has been denied her: she never had it. . . . Nothingness!" *(Sex, Literature, and Censorship,* pp. 49–50). ". . . marriage is no marriage that is not basically and permanently phallic, and that is not linked up with the sun and the earth, the moon and the fixed stars and the planets, in the rhythm of days, in the rhythm of months, in the rhythm of quarters, of years, of decades, of centuries. Marriage is no marriage that is not a correspondence of blood. . . . The phallus is a column of blood that fills the valley of blood of a woman" *(Sex, Literature, and Censorship,* p. 101). "Into

says that cocksucking is a form of human cannibalism; she decries the loss of the child who is the sperm.* Norman Mailer believes that lost ejaculations are lost sons and on that basis disparages male homosexuality, masturbation, and contraception.† But Anita Bryant is stupid and Norman Mailer is smart. Is the difference in the style with which these same ideas are delivered or in the penis? Mailer says that a great writer writes with his balls; novelist Cynthia Ozick asks Mailer in which color ink he dips his balls. Who is smart and who is stupid?

---

the womb of the primary darkness enters the ray of ultimate light, and time is begotten, conceived, there is the beginning of the end. We are the beginning of the end. And there, within the womb, we ripen upon the beginning, till we become aware of the end" *(Reflections on the Death of a Porcupine* [Bloomington: Indiana University Press, 1963], p. 7).

*For instance: "Why do you think the homosexuals are called fruits? It's because they eat the forbidden fruit of life. . . . That's why homosexuality is an abomination of God, because life is so precious to God and it is such a sacred thing when man and woman come together in one flesh and the seed is fertilized—that's the sealing of life, that's the beginning of life. To interfere with that in any way—especially the eating of the forbidden fruit, the eating of the sperm—that's why it's such an abomination. . . . it makes the sin of homosexuality all the more hideous because it's antilife, degenerative" *(Playboy*, May 1978).

†For instance: ". . . but if you're not ready to make a baby with that marvelous sex, then you may also be putting something down the drain forever, which is the ability that you had to make a baby; the most marvelous thing that was in you may have been shot into a diaphragm or wasted on a pill. One might be losing one's future" *(The Presidential Papers* [New York: Bantam Books, 1964], p. 142). "Of the million spermatozoa, there may be only two or three with any real chance of reaching the ovum . . . [The others] go out with no sense at all of being real spermatozoa. They may appear to be real spermatozoa under the microscope, but after all, a man from Mars who's looking at us through a telescope might think that Communist bureaucrats and FBI men look exactly the same. . . . Even the electron microscope can't measure the striation of passion in a spermatozoon. Or the force of its will" *(The Presidential Papers*, p. 143). "I hate contraception. . . . There's nothing I abhor more than planned parenthood. Planned parenthood is an abomination. I'd rather have those fucking Communists over here" *(The Presidential Papers*, p. 131). "I think

(Footnote continues overleaf)

If an idea is stupid, presumably it is stupid whether the one who articulates it is male or female. But that is not the case. Women, undereducated as a class, do not have to read Aeschylus to know that a man plants the sperm, the child, the son; women are the soil; she brings forth the human he created; he is the originator, the father of life. Women can have their own provincial, moralistic sources for this knowledge: clergy, movies, gym teachers. The knowledge is common knowledge: respected in the male writers because the male writers are respected; stupid in women because women are stupid as a condition of birth. Women articulate received knowledge and are laughed at for doing so. But male writers with the same received ideas are acclaimed as new, brilliant, interesting, even rebellious, brave, facing the world of sin and sex forthrightly. Women have ignorant, moralistic prejudices; men have ideas. To call this a double standard is to indulge in cruel euphemism. This gender system of evaluating ideas is a sledgehammer that bangs female intelligence to a pulp, annihilating it. Mailer and Lawrence have taken on the world always; they knew they had a right to it; their prose takes that right for granted; it is the gravitational field in which they move. Marabel Morgan and Anita Bryant come to the world as middle-aged women and try to act in it; of course they are juvenile and imprecise in style, ridiculous even. Both Mailer and Lawrence have written volumes that are as ridiculous, juvenile, despite what they can take for granted as men, despite their sometimes mastery of the language, despite their

(Footnote continued from previous page)
one of the reasons that homosexuals go through such agony when they're around 40 or 50 is that their lives have nothing to do with procreation. They realize with great horror that all that wonderful sex they had in the past is gone—where is it now? They've used up their being" *(The Presidential Papers*, p. 144). "It's better to commit rape than masturbate" *(The Presidential Papers*, p. 140). "what if the seed be already a being? So desperate that it / claws, bites, cuts and lies, / burns, and betrays / desperate to capture the oven . . ." ("I Got Two Kids and Another in the Oven," *Advertisements for Myself* [New York: Perigee, 1981], p. 397).

genuine accomplishments, despite the beauty of a story or novel. But they are not called stupid even when they are ridiculous. When the ideas of Lawrence cannot be distinguished from the ideas of Morgan, either both are smart or both are stupid; and similarly with Mailer and Bryant. Only the women, however, deserve and get our contempt. Are Anita Bryant's ideas pernicious? Then so are Norman Mailer's. Are Marabel Morgan's ideas side-slappingly funny? Then so are D. H. Lawrence's.

A woman must keep her intelligence small and timid to survive. Or she must hide it altogether or hide it through style. Or she must go mad like clockwork to pay for it. She will try to find the nice way to exercise intelligence. But intelligence is not ladylike. Intelligence is full of excesses. Rigorous intelligence abhors sentimentality, and women must be sentimental to value the dreadful silliness of the men around them. Morbid intelligence abhors the cheery sunlight of positive thinking and eternal sweetness; and women must be sunlight and cheery and sweet, or the woman could not bribe her way with smiles through a day. Wild intelligence abhors any narrow world; and the world of women must stay narrow, or the woman is an outlaw. No woman could be Nietzsche or Rimbaud without ending up in a whorehouse or lobotomized. Any vital intelligence has passionate questions, aggressive answers: but women cannot be explorers; there can be no Lewis and Clark of the female mind. Even restrained intelligence is restrained not because it is timid, as women must be, but because it is cautiously weighing impressions and facts that come to it from an outside that the timid dare not face. A woman must please, and restrained intelligence does not seek to please; it seeks to know through discernment. Intelligence is also ambitious: it always wants more: not more being fucked, not more pregnancy; but more of a bigger world. A woman cannot be ambitious in her own right without also being damned.

We take girls and send them to schools. It is good of us, because girls are not supposed to know anything much, and in many other societies girls are not sent to school or taught to read and write. In our society, such a generous one to women, girls are taught some facts, but not inquiry or the passion of knowing. Girls are taught in order to make them compliant: intellectual adventurousness is drained, punished, ridiculed out of girls. We use schools first to narrow the girl's scope, her curiosity, then to teach her certain skills, necessary to the abstract husband. Girls are taught to be passive in relation to facts. Girls are not seen as the potential originators of ideas or the potential searchers into the human condition. Good behavior is the intellectual goal of a girl. A girl with intellectual drive is a girl who has to be cut down to size. An intelligent girl is supposed to use that intelligence to find a smarter husband. Simone de Beauvoir settled on Sartre when she determined that he was smarter than she was. In a film made when both were old, toward the end of his life, Sartre asks de Beauvoir, the woman with whom he has shared an astonishing life of intellectual action and accomplishment: how does it feel, to have been a literary lady?

Carolina Maria de Jesus wrote in her diary: "Everyone has an ideal in life. Mine is to be able to read."[5] She is ambitious, but it is a strange ambition for a woman. She wants learning. She wants the pleasure of reading and writing. Men ask her to marry but she suspects that they will interfere with her reading and writing. They will resent the time she takes alone. They will resent the focus of her attention elsewhere. They will resent her concentration and they will resent her self-respect. They will resent her pride in herself and her pride in her unmediated relationship to a larger world of ideas, descriptions, facts. Her neighbors see her poring over books, or with pen and paper in hand, amidst the garbage and hunger of the *favela*. Her ideal makes her a pariah: her desire to read makes her more an outcast than if she sat in the street putting fistfuls of nails into her mouth. Where did she get her ideal? No one offered it to her. Two thirds of the world's illiterates are women. To be fucked, to birth children, one need not know how to read. Women are for sex and reproduction, not for literature. But women have stories to tell. Women want to know. Women have questions, ideas, arguments, answers. Women have dreams of being in the world, not merely passing blood and heaving wet infants out of laboring wombs. "Women dream," Florence Nightingale wrote in *Cassandra*, "till they have no longer the strength to dream; those dreams against which they so struggle, so honestly, vigorously, and conscientiously, and so in vain, yet which are their life, without which they could not have lived; those dreams go at last. . . . Later in life, they neither desire nor dream, neither of activity, nor of love, nor of intellect."[6]

Virginia Woolf, the most splendid modern writer, told us over and over how awful it was to be a woman of creative intelligence. She told us when she loaded a large stone into her pocket and walked into the river; and she told us each time a book was published and she went mad—don't hurt me for what I have done, I will hurt myself first, I will be incapacitated and I will suffer and I will be punished and then perhaps you need not destroy me, perhaps you will pity me, there is such contempt in pity and I am so proud, won't that be enough? She told us over and over in her prose too: in her fiction she showed us, ever so delicately so that we would not take offense; and in her essays she piled on the charm, being polite to keep us polite. But she did write it straight out too, though it was not published in her lifetime, and she was right:

> A certain attitude is required—what I call the pouring-out-tea attitude—the clubwoman, Sunday afternoon attitude. I don't know. I think that the angle is almost as important as the thing. What I value is the naked contact of a mind. Often one cannot say anything valuable about a writer—except what one thinks. Now I found my angle incessantly obscured, quite unconsciously no doubt, by the desire of the editor and of the public that a woman should see things from the chary feminine angle. My article, written from that oblique point of view, always went down.[7]

To value "the naked contact of a mind" is to have a virile intelligence, one not shrouded in dresses and pretty gestures. Her work did always go down, with the weight of what being female demanded. She became a master of exquisite indirection. She hid her meanings and her messages in a feminine style. She labored under that style and hid behind that mask: and she was less than she could have been. She died not only from what she did dare, but also from what she did not dare.

These three things are indissolubly linked: literacy, intellect, and creative intelligence. They distinguish, as the cliché goes, man from the animals. He who is denied these three is denied a fully human life and has been robbed of a right to human dignity. Now change the gender. Literacy, intellect, and creative intelligence distinguish woman from the animals: no. Woman is not distinguishable from the animals because she has been condemned by virtue of her sex class to a life of animal functions: being fucked, reproducing. For her, the animal functions are her meaning, her so-called humanity, as human as she gets, the highest human capacities in her because she is female. To the orthodox of male culture, she is animal, the antithesis of soul; to the liberals of male culture, she is nature. In discussing the so-called biological origins of male dominance, the boys can afford to compare themselves to baboons and insects: they are writing books or teaching in universities when they do it. A Harvard professor does not refuse tenure because a baboon has never been granted it. The biology of power is a game boys play. It is the male way of saying: she is more like the female baboon than she is like me; she cannot be an éminence grise at Harvard because she bleeds, we fuck her, she bears our young, we beat her up, we rape her; she is an animal, her function is to breed. I want to see the baboon, the ant, the wasp, the goose, the cichlid, that has written *War and Peace*. Even more I want to see the animal or insect or fish or fowl that has written *Middlemarch*.

Literacy is a tool, like fire. It is a more advanced tool than fire, and it has done as much or more to change the complexion of the natural and social worlds. Literacy, like fire, is a tool that must be used by intelligence. Literacy is also a capacity: the capacity to be literate is a human capacity; the capacity exists and it can be used or it can be denied, refuted, made to atrophy. In persons socially despised, it is denied. But denial is not enough, because people insist on meaning. Humankind finds meaning in experiences, events, objects, communications, relationships, feelings. Literacy functions as part of the search for meaning; it helps to make that search possible. Men can deny that women have the capacity to learn ancient Greek, but some women will learn it nevertheless. Men can deny that poor women or working-class women or prostituted women have the capacity to read or write their own language, but some of those women will read or write their own language anyway; they will risk everything to learn it. In the slaveholding South in the United States, it was forbidden by law to teach slaves to read or write; but some slaveowners taught, some slaves learned, some slaves taught themselves, and some slaves taught other slaves. In Jewish law, it is forbidden to teach women Talmud, but some women learned Talmud anyway. People know that literacy brings dignity and a wider world. People are strongly motivated to experience the world they live in through language: spoken, sung, chanted, and written. One must punish people terribly to stop them from wanting to know what reading and writing bring, because people are curious and driven toward both experience and the conceptualization of it. The denial of literacy to any class or category of people is a denial of fundamental humanity. Humans viewed as animal, not human, are classically denied literacy: slaves in slave-owning societies; women in woman-owning societies; racially degraded groups in racist societies. The male slave is treated as a beast of burden; he cannot be allowed to read or write. The woman is treated as a beast of breeding; she must not read or write. When women as a class are denied the right to read and write, those who learn are shamed by their knowledge: they are masculine, deviant; they have denied their wombs, their cunts; in their literacy they repudiate the definition of their kind.

Certain classes of women have been granted some privileges of literacy—not rights, privileges. The courtesans of ancient Greece were educated when other women were kept ignorant, but they were not philosophers, they were whores. Only by accepting their function as whores could they exercise the privilege of literacy. Upper-class women are traditionally taught some skills of literacy (distinctly more circumscribed than the skills taught the males of their mating class): they can exercise the privilege of literacy if they accept their decorative function. After all, the man does not want the breeding, bleeding bitch at the dinner table or the open cunt in the parlor while he reads his newspaper or smokes his cigar. Language is refinement: proof that he is human, not she.

The increase in illiteracy among the urban poor in the United States is consonant with a new rise in overt racism and contempt for the poor. The illiteracy is programmed into the system: an intelligent child can go to school and not be taught how to read or write. When the educational system abandons reading and writing for particular subgroups, it abandons human dignity for those groups: it becomes strictly custodial, keeping the animals penned in; it does not bring human life to human beings.

Cross-culturally, girls and women are the illiterates, with two thirds of the world's illiterates women and the rate rising steadily. Girls need husbands, not books. Girls need houses or shacks to keep clean, or street corners to stand on, not the wide world in which to roam. Refusal to give the tool of literacy is refusal to give access to the world. If she can make her own fire, read a book herself, write a letter or a record of her thoughts or an essay or a story, it will be harder to get her to tolerate the unwanted fuck, to bear the unwanted children, to see him as life and life through him. She might get ideas. But even worse, she might know the value of the ideas she gets. She must not know that ideas have value, only that being fucked and reproducing are her value.

It has been hard, in the United States, to get women educated: there are still many kinds of education off limits to women. In England, it was hard for Virginia Woolf to use a university library. Simple literacy is the first step, and, as Abby Kelley told a women's rights convention in 1850, "Sisters, bloody feet have worn smooth the path by which you came here."[8] Access to the whole language has been denied women; we are only supposed to use the ladylike parts of it. Alice James noted in her diary that "[i]t is an immense loss to have all robust and sustaining expletives refined away from one!"[9]

But it is in the actual exercise of literacy as a tool and as a capacity that women face punishment, ostracization, exile, recrimination, the most virulent contempt. To read and be feminine simultaneously she reads Gothic romances, not medical textbooks; cookbooks, not case law; mystery stories, not molecular biology. The language of mathematics is not a feminine language. She may learn astrology, not astronomy. She may teach grammar, not invent style or originate ideas. She is permitted to write a little book about neurotic women, fiction or nonfiction, if the little book is trite and sentimental enough; she had better keep clear of philosophy altogether. In fiction, she had better be careful not to overstep the severe limits imposed by femininity. "This then," wrote Virginia Woolf, "is another incident, and quite a common incident in the career of a woman novelist. She has to say I will wait. I will wait until men have become so civilised that they are not shocked when a woman speaks the truth about her body. The future of fiction depends very much upon what extent men can be educated to stand free speech in women."[10] The constraint is annihilation: language that must avoid one's own body is language that has no place in the world. But speaking the truth about a woman's body is not the simple explication of body parts—it is instead the place of that particular body in this particular world, its value, its use, its place in power, its political and economic life, its capacities both potentially realized and habitually abused.

In a sense intellect is the combination of literacy and intelligence: literacy disciplines intelligence and intelligence expands the uses of literacy; there is a body of knowledge that changes and increases and also a skill in acquiring knowledge; there is a memory filled with ideas, a storehouse of what has gone before in the world. Intellect is mastery of ideas, of culture, of the products and processes of other intellects. Intellect is the capacity to learn language disciplined into learning. Intellect must be cultivated: even in men, even in the smartest. Left alone in a private world of isolation, intellect does not develop unless it has a private cultivator: a teacher, a father of intellect, for instance. But the intellect in the female must not exceed that of the teacher—or the female will be rebuked and denied. Walt Whitman wrote that a student necessarily disowns and overthrows a teacher; but the female student must always stay smaller than the teacher, always meeker; her intelligence is never supposed to become mastery. Intellect in a woman is always a sign of privilege: she has been raised up above her kind, usually because of the beneficence of a man who has seen fit to educate her. The insults to females of intellect are legion: so-called bluestockings are a laughingstock; women of intellect are ugly or they would not bother to have ideas; the pleasure of cultivating the mind is sexual perversion in the female; the works of literate men are strewn with vicious remarks against intellectual women. Intellect in a woman is malignant. She is not ennobled by a fine mind; she is deformed by it.

The creative mind is intelligence in action in the world. The world need not be defined as rivers, mountains, and plains. The world is anywhere that thought has consequences. In the most abstract philosophy, thought has consequences; philosophy is part of the world, sometimes its own self-contained world. Thinking is action; so are writing, composing, painting; creative intelligence can be used in the material world to make products of itself. But there is more to creative intelligence than what it produces. Creative intelligence is searching intelligence: it demands to know the world, demands its right to consequence. It is not contemplative: creative intelligence is too ambitious for that; it almost always announces itself. It may commit itself to the pure search for knowledge or truth, but almost always it wants recognition, influence, or power; it is an accomplishing intelligence. It is not satisfied by recognition of the personality that carries it; it wants respect in its own right, respect for itself. Sometimes this respect can be shown toward its product. Sometimes, when this intelligence exercises itself in the more ephemeral realm of pure talk or mundane action, respect for creative intelligence must be shown through respect for the person manifesting it. Women are consistently and systematically denied the respect creative intelligence requires to be sustained: painfully denied it, cruelly denied it, sadistically denied it. Women are not supposed to have creative intelligence, but when they do they are supposed to renounce it. If they want the love of men, without which they are not really women, they had better not hold on to an intelligence that searches and that is action in the world; thought that has consequences is inimical to fettered femininity. Creative intelligence is not animal: being fucked and reproducing will not satisfy it, ever; and creative intelligence is not decorative—it is never merely ornamental as, for instance, upper-class women however well educated must be. To stay a woman in the male-supremacist meaning of that word, women must renounce creative intelligence: not just verbally renounce it, though women do that all the time, but snuff it out in themselves at worst, keep it timid and restrained at best. The price for exercising creative intelligence for those born female is unspeakable suffering. "All things on earth have their price," wrote Olive Schreiner, "and for truth we pay the dearest. We barter it for love and sympathy. The road to honour is paved with thorns; but on the path to truth, at every step you set your foot down on your heart."[11] Truth is the goal of creative intelligence, whatever its kind and path; tangling with the world is tangling with the problem of truth. One confronts the muck of the world, but one's search is for the truth. The particular truth or the ultimate character of the truth one finds is not the issue. The intrusion of an intelligent, creative self into the world to find the truth is the issue. There is nothing here for women, except intimidation and contempt. In isolation, in private, a woman may have pleasure from the exercise of creative intelligence, however restrained she is in the exercise of it; but that intelligence will have to be turned against herself because there is no further, complex, human world in which it can be used and developed. Whatever of it leaks out will entitle all and sundry to criticize her womanhood, which is the sole identity available to her; her womanhood is deficient, because her intelligence is virile.

"Why have women passion, intellect, moral activity . . ." Florence Nightingale asked in 1852, "and a place in society where no one of these three can be exercised?"[12] When she referred to moral activity, she did not mean moralism; she meant moral intelligence. Moralism is the set of rules learned by rote that keeps women locked in, so that intelligence can never meet the world head on. Moralism is a defense against experiencing the world. Moralism is the moral sphere designated to women, who are supposed to learn the rules of their own proper, circumscribed behavior by rote. Moral intelligence is active; it can only be developed and refined by being used in the realm of real and direct experience. Moral activity is the use of that intelligence, the exercise of moral discernment. Moralism is passive: it accepts the version of the world it has been taught and shudders at the threat of direct experience. Moral intelligence is characterized by activity, movement through ideas and history: it takes on the world and insists on participating in the great and terrifying issues of right and wrong, tenderness and cruelty. Moral intelligence constructs values; and because those values are exercised in the real world, they have consequences. There is no moral intelligence that does not have real consequences in a real world, or that is simply and passively received, or that can live in a vacuum in which there is no action. Moral intelligence cannot be expressed only through love or only through sex or only through domesticity or only through ornamentation or only through obedience; moral intelligence cannot be expressed only through being fucked or reproducing. Moral intelligence must act in a public world, not a private, refined, rarefied relationship with one other person to the exclusion of the rest of the world. Moral intelligence demands a nearly endless exercise of the ability to make decisions: significant decisions; decisions inside history, not peripheral to it; decisions about the meaning of life; decisions that arise from an acute awareness of one's own mortality; decisions on which one can honestly and willfully stake one's life. Moral intelligence is not the stuff of which cunts are made. Moralism is the cunt's effort to find some basis for self-respect, a pitiful gesture toward being human at which men laugh and for which women pity other women.

There is also, possibly, sexual intelligence, a human capacity for discerning, manifesting, and constructing sexual integrity. Sexual intelligence could not be measured in numbers of orgasms, erections, or partners; nor could it show itself by posing painted clitoral lips in front of a camera; nor could one measure it by the number of children born; nor would it manifest as addiction. Sexual intelligence, like any other kind of intelligence, would be active and dynamic; it would need the real world, the direct experience of it; it would pose not buttocks but questions, answers, theories, ideas—in the form of desire or act or art or articulation. It would be in the body, but it could never be in an imprisoned, isolated body, a body denied access to the world. It would not be mechanical; nor could it stand to be viewed as inert and stupid; nor could it be exploited by another without diminishing in vigor; and being sold on the marketplace as a commodity would necessarily be anathema to it, a direct affront to its intrinsic need to confront the world in self-defined and self-determining terms. Sexual intelligence would probably be more like moral intelligence than like anything else: a point that women for centuries have been trying to make. But since no intelligence in a woman is respected, and since she is condemned to moralism because she is defined as being incapable of moral intelligence, and since she is defined as a sexual thing to be used, the meaning of women in likening moral and sexual intelligence is not understood. Sexual intelligence asserts itself through sexual integrity, a dimension of values and action forbidden to women. Sexual intelligence would have to be rooted first and foremost in the honest possession of one's own body, and women exist to be possessed by others, namely men. The possession of one's own body would have to be absolute and entirely realized for the intelligence to thrive in the world of action. Sexual intelligence, like moral intelligence, would have to confront the great issues of cruelty and tenderness; but where moral intelligence must tangle with questions of right and wrong, sexual intelligence would have to tangle with questions of dominance and submission. One preordained to be fucked has no need to exercise sexual intelligence, no opportunity to exercise it, no argument that justifies exercising it. To keep the woman sexually acquiescent, the capacity for sexual intelligence must be prohibited to her; and it is. Her clitoris is denied; her capacity for pleasure is distorted and defamed; her erotic values are slandered and insulted; her desire to value her body as her own is paralyzed and maimed. She is turned into an occasion for male pleasure, an object of male desire, a thing to be used; and any willful expression of her sexuality in the world unmediated by men or male values is punished. She is used as a slut or as a lady; but sexual intelligence cannot manifest in a human being whose predestined purpose is to be exploited through sex, by sex, in sex, as sex. Sexual intelligence constructs its own use: it begins with a whole body, not one that has already been cut into parts and fetishized; it begins with a self-respecting body, not one that is characterized by class as dirty, wanton, and slavish; it acts in the world, a world it enters on its own, with freedom as well as with passion. Sexual intelligence cannot live behind locked doors, any more than any other kind of intelligence can. Sexual intelligence cannot exist defensively, keeping out rape. Sexual intelligence cannot be decorative or pretty or coy or timid, nor can it live on a diet of contempt and abuse and hatred of its human form. Sexual intelligence is not animal, it is human; it has values; it sets limits that are meaningful to the whole person and personality, which must live in history and in the world. Women have found the development and exercise of sexual intelligence more difficult than any other kind: women have learned to read; women have acquired intellect; women have had so much creative intelligence that even despisal and isolation and punishment have not been able to squeeze it out of them; women have struggled for a moral intelligence that by its very existence repudiates moralism; but sexual intelligence is cut off at its roots, because the woman's body is not her own. The incestuous use of a girl murders it. The sexual intimidation or violation of a girl murders it. The enforced chastity of a girl murders it. The separation of girl from girl murders it. The turning over of a girl to a man as wife murders it. The selling of a girl into prostitution murders it. The use of a woman as a wife murders it. The use of a woman as a sexual thing murders it. The selling of a woman as a sexual commodity, not just on the street but in media, murders it. The economic value given to a woman's body, whether high or low, murders it. The keeping of a woman as a toy or ornament or domesticated cunt murders it. The need to be a mother so that one is not perceived as a whore murders it. The requirement that one bear babies murders it. The fact that the sexuality of the female is predetermined and that she is forced to be what men say she is murders sexual intelligence: there is nothing for her to discern or to construct; there is nothing for her to find out except what men will do to her and what she will have to pay if she resists or gives in. She lives in a private world—even a street corner is a private world of sexual usage, not a public world of honest confrontation; and her private world of sexual usage has narrow boundaries and a host of givens. No intelligence can function in a world that consists fundamentally of two rules that by their very nature prohibit the invention of values, identity, will, desire: be fucked, reproduce. Men have constructed female sexuality and in so doing have annihilated the chance for sexual intelligence in women. Sexual intelligence cannot live in the shallow, predestined sexuality men have counterfeited for women.

*

> I respect and honor the needy woman who, to procure food for herself and child, sells her body to some stranger for the necessary money; but for that legal virtue which sells itself for a lifetime for a home, with an abhorrence of the purchaser, and which at the same time says to the former, "I am holier than thou," I have only the supremest contempt.
>
> Victoria Woodhull, 1874

The argument between wives and whores is an old one; each one thinking that whatever she is, at least she is not the other. And there is no doubt that the wife envies the whore—or Marabel Morgan's ladies would not be wrapping themselves in Saran Wrap or wearing black boots with lacy neon nighties—and that the whore envies the domesticity of the wife—especially her physical sheltering and her relative sexual privacy. Both categories of women—specious as the categories finally turn out to be—need what men have to give: they need the material solicitude of men, not their cocks but their money. The cock is the inevitable precondition; without it there is no man, no money, no shelter, no protection. With it there may not be much, but women prefer men to silence, exile, to being pariahs, to being lone refugees, to being outcasts: defenseless. Victoria Woodhull—the first woman stockbroker on Wall Street, the first woman to run for president of the United States (1870), the publisher of the first translation of the *Communist*

Manifesto in the United States (1871), the first person ever arrested under the notoriously repressive Comstock Law (1872)*—crusaded against the material dependency of women on men because she knew that anyone who bartered her body bartered her human dignity. She hated the hypocrisy of married women; she hated the condition of prostitution, which degraded both wives and whores; and especially she hated the men who profited sexually and economically from marriage:

> It's a sharp trick played by men upon women, by which they acquire the legal right to debauch them without cost, and to make it unnecessary for them to visit professional prostitutes, whose sexual services can only be obtained for money. Now, isn't this true? Men know it is.[13]

Woodhull did not romanticize prostitution; she did not advocate it as freedom from marriage or freedom in itself or sexual freedom. Prostitution, she made clear, was for money, not for fun; it was survival, not pleasure. Woodhull's passion was sexual freedom, and she knew that the prostitution and rape of women were antithetical to it. She was a mass organizer, and the masses of women were married, sexually subordinated to men in marriage. At a time when feminists did not analyze sex directly or articulate ideas explicitly antagonistic to sex as practiced, Woodhull exposed marital rape and compulsory intercourse as the purpose, meaning, and method of marriage:

> Of all the horrid brutalities of this age, I know of none so horrid as those that are sanctioned and defended by marriage.

*Woodhull wrote an exposé of Henry Ward Beecher's adulterous affair with Elizabeth Tilton, the wife of his best friend. Beecher was an eminent minister. His hypocrisy was the main issue for Woodhull. The exposé was published by Woodhull in her own paper, *Woodhull and Clafin's Weekly*. She was arrested, as was her sister and co-publisher, Tennessee Clafin, for sending obscene literature through the mails. She was imprisoned for four weeks without trial.

> Night after night there are thousands of rapes committed, under cover of this accursed license; and millions—yes, I say it boldly, knowing whereof I speak—millions of poor, heart-broken, suffering wives are compelled to minister to the lechery of insatiable husbands, when every instinct of body and sentiment of soul revolts in loathing and disgust. All married persons know this is truth, although they may feign to shut their eyes and ears to the horrid thing, and pretend to believe it is not. The world has got to be startled from this pretense into realizing that there is nothing else now existing among pretendedly enlightened nations, except marriage, that invests men with the right to debauch women, sexually, against their wills. Yet marriage is held to be synonymous with morality! I say, eternal damnation sink such morality! [14]

Wives were the majority, whores the minority, prostitution the condition of each, rape the underbelly of prostitution. Woodhull's aggressive repudiation of the good woman/bad woman syndrome (with which women, then as now, were so very comfortable), her relentless attacks on the hypocrisy of the "good woman," and her rude refusal to call the sufferance of rape "virtue" had one purpose: to unite women in a common perception of their common condition. Selling themselves was women's desperate, necessary, unforgivable crime; not acknowledging the sale divided women and obscured how and why women were used sexually by men; marriage, women's only refuge, was the place of mass rape. Woodhull proclaimed herself a "Free Lover," by which she meant that she could not be bought, not in marriage, not in prostitution as commonly understood. In telling married women that they had indeed sold their sex for money, she was telling them that they had bartered away more than the prostitute ever could: all privacy, all economic independence, all legal individuality, every shred of control over their bodies in sex and in reproduction both.

Woodhull herself was widely regarded as a whore because she proclaimed herself sexually self-determining, sexually active; she spit in the face of the sexual double standard. Called a prostitute by a man at a public meeting, Woodhull responded: "A man questioning my virtue! Have I any right as a woman to answer him? I hurl the intention back in your face, sir, and stand boldly before you and this convention, and declare that I never had sexual intercourse with any man of whom I am ashamed to stand side by side before the world with the act. I am not ashamed of any act of my life. At the time it was the best I knew. Nor am I ashamed of any desire that has been gratified, nor of any passion alluded to. Every one of them are a part of my own soul's life, for which, thank God, I am not accountable to you."[15] Few feminists appreciated her (Elizabeth Cady Stanton was an exception, as usual) because she confronted women with her own sexual vitality, the political meaning of sex, the sexual and economic appropriation of women's bodies by men, the usurpation of female desire by men for the purposes of their own illegitimate power. She was direct and impassioned and she made women remember: that they had been raped. In focusing on the apparent and actual sexual worth of wives and whores, she made the basic claim of radical feminism: all freedom, including sexual freedom, begins with an absolute right to one's own body—physical self-possession. She knew too, in practical as well as political terms, that forced sex in marriage led to forced pregnancy in marriage: "I protest against this form of slavery, I *protest* against the custom which compels women to give the control of their maternal functions over to anybody."[16]

Victoria Woodhull exercised sexual intelligence in public discourse, ideas, and activism. She is one of the few women to have done so. This effort required all the other kinds of intelligence that distinguish humans from animals: literacy, intellect, creative intelligence, moral intelligence. Some consequences of sexual intelligence become clear in Woodhull's exercise of it: she made the women she addressed in person and in print face the sexual and economic system built on their bodies. She was one of the great philosophers of and agitators for sexual freedom—but not as men understand it, because she abhorred rape and prostitution, knew them when she saw them inside marriage or outside it, would not accept or condone the violence against women implicit in them.

"I make the claim boldly," she dared to say, "that from the very moment woman is emancipated from the necessity of yielding the control of her sexual organs to man to insure a home, food and clothing, the doom of sexual demoralization will be sealed."[17] Since women experienced sexual demoralization most abjectly in sexual intercourse, Woodhull did not shy away from the inevitable conclusion: "From that moment there will be no intercourse except such as is desired by women. It will be a complete revolution in sexual matters . . ."[18] Intercourse not willed and initiated by the woman was rape, in Woodhull's analysis. She anticipated current feminist critiques of intercourse—modest and rare as they are—by a century. As if to celebrate the centennial of Woodhull's repudiation of male-supremacist sexual intercourse, Robin Morgan in 1974 transformed Woodhull's insight into a firm principle: "*I claim that rape exists any time sexual intercourse occurs when it has not been initiated by the woman, out of her own genuine affection and desire.*"[19] This shocks, bewilders—who can imagine it, what can it mean? Now as then, there is one woman speaking, not a movement.*

Woodhull was not taken seriously as a thinker, writer, publisher, journalist, activist, pioneer, by those who followed her—not by the historians, teachers, intellectuals, revolutionaries, reformers; not by the lovers or rapists; not by the women. Had she been part of the cultural dialogue on sexual issues, the whole subsequent development of movements for sexual freedom would have been different in character: because she hated rape and prostitution and

*In a recent essay, novelist Alice Walker wrote: ". . . I submit that any sexual intercourse between a free man and a human being he owns or controls is rape." (See "Embracing the Dark and the Light," *Essence*, July 1982, p. 117.) This definition has the advantage of articulating the power that is the context for as well as the substance of the act.

understood them as violations of sexual freedom, which male liberationists did not. But then, this was why she was excluded: the men wanted the rape and prostitution. She threatened not only those sacred institutions but the male hallucinations that prettify those institutions: those happy visions of happy women, caged, domesticated or wanton, numb to rape, numb to being bought and sold. Her sexual intelligence was despised, then ignored, because of what it revealed: he who hates the truth hates the intelligence that brings it.

Sexual intelligence in women, that rarest intelligence in a male-supremacist world, is necessarily a revolutionary intelligence, the opposite of the pornographic (which simply reiterates the world as it is for women), the opposite of the will to be used, the opposite of masochism and self-hatred, the opposite of "good woman" and "bad woman" both. It is not in being a whore that a woman becomes an outlaw in this man's world; it is in the possession of herself, the ownership and effective control of her own body, her separateness and distinctness, the integrity of her body as hers, not his. Prostitution may be against the written law, but no prostitute has defied the prerogatives or power of men as a class through prostitution. No prostitute provides any model for freedom or action in a world of freedom that can be used with intelligence and integrity by a woman; the model exists to entice counterfeit female sexual revolutionaries, gullible liberated girls, and to serve the men who enjoy them. The prostitute is no honest woman. She manipulates as the wife manipulates. So too no honest woman can live in marriage: no woman honest in her will to be free. Marriage delivers her body to another to use: and there is no basis for self-respect in this carnal arrangement, however sanctified it may be by church and state.

Wife or whore: she is defined by what men want; sexual intelligence is stopped dead. Wife or whore: to paraphrase Thackeray, her heart is dead ("Her heart was dead long before her body. She had sold it to become Sir Pitt Crawley's wife. Mothers and daughters are making the same bargain every day in Vanity Fair"[20]). Wife or whore: both are fucked, bear children, resent, suffer, grow numb, want more. Wife or whore: both are denied a human life, forced to live a female one. Wife or whore: intelligence denied, annihilated, ridiculed, obliterated, primes her to surrender—to her female fate. Wife or whore: the two kinds of women whom men recognize, whom men let live. Wife or whore: battered, raped, prostituted; men desire her. Wife or whore: the whore comes in from the cold to become the wife if she can; the wife thrown out into the cold becomes the whore if she must. Is there a way out of the home that does not lead, inevitably and horribly, to the street corner? This is the question right-wing women face. This is the question all women face, but right-wing women know it. And in the transit—home to street, street to home—is there any place, reason, or chance for female intelligence that is not simply looking for the best buyer?

> So ladies, ye who prefer labor to prostitution, who pass days and nights in providing for the wants of your family, it is understood of course that you *are degraded;* a woman ought not to do anything; respect and honor belong to idleness.
>
> You, Victoria of England, Isabella of Spain—you command, therefore you *are radically degraded.*
>
> Jenny P. D'Hericourt, *A Woman's Philosophy of Woman; or Woman Affranchised*, 1864

The sex labor of women for the most part is private—in the bedroom—or secret—prostitutes may be seen, but how the johns use them may not. Ideally women do nothing; women simply are women. In truth women get used up in private or in secret being women. In the ideal conception of womanhood, women do not do work that can be seen: women only do hidden sex labor. In the real world, women who work for wages outside of sex are dangerously outside the female sphere; and women are denigrated for not being ideal—apparently idle, untouched by visible labor.

Behind the smoke screen of ideal idleness, there is always women's work. Women's work, first, is marriage. "In the morning I'm always nervous," Carolina de Jesus wrote. "I'm afraid of not getting money to buy food to eat. . . . Senhor Manuel showed up saying he wanted to marry me. But I don't want to . . . a man isn't going to like a woman who can't stop reading and gets out of bed to write and sleeps with paper and pencil under her pillow. That's why I prefer to live alone, for my ideals."[21]

The woman in marriage is often in marriage because her ideal is eating, not writing.

Women's work, second, is prostitution: sexual service outside of marriage for money. "I'd like so much to have the illusion that I had some freedom of choice," said J. in Kate Millett's *The Prostitution Papers*. "Maybe it's just an illusion, but I need to think I had some freedom. Yet then I realize how much was determined in the way I got into prostitution, how determined my life had been, how fucked over I was . . . So I believed I'd chosen it. What's most terrifying is to look back, to realize what I went through and that I endured it."[22]

The woman in prostitution learns, as Linda Lovelace said in *Ordeal*, "to settle for the smallest imaginable triumphs, the absence of pain or the momentary lessening of terror."[23] The woman in prostitution is often in prostitution because her ideal is physical survival—surviving the pimp, surviving poverty, having nowhere to go.

Women's social condition is built on a simple premise: women can be fucked and bear babies, therefore women must be fucked and bear babies. Sometimes, especially among the sophisticated, "penetrated" is substituted for "fucked": women can be penetrated, therefore women must be penetrated. This logic does not apply to men, whichever word is used: men can be fucked, therefore men must be fucked; men can be penetrated, therefore men must be penetrated. This logic applies only to women and sex. One does not say, for instance, women have delicate hands, therefore women must be surgeons. Or women have legs, therefore women must run, jump, climb. Or women have minds, therefore women must use them. One does learn, however, that women have sex organs that must be used by men, or the women are not women: they are somehow less or more, either of which is bad and thoroughly discouraged. Women are defined, valued, judged, in one way only: as women—that is, with sex organs that must be used. Other parts of the body do not signify, unless used in sex or as an indicator of sexual availability or desirability. Intelligence does not count. It has nothing to do with what a woman *is*.

Women are born into the labor pool specific to women: the labor is sex. Intelligence does not modify, reform, or revolutionize this basic fact of life for women.

Women are marked for marriage and prostitution by a wound between the legs, acknowledged as such when men show their strange terror of women. Intelligence neither creates nor destroys this wound; nor does it change the uses of the wound, the woman, the sex.

Women's work is done below the waist; intelligence is higher. Women are lower; men are higher. It is a simple, dull scheme; but women's sex organs in and of themselves are apparently appalling enough to justify the scheme, make it self-evidently true.

The natural intelligence of women, however expanded by what women manage to learn despite their low status, manifests in surviving: enduring, marking time, bearing pain, becoming numb, absorbing loss—especially loss of self. Women survive men's use of them—marriage, prostitution, rape; women's intelligence expresses itself in finding ways to endure and find meaning in the unendurable, to endure being used because of one's sex. "Sex with men, how can I say, lacks the personal,"[24] wrote Maryse Holder in *Give Sorrow Words*.

Some women want to work: not sex labor; real work; work that men, those real humans, do for a living wage. They want an honest wage for honest work. One of the prostitutes Kate Millett interviewed made $800 a week in her prime. "With a Ph.D. and after ten years' experience in teaching," Millet wrote, "I was permitted to make only $60 a week."[25]

Women's work that is not marriage or prostitution is mostly segregated, always underpaid, stagnant, sex-stereotyped. In the United States in 1981 women earned 56 to 59 percent of what men earned. Women are paid significantly less than men for doing comparable work. It is not easy to find comparable work. The consequences of this inequity—however the percentages read in any given year, in any given country—are not new for women. Unable to sell sex-neutral labor for a living wage, women must sell sex. "To subordinate women in a social order in which she must *work in order to live*," Jenny D'Hericourt wrote French socialist Joseph Proudhon in the mid-1800s, "is to *desire prostitution;* for disdain of the producer extends to the value of the product; . . . The woman who cannot live by working, can only do so by prostituting herself; the equal of man or a courtesan, such is the alternative."[26] Proudhon's egalitarian vision could not be stretched to include women. He wrote D'Hericourt:

> . . . I do not admit that, whatever reparation may be due to woman, of joint thirds with her husband (or father) and her children, the most rigorous justice can ever make her the EQUAL of man; . . . neither do I admit that this inferiority of the female sex constitutes for it either servitude, or humiliation, or a diminution of dignity, liberty, or happiness. I maintain that the contrary is true.[27]

D'Hericourt's argument constructs the world of women: women must work for fair wages in nonsexual labor or they must sell themselves to men; the disdain of men for women makes the work of women worth less simply because women do it; the devaluation of women's work is predetermined by the devaluation of women as a sex class; women end up having to sell themselves because men will not buy labor from them that is not sex labor at wages that will enable women to divest themselves of sex as a form of labor.

Proudhon's answer constructs the world of men: in the best of all possible worlds—acknowledging that some economic discrimination against women has taken place—no justice on earth can make women equal to men because women are inferior to men: this inferiority does not humiliate or degrade women; women find happiness, dignity, and liberty in this inequality precisely because they are women—that is the nature of women; women are being treated justly and are free when they are treated as women—that is, as the natural inferiors of men.

The brave new world Proudhon wanted was, for women, the same old world women already knew.

D'Hericourt recognized what Victoria Woodhull would not: "disdain of the producer extends to the value of the product." Work for wages outside sex labor would not effectively free women from the stigma of being female because the stigma precedes the woman and predetermines the undervaluing of her work.

This means that right-wing women are correct when they say that they are worth more in the home than outside it. In the home their value is recognized and in the workplace it is not. In marriage, sex labor is rewarded: the woman is generally "given" more than she herself could earn at a job. In the marketplace, women are exploited as cheap labor. The argument that work outside the home makes women sexually and economically independent of men is simply untrue. Women are paid too little. And right-wing women know it.

Feminists know that if women are paid equal wages for equal work, women will gain sexual as well as economic independence. But feminists have refused to face the fact that in a woman-hating social system, women will never be paid equal wages. Men in all their institutions of power are sustained by the sex labor and sexual subordination of women. The sex labor of women must be maintained; and systematic low wages for sex-neutral work effectively force women to sell sex to survive. The economic system that pays women lower wages than it pays men actually punishes women for working outside marriage or prostitution, since women work hard for low wages and still must sell sex. The economic system that punishes women for working outside the bedroom by paying low wages contributes significantly to women's perception that the sexual serving of men is a necessary part of any woman's life: or how else could she live? Feminists appear to think that equal pay for equal work is a simple reform, whereas it is no reform at all; it is revolution. Feminists have refused to face the fact that equal pay for equal work is impossible as long as men rule women, and right-wing women have refused to forget it. Devaluation of women's labor outside the home pushes women back into the home and encourages women to support a system in which, as she sees it, he is paid for both of them—her share of his wage being more than she could earn herself.

In the workplace, sexual harassment fixes the low status of women irreversibly. Women are sex; even filing or typing, women are sex. The debilitating, insidious violence of sexual harassment is pervasive in the workplace. It is part of nearly every working environment. Women shuffle; women placate; women submit; women leave; the rare, brave women fight and are tied up in the courts, often without jobs, for years. There is also rape in the workplace.

Where is the place for intelligence—for literacy, intellect, creativity, moral discernment? Where in this world in which women live, circumscribed by the uses to which men put women's sexual organs, is the cultivation of skills, the cultivation of gifts, the cultivation of dreams, the cultivation of ambition? Of what use is human intelligence to a woman?

"Of course," wrote Virginia Woolf, "the learned women were very ugly; but then they were very poor. She would like to feed

Chuffy for a term on Lucy's rations and see what he said then about Henry the Eighth."[28]

"No, it would not do the slightest good if he read my manuscript . . . ," wrote Ellen Glasgow in her memoir. "'The best advice I can give you,' he said, with charming candor, 'is to stop writing, and go back to the South and have some babies.' And I think, though I may have heard this ripe wisdom from other men, probably from many, that he added: 'The greatest woman is not the woman who has written the finest book, but the woman who has had the finest babies.' That might be true. I did not stay to dispute it. However, it was true also that I wanted to write books, and not ever had I felt the faintest wish to have babies."[29]

Woodhull thought that freedom from sexual coercion would come with work in the marketplace. She was wrong; the marketplace became, as men would have it, another place for sexual intimidation, another arena of danger to women burdened already with too many such arenas. Woolf put her faith in education and art. She too was wrong. Men erase; misogyny distorts; the intelligence of women is still both punished and despised.

Right-wing women have surveyed the world: they find it a dangerous place. They see that work subjects them to more danger from more men; it increases the risk of sexual exploitation. They see that creativity and originality in their kind are ridiculed; they see women thrown out of the circle of male civilization for having ideas, plans, visions, ambitions. They see that traditional marriage means selling to one man, not hundreds: the better deal. They see that the streets are cold, and that the women on them are tired, sick, and bruised. They see that the money they can earn will not make them independent of men and that they will still have to play the sex games of their kind: at home and at work too. They see no way to make their bodies authentically their own and to survive in the world of men. They know too that the Left has nothing better to offer: leftist men also want wives and whores; leftist men value whores too much and wives too little. Right-wing women are not wrong. They fear that the Left, in stressing impersonal sex and promiscuity as values, will make them more vulnerable to male sexual aggression, and that they will be despised for not liking it. They are not wrong. Right-wing women see that within the system in which they live they cannot make their bodies their own, but they can agree to privatized male ownership: keep it one-on-one, as it were. They know that they are valued for their sex—their sex organs and their reproductive capacity—and so they try to up their value: through cooperation, manipulation, conformity; through displays of affection or attempts at friendship; through submission and obedience; and especially through the use of euphemism—"femininity," "total woman," "good," "maternal instinct," "motherly love." Their desperation is quiet; they hide their bruises of body and heart; they dress carefully and have good manners; they suffer, they love God, they follow the rules. They see that intelligence displayed in a woman is a flaw, that intelligence realized in a woman is a crime. They see the world they live in and they are not wrong. They use sex and babies to stay valuable because they need a home, food, clothing. They use the traditional intelligence of the female—animal, not human: they do what they have to to survive.

3

Abortion

> I have never regretted the abortion. I *have* regretted both my marriage and having children.
>
> A witness on forced motherhood, International Tribunal on Crimes Against Women,* March 1976

Before the 1973 Supreme Court decision legalizing abortion in the United States, abortion was a crime. Some abortions were medically licensed, but they were a minute percentage of the abortions actually undergone by women. This meant that there were no records of the illegal abortions performed (each abortion was a crime, each abortion was clandestine), no medical histories or records, no statistics. Information on illegal abortions came from these sources: (1) the testimonies of women who had had such abortions and survived; (2) the physical evidence of the botched abortions, evidence that showed up in hospital emergency rooms all over the country every single day—perforated uteruses, infections including gangrene, severe hemorrhaging, incomplete abortions (in which fetal tissue is left in the womb, always fatal if not removed); (3) the physical evidence of the dead bodies (for instance, nearly one half

*See testimony on forced motherhood, forced sterilization, and forced sex in *Crimes Against Women: Proceedings of the International Tribunal*, ed. Diana E. H. Russell and Nicole Van de Ven (Millbrae, Calif.: Les Femmes, 1976).

of the maternal deaths in New York State resulted from illegal abortions); (4) the anecdotal reminiscences of doctors who were asked for "help" by desperate women. These sources provide a profile of the average woman who wanted and got an illegal abortion. Indisputably, she was married and had children: ". . . it has been repeatedly demonstrated that most criminal abortions today are obtained by married women with children,"[1] wrote Jerome E. Bates and Edward S. Zawadzki in *Criminal Abortion*, published in 1964. An estimated two thirds of the women who got criminal abortions were married.* This means that up to two thirds of the botched abortions were done on married women; up to two thirds of the dead were married women; perhaps two thirds of the survivors are married women. This means that most of the women who risked death or maiming so as not to bear a child were married—perhaps one million married women each year. They were not shameless sluts, unless all women by definition are. They were not immoral in traditional terms—though, even then, they were thought of as promiscuous and single. Nevertheless, they were not women from the streets, but women from homes; they were not daughters in the homes of fathers, but wives in the homes of husbands. They were, quite simply, the good and respectable women of Amerika. The absolute equation of abortion with sexual promiscuity is a bizarre distortion of the real history of women and abortion—too distorted to be acceptable even in the United States, where historical memory

---

*Bates and Zawadzki, in their 1964 study of 111 convicted abortionists, place the percentage of married women at 67.6 percent. Other studies range from the conservative 49.6 percent (based on the records of two abortionists in a single year, 1948; arguably, the figure is low compared to other findings and estimates because women lied about marital status when committing the criminal act of getting an abortion) to 75 percent (the sample being composed of women in charity hospitals from botched abortions). Bates and Zawadzki, who discuss both the 49.6 percent figure and the 75 percent figure, conclude that they "could find no authority or piece of research purporting to demonstrate that the majority of women undergoing abortion today are unmarried" *(Criminal Abortion*, p. 44).

reaches back one decade. Abortion has been legalized just under one decade.* The facts should not be obliterated yet. Millions of respectable, God-fearing, married women have had illegal abortions. They thank their God that they survived; and they keep quiet.

Their reasons for keeping quiet are women's reasons. Because they are women, their sexuality or even perceptions of it can discredit or hurt or destroy them—inexplicably shame them; provoke rage, rape, and ridicule in men. Dissociation from other women is always the safest course. They are not sluttish, but other women who have had abortions probably are. They tried not to get pregnant (birth control being illegal in many parts of the country before 1973), but other women who had abortions probably did not. They love their children, but other women who have had abortions may well be the cold mothers, the cruel mothers, the vicious women. They are individuals of worth and good morals who had compelling reasons for aborting, but the other women who had abortions must have done something wrong, were wrong, are somehow indistinct (not emerged from the primal female slime as individuals), were sex not persons. In keeping the secret they cut themselves off from other women to escape the shame of other women, the shame of being the same as other women, the shame of being female. They are ashamed of having had this bloody experience, of having this female body that gets torn into again and again and bleeds and can die from the tearing and the bleeding, the pain and the mess, of having this body that was violated again, this time by abortion. Admitting to an illegal abortion is like admitting to having been raped: whoever you tell can see you, undress you, spread your legs, see the thing go in, see the blood, watch the pain, almost touch the fear, almost taste the desperation. The woman

*As this book is published, abortion has been legalized not quite one decade, but never without restrictions permitted by the Supreme Court and imposed by state legislatures and often with unconstitutional restrictions imposed by state or local governments until overturned by federal courts (paternal and parental consent requirements, for instance).

who admits to having had an illegal abortion allows whoever hears her to picture her—her as an individual in that wretched body—in unbearable vulnerability, as close to being punished purely for being female as anyone ever comes. It is the picture of a woman being tortured for having had sex.

There is the fear of having murdered: not someone, not real murder; but of having done something hauntingly wrong. She has learned (*learned* is a poor word for what has happened to her) that every life is more valuable than her own; her life gets value through motherhood, a kind of benign contamination. She has been having children in her mind, and getting her value through them, since she herself was a baby. Little girls believe that dolls are real babies. Little girls put dolls to sleep, feed them, bathe them, diaper them, nurse them through illnesses, teach them how to walk and how to talk and how to dress—love them. Abortion turns a woman into a murderer all right: she kills that child pregnant in her since her own childhood; she kills her allegiance to Motherhood First. This is a crime. She is guilty: of not wanting a baby.

There is the fear of having murdered because so many men believe so passionately that she has. To many men, each aborted pregnancy is the killing of a son—and he is the son killed. His mother would have killed him if she had had the choice. These men have a peculiarly retroactive and abstract sense of murder: if she had had a choice, *I* would not have been born—which is murder. The male ego, which refuses to believe in its own death, now pushes backward, before birth. *I* was once a fertilized egg; therefore to abort a fertilized egg is to kill *me*. Women keep abortions secret because they are afraid of the hysteria of men confronted with what they regard as the specter of their own extinction. If you had your way, men say to feminists, my mother would have aborted *me*. Killed *me*. ". . . I was born out of wedlock (and against the advice that my mother received from her doctor)," Jesse Jackson writes in fervent opposition to abortion, "and therefore abortion is a personal issue for me."[2] The woman's responsibility to the fertilized egg is imaginatively and with great conviction construed to be her relation to the adult male. At the very least, she must not murder him; nor should she outrage his existence by an assertion of her separateness from him, her distinctness, her importance as a person independent of him. The adult male's identification with the fertilized egg as being fully himself can even be conceptualized in terms of power: his rightful power over an impersonal female (all females being the same in terms of function). "The *power* I had as *one* cell to affect my environment I shall never have again,"[3] R. D. Laing laments in an androcentric meditation on prebirth ego. "My environment" is a woman; the adult male, even as a fertilized egg, one cell, has the right of occupation with respect to her—he has the right to be inside her and the rightful power to change her body for his sake. This relation to gestation is specifically male. Women do not think of themselves in utero when they think either of being pregnant or of aborting; men think of pregnancy and abortion primarily in terms of themselves, including what happened or might have happened to them back in the womb when, as one cell, they were themselves.

Women keep quiet about abortions they have had, illegal abortions, because they are humiliated by the memory of those abortions; they are humiliated by the memory of their desperation, the panic, finding the money, finding the abortionist, the dirt, the danger, the secrecy. Women are humiliated when they remember asking for help, begging for help, when they remember those who turned away, left them out in the cold. Women are humiliated by the memory of the fear. Women are humiliated by the memory of the physical intrusion, the penetration, the pain, the violation; countless women were sexually assaulted by the abortionist before or after the abortion; they hate remembering. Women are humiliated because they hated themselves, their sex, their female bodies, they hated being female. Women hate remembering illegal abortions because they almost died, they could have died, they wanted to die, they hoped they would not die, they made promises to God begging him not to let them die, they were afraid of dying before and during and after; they have never again been so afraid of death or so alone; they had never before been so afraid of death or so alone. And women hate remembering illegal abortions because their husbands experienced none of this: which no woman forgives.

Women also keep quiet about illegal abortions precisely because they had married sex: their husbands mounted them, fucked them, impregnated them; their husbands determined the time and the place and the act; desire, pleasure, or orgasm were not necessarily experienced by the women, yet the women ended up on the butcher's block. The abortionist finished the job the husband had started. No one wants to remember this.

Women also keep quiet about abortions they have had because they wanted the child, but the man did not; because they wanted other children and could not have them; because they never regretted the abortion and did regret subsequent children; because they had more than one abortion, which, like more than one rape, fixes the woman's guilt. Women keep quiet about abortions because abortion inside marriage is selfish, ruthless, marks the woman as heartless, loveless—yet she did it anyway. Women also keep quiet about abortions they have had, illegal abortions, because the woman who has had one, or tried to induce one in herself, is never really trusted again: if she will do that to herself—hurt herself, tear up her own insides rather than have a child—she must be the frenzied female, the female gone mad, the lunatic female, the female in rebellion against her own body and therefore against man and God, the female who is most feared and abhorred, the Medea underneath the devoted wife and mother, the wild woman, the woman enraged with the sorrow between her legs, the woman grief-stricken by the way men use her uterus, the woman who has finally refused to be forced and so she must be punished by the pain and the blood, the tearing and the terror.

The law gives a married woman to her husband to be fucked at will, his will; the law forced the woman to bear any child that might result. Illegal abortion was a desperate, dangerous, last-ditch, secret, awful way of saying no. It is no wonder that so many respectable, married, God-fearing women hate abortion.

*

> An estimated 20 million illegal abortions are performed in the world each year and are a leading cause of death among women of child-bearing age, a study issued today said.
>
> The report by the Population Crisis Committee also said that another 20 million abortions were self-induced annually and that the number was growing.
>
> *The New York Times*, April 30, 1979

Women cannot be responsible for pregnancy, in the sense of acting to prevent it, because women do not control when, where, how, and on what terms they have intercourse. Intercourse is forced on women, both as a normal part of marriage and as the primary sex act in virtually any sexual encounter with a man. No woman needs intercourse; few women escape it.

In marriage a man has the sexual right to his wife: he can fuck her at will by right of law. The law articulates and defends this right. The state articulates and defends this right. This means that the state defines the intimate uses of a woman's body in marriage; so that a man acts with the protection of the state when he fucks his wife, regardless of the degree of force surrounding or intrinsic to the act. In the United States only five states have entirely abrogated the so-called marital rape exemption—the legal proviso that a man cannot be criminally charged for raping his wife because rape by definition cannot exist in the context of marriage, since marriage licenses the use of a woman's body by her husband against her will. Nearly three times that many states have *extended* the husband's right to forced intercourse to cohabiting men or, in some cases, even to so-called voluntary social companions. But even where marital rape is illegal, the husband has at his disposal the ordinary means of sexual coercion, including threat of physical violence, punitive economic measures, sexual or verbal humiliation in private or in public, violence against inanimate objects, and threats against children. In other words, eliminating the legal sanctioning of rape does not in itself eliminate sexual coercion in marriage; but the continued legal sanctioning of rape underlines the coercive character and purpose of marriage. Marriage law is irrefutable proof that women are not equal to men. No person can enter into an agreement in which her body is given to another and remain or become or act as or effectually be his equal.

The law takes the form it does with divine sanction: civil law reiterates religious dogma. The law enforces a relationship between men and women that has its origins in so-called divine law; the law enforces the divinely ordained subordination of women through its regulation of sex in marriage. The law is an instrument of religion, and it is precisely as an instrument of religion that law regulating marriage gets its special character: laws against assault and battery pale in importance when compared with the divine law giving a man authority over his wife's body. The man's authority over his wife's body is willed by God—even if the same relationship outside of marriage and without reference to gender would be described as slavery or torture. The laws of God are upheld by the laws of this republic, this proud secular democracy. The marriage laws fundamentally violate the civil rights of women as a class by forcing all married women to conform to a religious view of women's sexual function. These same laws violate the civil rights of women by compelling women to serve their husbands sexually whether they will it or not and by defining women as a class in terms of a sexual function that must be fulfilled.*

Women feel the pressure to submit in a myriad of ways, none of which have to do with marital law as such. The woman is likely to encounter marital law when she has been abused and seeks to act in her own behalf as if she had a right to the disposition of her own body. The point is that the law sets the standard for the disposition of her body: it belongs to her husband, not to her.

The good wife submits; the bad wife can be forced to submit. All women are supposed to submit.

One of the consequences of submission, whether conforming or forced, is pregnancy.

Women are required to submit to intercourse, and women may then be required to submit to the pregnancy.

Women are required to submit to the man, and women may then be required to submit to the fetus.

Since the law sets the standard for the control, use of, function of, purpose of, the wife's body, and since the law supports the right of the man to use force against his wife in order to have sex, women live in a context of forced sex. This is true outside the realm of subjective interpretation. If it were not true, the law would not be formulated to sanction the husband's forced penetra-

---

*The American Civil Liberties Union has a handbook on women's rights. In that handbook, laws against prostitution are discussed in terms of the right of women to have sex: "the central focus of all these laws is to punish *sexual activity*" (*The Rights of Women*, Susan C. Ross [New York: Avon, 1973], p. 176); equal right to sexual activity is seen to be the civil liberties issue of paramount importance and laws against prostitution are simply a cover for denying women the right to sexual activity. This is not a narrow discussion of laws on prostitution and their sex-discriminatory language or enforcement. It is a position on what rights are for women, what freedom is. There is no mention of marital rape or of the marital rape exemption as violations of civil liberties and no discussion whatsoever of sexual coercion in marriage sanctioned by law in letter and in practice as a violation of civil liberties. The discussion of rape also makes no reference to marital rape or the role of law in upholding it.

tion of his wife. Marriage is the common state of adult women; women live in a system in which sex is forced on them; and the sex is intercourse. Women, it is said, have a bad attitude toward sex. Women, it is not said often enough, have a long-lived resentment against forced sex and a longing for freedom, which is often expressed as an aversion to sex. It is a fact for women that they must come to terms with forced sex over and over in the course of a normal life.

Forced sex, usually intercourse, is a central issue in any woman's life. She must like it or control it or manipulate it or resist it or avoid it; she must develop a relationship to it, to the male insistence on intercourse, to the male insistence on her sexual function in relation to him. She will be measured and judged by the nature and quality of her relationship to intercourse. Her character will be assessed in terms of her relationship to intercourse, as men evaluate that relationship. All the possibilities of her body will be reduced to expressing her relationship to intercourse. Every sign on her body, every symbol—clothes, posture, hair, ornament—will have to signal her acceptance of his sex act and the nature of her relationship to it. His sex act, intercourse, explicitly announces his power over her: his possession of her interior; his right to violate her boundaries. His state promotes and protects his sex act. If she were not a woman, this intrusion by the state would be recognized as state coercion, or force. The act itself and the state that protects it call on force to exercise illegitimate power; and intercourse cannot be analyzed outside this system of force. But the force is hidden and denied by a barrage of propaganda, from pornography to so-called women's magazines, that seek to persuade that accommodation is pleasure, or that accommodation is femininity, or that accommodation is freedom, or that accommodation is a strategic means to some degree of self-determination.

The propaganda for femininity (femininity being the apparent acceptance of sex on male terms with goodwill and demonstrable good faith, in the form of ritualized obsequiousness) is produced according to the felt need of men to have intercourse. In a time of feminist resistance, such propaganda increases in bulk geometrically. The propaganda stresses that intercourse can give a woman pleasure if she does it right: especially if she has the right attitude toward it and toward the man. The right attitude is to want it. The right attitude is to desire men *because* they engage in phallic penetration. The right attitude is to want intercourse because men want it. The right attitude is not to be selfish: especially about orgasm. This prohibits a sexuality for women outside the boundaries of male dominance. This makes any woman-centered sexuality impossible. What it does make possible is a woman's continued existence within a system in which men control the valuation of her existence as an individual. This valuation is based on her sexual conformity within a sexual system based on his right to possess her. Women are brought up to conform: all the rules of femininity—dress, behavior, attitude—essentially break the spirit. Women are trained to need men, not sexually but metaphysically. Women are brought up to be the void that needs filling, the absence that needs presence. Women are brought up to fear men and to know that they must please men and to understand that they cannot survive without the help of men richer and stronger than they can be themselves, on their own. Women are brought up to submit to intercourse—and here the strategy is shrewd—by being kept ignorant of it. The rules are taught, but the act is hidden. Girls are taught "love," not "fuck." Little girls look between their legs to see if "the hole" is there, get scared thinking about what "the hole" is for; no one tells them either. Women use their bodies to attract men; and most women, like the little girls they were, are astonished by the brutality of the fuck. The importance of this ignorance about intercourse cannot be overstated: it is as if no girl would grow up, or accept the hundred million lessons on how to be a girl, or want boys to like her, if she knew what she was for. The propaganda for femininity assumes that the girl still lives inside the woman; that the lessons of femininity must be taught and retaught without letup; that the woman left to herself would repudiate the male use of her body, simply not accept it. The propaganda for femininity teaches women over and over, endlessly, that they must like intercourse; and the lesson must be taught over and over, endlessly, because intercourse does not express their own sexuality in general and the male use of women rarely has anything to do with the woman as an individual. The sexuality they are supposed to like does not recognize, let alone honor, their individuality in any meaningful way. The sexuality they must learn to like is not concerned with desire toward them as distinct personalities—at best they are "types"; nor is it concerned with their own desire toward others.

Despite the propaganda, the mountains of it, intercourse requires force; force is still essential to make women have intercourse—at least in a systematic, sustained way. Despite every single platitude about love, women and men, passion, femininity, intercourse as health or pleasure or biological necessity, it is forced sex that keeps intercourse central and it is forced sex that keeps women in sexual relation to men. If the force were not essential, the force would not be endemic. If the force were not essential, the law would not sanction it. If the force were not essential, the force itself would not be defined as intrinsically "sexy," as if in practicing force sex itself is perpetuated.

The first kind of force is physical violence: endemic in rape, battery, assault.

The second kind of force is the power differential between male and female that intrinsically makes any sex act an act of force: for instance, the sexual abuse of girls in families.

The third kind of force is economic: keeping women poor to keep women sexually accessible and sexually compliant.

The fourth kind of force is cultural on a broad scale: woman-hating propaganda that makes women legitimate and desirable sexual targets; woman-hating laws that either sanction or in their actual application permit sexual abuse of women; woman-hating practices of verbal harassment backed by the threat of physical violence on the streets or in the workplace; woman-hating textbooks used to teach doctors, lawyers, and other professionals misogyny as a central element of the practice of their profession; woman-hating art that romanticizes sexual assault, stylizes and celebrates sexual violence; woman-hating entertainment that makes women as a class ridiculous, stupid, despicable, and the sexual property of all men.

Because women are exploited as a sex class for sex, it is impossible to talk about women's sexuality outside the context of forced sex or, at the least, without reference to forced sex; and yet, to keep forced sex going and invisible simultaneously, it is discussed every other way, all the time.

The force itself is intrinsically "sexy," romanticized, described as a measure of the desire of an individual man for an individual woman. Force, duress, subterfuge, threat—all add "sex" to the sex act by intensifying the femininity of the woman, her status as a creature of forced sex.

It is through intercourse in particular that men express and maintain their power and dominance over women. The right of men to women's bodies for the purpose of intercourse remains the heart, soul, and balls of male supremacy: this is true whatever style of advocacy is used, Right or Left, to justify coital access.

Every woman—no matter what her sexual orientation, personal sexual likes or dislikes, personal history, political ideology—lives inside this system of forced sex. This is true even if she has never personally experienced any sexual coercion, or if she personally likes intercourse as a form of intimacy, or if she as an individual has experiences of intercourse that transcend, in her opinion, the dicta of gender and the institutions of force. This is true even if—for her—the force is eroticized, essential, central, sacred, meaningful, sublime. This is true even if—for her—she repudiates intercourse and forbids it: if she subjectively lives outside the laws of gravity, obviously the laws of gravity will intrude. Every woman is surrounded by this system of forced sex and is encapsulated by it. It acts on her, shapes her, defines her boundaries and her possibilities, tames her, domesticates her, determines the quality and nature of her privacy: it modifies her. She functions within it and with constant reference to it. This same system that she is inside is inside her—metaphorically and literally delivered into her by intercourse, especially forced intercourse, especially deep thrusting. Intercourse violates the boundaries of her body, which is why intercourse is so often referred to as violation. Intercourse as a sex act does not correlate with anything but male power: its frequency and centrality have nothing to do with reproduction, which does not require that intercourse be the central sexual act either in society at large or in any given sexual relationship or encounter; its frequency and centrality have nothing to do with sexual pleasure for the female or the male, in that pleasure does not prohibit intercourse but neither does pleasure demand it. Intercourse is synonymous with sex because intercourse is the most systematic expression of male power over women's bodies, both concrete and emblematic, and as such it is upheld as a male right by law (divine and secular), custom, practice, culture, and force. Because intercourse so consistently expresses illegitimate power, unjust power, wrongful power, it is intrinsically an expression of the female's subordinate status, sometimes a celebration of that status. The shame that women feel on being fucked and simultaneously experiencing pleasure in being possessed is the shame of having acknowledged, physically and emotionally, the extent to which one has internalized and eroticized the subordination. It is a shame that has in it the kernel of resistance. The woman who says no to her husband, whatever her reasons, also says no to the state, no to God, no to the power of men over her, that power being both personal and institutional. Intercourse is forced on the woman by a man, his state, his God, and through intercourse an individual is made into a woman: a woman is made. Whether a woman likes or does not like, desires or does not desire, to be made a woman does not change the meaning of the act. "There are many scarcely nubile girls," wrote Colette, "who dream of becoming the show, the plaything, the licentious masterpiece of some middle-aged man. It is an ugly dream that is punished by its fulfilment, a morbid thing, akin to the neuroses of puberty, the habit of eating chalk and coal, of drinking mouthwash, of reading dirty books and sticking pins into the palm of the hand."[4]

Forced intercourse in marriage—that is, the right to intercourse supported by the state in behalf of the husband—provides the context for both rape as commonly understood and incestuous rape. Marital sex and rape are opposite and opposing forms of sexual expression only when women are viewed as sexual property: when rape is seen as the theft of one man's property by another man. As soon as the woman as a human being becomes the central figure in a rape, that is, as soon as she is recognized as a human victim of an inhumane act, forced sex must be recognized as such, whatever the relation of the man to his victim. But if forced sex is sanctioned and protected in marriage, and indeed provides an empirical definition of what women are for, how then does one distinguish so-called consensual, normal sex (intercourse) from rape? There is no context that is both normal and protected in which the will of the woman is recognized as the essential precondition for sex. It has been the business of the state to regulate male use of sexual force against women, not to prohibit it. The state may allow a man to force his wife but not his daughter, or his wife but not his neighbor's wife. Rather than prohibiting the use of force against women per se, a male-supremacist state establishes a relationship between sexual force and normalcy: in marriage, a woman has no right to refuse her husband intercourse. Limits to the force men can use have been negotiated by men with one another in their own interests—and are renegotiated in every rape or incest case in which the man is held blameless because force is seen as intrinsically and properly sexual (that is, normal) when used to effect female sexual compliance. The society's opposition to rape is fake because the society's commitment to forced sex is real: marriage defines the normal uses to which women should be put, and marriage institutionalizes forced intercourse. Consent then logically becomes mere passive acquiescence; and passive compliance does become the standard of female participation in intercourse. Because passive acquiescence is the standard in normal intercourse, it becomes proof of consent in rape. Because force is sanctioned to effect intercourse in marriage, it becomes common sexual practice, so that its use in sex does not signify, prove, or even—especially to men—suggest rape. Forced intercourse in marriage, being both normal and state-sanctioned, provides the basis for the wider practice of forced sex, tacitly accepted most of the time. Forced intercourse in marriage as the norm sanctioned by the state makes it virtually impossible to identify (male) force or (female) consent; to say what they are so as to be able to recognize them in discrete instances. The state can and does make distinctions by category—for instance, sex with little girls is off limits—but no finer kind of distinction can be made because that would require a repudiation of force as a part of normal sex. Since the nearly universal acceptance of forced intercourse in marriage is a kind of universal callousness—an agreement as to the disposition of married women's bodies, thereby annihilating any conception of their civil or sexual rights or any sensitivity to force in sex as a violation of those women's rights—it is easy to extend the callous acceptance of men's civilly guaranteed right to use force to get sex to broader categories of women, also to girls, and this has happened. There is the belief that men use force because they are men. There is the belief that women like force and respond to it sexually. There is the belief that force is intrinsically sexy. There is the conceit that the married woman is the most protected of all women: if force is right with her, with whom can it be wrong? if a man does to another woman what he does to his wife, it may be adultery but how can it be rape when in fact it is simply—from his point of view—plain old sex? There is the definition of when a girl becomes a woman: a girl may be considered adult because she has menstruated (at the age of ten, for instance) or because she has a so-called provocative quality, which means that a man wants to fuck her and that therefore she is presumed to be a woman and to have adult knowledge of what sex is and what a woman is. There is the definition of the female in terms of her function, which is to be fucked; so it may be unfortunate that she is fucked too early, but once fucked she has fulfilled a preordained function as a woman and therefore is a woman and therefore can legitimately be fucked.

With respect to pregnancy, if a woman can be forced to bear a child conceived by force in marriage, there is no logic in differentiating pregnancy as a result of rape or incestuous rape. Force is the norm; pregnancy is the result; the woman has no claim to a respected identity not predicated on forced intercourse—that is, at best her dignity inheres in being a wife, subject to forced intercourse and therefore to forced pregnancy; why would any woman's body be entitled to more respect than the married woman's? Rape, rarely credited as such by men unless the display of force has been brutal almost beyond imagining, is in fact an exaggerated expression of a fully accepted sexual relation between men and women; and incestuous rape adds a new element of exaggeration, but the essential sexual relation—the relation of force to female—remains the same. Therefore, men—especially men responsible for maintaining the right and role of sexual force in marriage (lawmakers and theologians)—cannot consider pregnancy resulting from rape or incestuous rape as *significantly* different from pregnancy that results from the normal use of a married woman; and in their frame of reference regarding intercourse, it is not. The woman's function is to be fucked—and if she is pregnant, then she was fucked, no matter what the circumstance or the means. Being fucked did not violate her integrity as a woman because being fucked *is* her integrity as a woman. Force is intrinsic to fucking, and the state cannot allow women to determine when they have been raped (forced), because rape (force) in marriage is supported by the state. The willingness to consider rape or incestuous rape exceptions at all comes from the male recognition that a man might not want to accept the offspring of another man's rape as his own; a father may not want to be both father and grandfather to the daughter of his daughter. These exceptions, to the extent that they are or will be honored in legislation forbidding abortion, exist to protect men. Henry Hyde, author of the Hyde Amendment forbidding Medicaid money to poor women for abortions and opponent of all abortion under all circumstances without exception for rape, was asked by a television interviewer if he would insist that his daughter carry a pregnancy to term if she were pregnant as the result of rape. Yes, he answered solemnly. But the question he should have been asked was this one: suppose his wife were pregnant as the result of rape? This would impinge not on his sentimentality, but on his day-to-day right of sexual possession; he would have to live with the rape and with the carnal reality of the rape and with the pregnancy resulting from the rape and with the offspring or the damaged woman who would have to bear it and then give it up. Regardless of his answer to the hypothetical question, only the male sense of what is at stake for him in actually having to accept a pregnancy caused by rape or incestuous rape in his own life as a husband to the woman or girl involved could make the rape or the woman raped real. Abortion can protect men, and can be tolerated when it demonstrably does. In terms of the woman used, herself alone, she is her function; she has been used in accordance with her function; there is no reason to let her off the hook just because she was forced by a man not her husband.

Norman Mailer remarked during the sixties that the problem with the sexual revolution was that it had gotten into the hands of the wrong people. He was right. It was in the hands of men.

The pop idea was that fucking was good, so good that the more there was of it, the better. The pop idea was that people should fuck whom they wanted: translated for the girls, this meant that girls should want to be fucked—as close to all the time as was humanly possible. For women, alas, all the time is humanly possible with enough changes of partners. Men envision frequency with reference to their own patterns of erection and ejaculation. Women got fucked a lot more than men fucked.

Sexual-revolution philosophy predates the sixties. It shows up in Left ideologies and movements with regularity—in most countries, in many different periods, manifest in various leftist "tendencies." The sixties in the United States, repeated with different tonalities throughout Western Europe, had a particularly democratic character. One did not have to read Wilhelm Reich, though some did. It was simple. A bunch of nasty bastards who hated making love were making war. A bunch of boys who liked flowers were making love and refusing to make war. These boys were wonderful and beautiful. They wanted peace. They talked love, love, love, not romantic love but love of mankind (translated by women: humankind). They grew their hair long and painted their faces and wore colorful clothes and risked being treated *like girls.* In resisting going to war, they were cowardly and sissies and weak, *like girls.* No wonder the girls of the sixties thought that these boys were their special friends, their special allies, lovers each and every one.

The girls were real idealists. They hated the Viet Nam War and their own lives, unlike the boys', were not at stake. They hated the racial and sexual bigotry visited on blacks, in particular on black men who were the figures in visible jeopardy. The girls were not all white, but still the black man was the figure of empathy, the figure whom they wanted to protect from racist pogroms. Rape was seen as a racist ploy: not something real in itself used in a racist context to isolate and destroy black men in specific and strategic ways, but a fabrication, a figment of the racist imagination.

The girls were idealistic because, unlike the boys, many of them had been raped; their lives were at stake. The girls were idealists especially because they believed in peace and freedom *so much* that they even thought it was intended for them too. They knew that their mothers were not free—they saw the small, constrained, female lives—and they did not want to be their mothers. They accepted the boys' definition of sexual freedom because it, more than any other idea or practice, made them different from their mothers. While their mothers kept sex secret and private, with so much fear and shame, the girls proclaimed sex their right, their pleasure, their freedom. They decried the stupidity of their mothers and allied themselves on overt sexual terms with the long-haired boys who wanted peace, freedom, and fucking everywhere. This was a world vision that took girls out of the homes in which their mothers were dull captives or automatons and at the same time turned the whole world, potentially, into the best possible home. In other words, the girls did not leave home in order to find sexual adventure in a sexual jungle; they left home to find a warmer, kinder, larger, more embracing home.

Sexual radicalism was defined in classically male terms: number of partners, frequency of sex, varieties of sex (for instance, group sex), eagerness to engage in sex. It was all supposed to be essentially the same for boys and girls: two, three, or however many long-haired persons communing. It was especially the lessening of gender polarity that kept the girls entranced, even after the fuck had revealed the boys to be men after all. Forced sex occurred—it occurred often; but the dream lived on. Lesbianism was never accepted as lovemaking on its own terms but rather as a kinky occasion for male voyeurism and the eventual fucking of two wet women; still, the dream lived on. Male homosexuality was toyed with, vaguely tolerated, but largely despised and feared because heterosexual men however bedecked with flowers could not bear to be fucked "like women"; but the dream lived on. And the dream for the girls at base was a dream of a sexual and social empathy that negated the strictures of gender, a dream of sexual equality based on what men and women had in common, what the adults tried to kill in you as they made you grow up. It was a desire for a sexual community more like childhood—before girls were crushed under and segregated. It was a dream of sexual transcendence: transcending the absolutely dichotomized male-female world of the adults who made war not love. It was—for the girls—a dream of being less female in a world less male; an eroticization of sibling equality, not the traditional male dominance.

Wishing did not make it so. Acting as if it were so did not make it so. Proposing it in commune after commune, to man after man, did not make it so. Baking bread and demonstrating against the war together did not make it so. The girls of the sixties lived in what Marxists call, but in this instance do not recognize as, a "contradiction." Precisely in trying to erode the boundaries of gender through an apparent single standard of sexual-liberation practice, they participated more and more in the most gender-reifying act: fucking. The men grew more manly; the world of the counterculture became more aggressively male-dominated. The girls became women—found themselves possessed by a man or a man and his buddies (in the parlance of the counterculture, his brothers and hers too)—traded, gang-fucked, collected, collectivized, objectified, turned into the hot stuff of pornography, and socially resegregated into traditionally female roles. Empirically speaking, sexual liberation was practiced by women on a wide scale in the sixties and it did not work: that is, it did not free women. Its purpose—it turned out—was to free men to use women without bourgeois constraints, and in that it was successful. One consequence for the women was an intensification of the experience of being sexually female—the precise opposite of what those idealistic girls had envisioned for themselves. In experiencing a wide variety of men in a wide variety of circumstances, women who were not prostitutes discovered the impersonal, class-determined nature of their sexual function. They discovered the utter irrelevance of their own individual, aesthetic, ethical, or political sensitivities (whether those sensitivities were characterized by men as female or bourgeois or puritanical) in sex as men practiced it. The sexual standard was the male-to-female fuck, and women served it—it did not serve women.

In the sexual-liberation movement of the sixties, its ideology and practice, neither force nor the subordinate status of women was an issue. It was assumed that—unrepressed—everyone wanted intercourse all the time (men, of course, had other important things to do; women had no legitimate reason not to want to be fucked); and it was assumed that in women an aversion to intercourse, or not climaxing from intercourse, or not wanting intercourse at a particular time or with a particular man, or wanting fewer partners than were available, or getting tired, or being cross, were all signs of and proof of sexual repression. Fucking per se was freedom per se. When rape—obvious, clear, brutal rape—occurred, it was ignored, often for political reasons if the rapist was black and the woman white. Interestingly, in a racially constructed rape, the rape was likely to be credited as such, even when ultimately ignored. When a white man raped a white woman, there was no vocabulary to describe it. It was an event that occurred outside the political discourse of the generation in question and therefore it did not exist. When a black woman was raped by a white man, the degree of recognition depended on the state of alliances between black and white men in the social territory involved: whether, at any given time, they were sharing women or fighting territorially over them. A black woman raped by a black man had the special burden of not jeopardizing her own race, endangered especially by charges of rape, by calling attention to any such brutality committed against her. Beatings and forced intercourse were commonplace in the counterculture. Even more widespread was the social and economic coercion of women to engage in sex with men. Yet no antagonism was seen to exist between sexual force and sexual freedom: one did not preclude the other. Implicit was the conviction that force would not be necessary if women were not repressed; women would want to fuck and would not have to be forced to fuck; so that it was repression, not force, that stood in the way of freedom.

Sexual-liberation ideology, whether pop or traditionally leftist-intellectual, did not criticize, analyze, or repudiate forced sex, nor did it demand an end to the sexual and social subordination of women to men: neither reality was recognized. Instead, it posited that freedom for women existed in being fucked more often by more men, a sort of lateral mobility in the same inferior sphere. No persons were held responsible for forced sex acts, rapes, beatings of women, unless the women themselves were blamed—usually for not complying in the first place. These were in the main women who wanted to comply—who wanted the promised land of sexual freedom—and still they had limits, preferences, tastes, desires for intimacy with some men and not others, moods not necessarily related to menstruation or the phases of the moon, days on which they would rather work or read; and they were punished for all these puritanical repressions, these petit bourgeois lapses, these tiny exercises of tinier wills not in conformity with the wills of their brother-lovers: force was frequently used against them, or they were threatened or humiliated or thrown out. No diminution of flower power, peace, freedom, political correctness, or justice was seen to be implicit in the use of coercion in any form to get sexual compliance.

In the garden of earthly delights known as the sixties counterculture, pregnancy did intrude, almost always rudely; and even then and there it was one of the real obstacles to female fucking on male demand. It made women ambivalent, reluctant, concerned, cross, preoccupied; it even led women to say no. Throughout the sixties, the birth control pill was not easy to get, and nothing else was sure. Unmarried women had an especially hard time getting access to contraceptive devices, including the diaphragm, and abortion was illegal and dangerous. Fear of pregnancy provided a reason for saying no: not just an excuse but a concrete reason not easily seduced or persuaded away, even by the most astute or dazzling argument in behalf of sexual freedom. Especially difficult to sway were the women who had had illegal abortions already. Whatever they thought of fucking, however they experienced it, however much they loved or tolerated it, they knew that for them it had consequences in blood and pain and they knew that it cost the men nothing, except sometimes money. Pregnancy was a material reality, and it could not be argued away. One tactic used to counterbalance the high anxiety caused by the possibility of pregnancy was the esteem in which "natural" women were held—women who were "natural" in all respects, who wanted organic fucking (no birth control, whatever children resulted) and organic vegetables too. Another tactic was to stress the communal raising of children, to promise it. Women were not punished in the conventional ways for bearing the children—they were not labeled "bad" or shunned—but they were frequently abandoned. A woman and her child—poor and relatively outcast—wandering within the counterculture changed the quality of the hedonism in the communities in which they intruded: the mother-and-child pair embodied a different strain of reality, not a welcome one for the most part. There were lone women struggling to raise children "freely" and they got in the way of the males who saw freedom as the fuck—and the fuck ended for the males when the fuck ended. These women with children made the other women a little somber, a little concerned, a little careful. Pregnancy, the fact of it, was antiaphrodisiacal. Pregnancy, the burden of it, made it harder for the flower boys to fuck the flower girls, who did not want to have to claw out their own insides or pay someone else to do it; they also did not want to die.

It was the brake that pregnancy put on fucking that made abortion a high-priority political issue for men in the 1960s—not only for young men, but also for the older leftist men who were skimming sex off the top of the counterculture and even for more traditional men who dipped into the pool of hippie girls now and then. The decriminalization of abortion—for that was the political goal

—was seen as the final fillip: it would make women absolutely accessible, absolutely "free." The sexual revolution, in order to work, required that abortion be available to women on demand. If it were not, fucking would not be available to men on demand. Getting laid was at stake. Not just getting laid, but getting laid the way great numbers of boys and men had always wanted—lots of girls who wanted it all the time outside marriage, free, giving it away. The male-dominated Left agitated for and fought for and argued for and even organized for and even provided political and economic resources for abortion rights for women. The Left was militant on the issue.

Then, at the very end of the sixties, women who had been radical in counterculture terms—women who had been both politically and sexually active—became radical in new terms: they became feminists. They were not Betty Friedan's housewives. They had fought out on the streets against the Viet Nam War; some of them were old enough to have fought in the South for black civil rights, and all had come into adulthood on the back of that struggle; and lord knows, they had been fucked. As Marge Piercy wrote in a 1969 exposé of sex and politics in the counterculture:

> Fucking a staff into existence is only the extreme form of what passes for common practice in many places. A man can bring a woman into an organization by sleeping with her and remove her by ceasing to do so. A man can purge a woman for no other reason than that he has tired of her, knocked her up, or is after someone else: and that purge is accepted without a ripple. There are cases of a woman excluded from a group for no other reason than that one of its leaders proved impotent with her. If a *macher* enters a room full of *machers*, accompanied by a woman and does not introduce her, it is rare indeed that anyone will bother to ask her name or acknowledge her presence. The etiquette that governs is one of master-servant.[5]

Or, as Robin Morgan wrote in 1970: "We have met the enemy and he's our friend. And dangerous."[6] Acknowledging the forced sex so pervasive in the counterculture in the language of the counterculture, Morgan wrote: "It hurts to understand that at Woodstock or Altamont a woman could be declared uptight or a poor sport if she didn't want to be raped."[7] These were the beginnings: recognizing that the brother-lovers were sexual exploiters as cynical as any other exploiters—they ruled and demeaned and discarded women, they used women to get and consolidate power, they used women for sex and for menial labor, they used women up; recognizing that rape was a matter of utter indifference to these brother-lovers—they took it any way they could get it; and recognizing that all the work for justice had been done on the backs of sexually exploited women within the movement. "But surely," wrote Robin Morgan in 1968, "even a male reactionary on this issue can realize that it is *really* mind-blowing to hear some young male 'revolutionary'—supposedly dedicated to building a new, free social order to replace this vicious one under which we live—turn around and absent-mindedly order his 'chick' to shut up and make supper or wash his socks—*he's* talking now. We're used to such attitudes from the average American clod, but from this brave new radical?"[8]

It was the raw, terrible realization that sex was not brother-sister but master-servant—that this brave new radical wanted to be not only master in his own home but pasha in his own harem—that proved explosive. The women ignited with the realization that they had been sexually used. Going beyond the male agenda on sexual liberation, these women discussed sex and politics with one another—something not done even when they had shared the same bed with the same man—and discovered that their experiences had been staggeringly the same, ranging from forced sex to sexual humiliation to abandonment to cynical manipulation as both menials and pieces of ass. And the men were entrenched in sex as power: they wanted the women for fucking, not revolution: the two were revealed to be different after all. The men refused to change but even more important they hated the women for refusing to service them anymore on the old terms—there it was, revealed for what it was. The women left the men—in droves. The women formed an autonomous women's movement, a militant feminist movement, to fight against the sexual cruelty they had experienced and to fight for the sexual justice they had been denied.

From their own experience—especially in being coerced and in being exchanged—the women found a first premise for their political movement: that freedom for a woman was predicated on, and could not exist without, her own absolute control of her own body in sex and in reproduction. This included not only the right to terminate a pregnancy but also the right to not have sex, to say no, to not be fucked. For women, this led to many areas of sexual discovery about the nature and politics of their own sexual desire, but for men it was a dead end—most of them never recognized feminism except in terms of their own sexual deprivation; feminists were taking away the easy fuck. They did everything they could to break the back of the feminist movement—and in fact they have not stopped yet. Especially significant has been their change of heart and politics on abortion. The right to abortion defined as an intrinsic part of the sexual revolution was essential to them: who could bear the horror and cruelty and stupidity of illegal abortion? The right to abortion defined as an intrinsic part of a woman's right to control her own body, in sex too, was a matter of supreme indifference.

Material resources dried up. Feminists fought the battle for decriminalized abortion—no laws governing abortion—on the streets and in the courts with severely diminished male support. In 1973, the Supreme Court gave women legalized abortion: abortion regulated by the state.

If before the Supreme Court decision in 1973 leftist men expressed a fierce indifference to abortion rights on feminist terms, after 1973 indifference changed to overt hostility: feminists had the right to abortion and were still saying no—no to sex on male terms and no to politics dominated by these same men. Legalized abortion did not make these women more available for sex; on the contrary, the women's movement was growing in size and importance and male sexual privilege was being challenged with more intensity, more commitment, more ambition. The leftist men turned from political activism: without the easy lay, they were not prepared to engage in radical politics. In therapy they discovered that they had had personalities in the womb, that they had suffered traumas in the womb. Fetal psychology—tracing a grown man's life back into the womb, where, as a fetus, he had a whole human self and psychology—developed on the therapeutic Left (the residue of the male counterculture Left) before any right-wing minister or lawmaker ever thought to make a political stand on the right of fertilized eggs as persons to the protection of the Fourteenth Amendment, which is in fact the goal of antiabortion activists.* The argument that abortion was a form of genocide directed particularly at blacks gained political currency, even though feminists from the first based part of the feminist case on the real facts and figures—black and Hispanic women died and were hurt disproportionately in illegal abortions. As early as 1970, these figures were

---

*The Fourteenth Amendment, ratified in 1868, has five sections, the first of which is crucial here, the second of which is interesting. Section 1: "All persons born or naturalized in the United States, and subject to the jurisdiction thereof, are citizens of the United States and of the State wherein they reside. No State shall make or enforce any law which shall abridge the privileges or immunities of citizens of the United States; nor shall any State deprive any person of life, liberty, or property, without due process of law; nor deny to any person within its jurisdiction the equal protection of the laws." The second section guarantees the vote to all males. It was purposely written to exclude women. Even though women have subsequently been given the vote, laws in the United States routinely abridge the privileges and immunities of women and deprive women of liberty and property (there are still states in which married women cannot own property on their own)—and women do not have equal protection of the laws. The fetus, once legally a "person," would have all the protections guaranteed by this amendment but not in practice extended to women. The Equal Rights Amendment was in large part an effort to extend the protections of the Fourteenth Amendment to women.

available in *Sisterhood Is Powerful:* "4.7 times as many Puerto Rican women, and 8 times as many black women die of the consequences of illegal abortions as do white women . . . In New York City, 80 percent of the women who die from abortions are black and brown."[9] And on the nonviolent Left, abortion was increasingly considered murder—murder in the most grandiose terms. "Abortion is the domestic side of the nuclear arms race,"[10] wrote one male pacifist in a 1980 tract not at all singular in the scale and tone of its denunciation. Without the easy fuck, things sure had changed on the Left.

The Democratic Party, establishment home of many Left groups, especially since the end of the 1960s ferment, had conceded abortion rights as early as 1972, when George McGovern ran against Richard Nixon and refused to take a stand for abortion so that he could fight against the Viet Nam War and for the presidency without distraction. When the Hyde Amendment cutting off Medicaid funding for abortions was passed in 1976,* it had Jesse Jackson's support: he had sent telegrams to all members of Congress supporting the cutoff of funds. Court challenges delayed the implementation of the Hyde Amendment, but Jimmy Carter, elected with the help of feminist and leftist groups in the Democratic Party, had his man, Joseph A. Califano, Jr., head of the then Department of Health, Education, and Welfare, halt federal funding of abortion by administrative order. By 1977 the first documented death of a poor woman (Hispanic) from an illegal abortion had occurred: illegal abortion and death were again realities for women in the United States. In the face of the so-called human-life amendment and human-life statute—respectively a constitutional amendment and a bill of law defining a fertilized egg as a human being—the male Left has simply played dead.

The male Left abandoned abortion rights for genuinely awful

---

*Except when the mother's life is at stake in the original version (Hyde's version); as amended in the Senate, also in cases of rape and incest.

reasons: the boys were not getting laid; there was bitterness and anger against feminists for ending a movement (by withdrawing from it) that was both power and sex for the men; there was also the familiar callous indifference of the sexual exploiter—if he couldn't screw her she wasn't real.

The hope of the male Left is that the loss of abortion rights will drive women back into the ranks—even fear of losing might do that; and the male Left has done what it can to assure the loss. The Left has created a vacuum that the Right has expanded to fill—this the Left did by abandoning a just cause, by its decade of quietism, by its decade of sulking. But the Left has not just been an absence; it has been a presence, outraged at women's controlling their own bodies, outraged at women's organizing against sexual exploitation, which by definition means women also organizing against the sexual values of the Left. When feminist women have lost legal abortion altogether, leftist men expect them back—begging for help, properly chastened, ready to make a deal, ready to spread their legs again. On the Left, women will have abortion on male terms, as part of sexual liberation, or women will not have abortion except at risk of death.

And the boys of the sixties did grow up too. They actually grew older. They are now men in life, not just in the fuck. They want babies. Compulsory pregnancy is about the only way they are sure to get them.

> Every mother is a judge who sentences the children for the sins of the father.
>
> Rebecca West, *The Judge*

The girls of the sixties had mothers who predicted, insisted, argued that those girls would be hurt; but they would not say how or why. In the main, the mothers appeared to be sexual conservatives: they upheld the marriage system as a social ideal and were silent about the sex in it. Sex was a duty inside marriage; a wife's attitude toward it was irrelevant unless she made trouble, went crazy, fucked around. Mothers had to teach their daughters to like men as a class—be responsive to men as men, warm to men as men—and at the same time to not have sex. Since males mostly wanted the girls for sex, it was hard for the girls to understand how to like boys and men without also liking the sex boys and men wanted. The girls were told nice things about human sexuality and also told that it would cost them their lives—one way or another. The mothers walked a tough line: give the girls a good attitude, but discourage them. The cruelty of the ambivalence communicated itself, but the kindness in the intention did not: mothers tried to protect their daughters from many men by directing them toward one; mothers tried to protect their daughters by getting them to do what was necessary inside the male system without ever explaining why. They had no vocabulary for the why—why sex inside marriage was good but outside marriage was bad, why more than one man turned a girl from a loving woman into a whore, why leprosy or paralysis were states preferable to pregnancy outside marriage. They had epithets to hurl, but no other discourse. Silence about sex in marriage was also the only way to avoid revelations bound to terrify—revelations about the quality of the mothers' own lives. Sexual compliance or submission was presented as the wife's natural function and also her natural response to her sexual circumstance. That compliance was never seen or presented as the result of actual force, threatened force, possible force, or a sexual and social cul-de-sac. It has always been essential to keep women riveted on the details of submission so as to divert women from thinking about the nature of force—especially the sexual force that necessitates sexual submission. The mothers could not ward off the enthusiasm of sexual liberation—its energy, its hope, its bright promise of sexual equality—because they could not or would not tell what they knew about the nature and quality of male sexuality as they had experienced it, as practiced on them in marriage. They knew the simple logic of promiscuity, which the girls did not: that what one man could do, ten men could do ten times over. The girls did not understand that logic because the girls did not know fully what one man could do. And the mothers failed to convince also because the only life they offered was a repeat version of their own: and the girls were close enough to feel the inconsolable sadness and the dead tiredness of those lives, even if they did not know how or why mother had gotten the way she was. The girls, having been taught well by their mothers to like men because they were men, picked flower-children boys over their mothers: they did not look for husbands (fathers) as dictated by convention but for brothers (lovers) as dictated by rebellion. The daughters saw the strained silence of their mothers on sex as a repudiation of the pleasure of sex, not as an honest though inarticulate assessment of it. The disdain, disapproval, repugnance for sex was not credited as having any objective component. What their mothers would not tell them they could not know. They repudiated the putative sexual conservatism of their mothers for so-called sexual radicalism: more men, more sex, more freedom.

The girls of the counterculture Left were wrong: not about civil rights or the Viet Nam War or imperial Amerika, but about sex and men. It is fair to say that the silence of the mothers hid a real, tough, unsentimental knowledge of men and intercourse, and that the noisy sexuality of the daughters hid romantic ignorance.

Times have changed. The silence has been shattered—or parts of it have been shattered. Right-wing women defending the traditional family are public; they are loud and they are many. Especially they are loud about legal abortion, which they abhor; and what they have to say about legal abortion is connected to what they know about sex. They know some terrible things. Right-wing women consistently denounce abortion because they see it as inextricably linked to the sexual degradation of women. The sixties did not simply pass them by. They learned from what they saw. They saw the cynical male use of abortion to make women easier fucks—

first the political use of the issue and then, after legalization, the actual use of the medical procedure. When abortion was legal, they saw a massive social move to secure sexual access to all women on male terms—the glut of pornography; and indeed, they link the two issues, and not for reasons of hysteria. Abortion, they say, flourishes in a pornographic society; pornography, they say, flourishes in what they call an abortion society. What they mean is that both reduce women to the fuck. They have seen that the Left only champions women on its own sexual terms—as fucks; they find the right-wing offer a tad more generous. They are not dazzled by the promise of abortion as choice, as sexual self-determination, as woman's control of her own body, because they know that the promise is crap: as long as men have power over women, men will not allow abortion or anything else on those terms.

Right-wing women see in promiscuity, which legal abortion makes easier, the generalizing of force. They see force in marriage as essentially containable—contained within the marriage, limited to one man at a time. They try to "handle" him. They see that limitation—one man at a time—as necessary protection from the many men who would do the same and to whom they would be available on sexual-liberation terms—terms fortified and made genuinely possible by abortion rights. With all their new public talk, they continue the traditional silence of women in that they are silent about forced sex in marriage: but all they do is predicated on a knowledge of it, and they do not see how more force is better than less force—and more men means more force to them.

Right-wing women accuse feminists of hypocrisy and cruelty in advocating legal abortion because, as they see it, legal abortion makes them accessible fucks without consequence to men. In their view, pregnancy is the only consequence of sex that makes men accountable to women for what men do to women. Deprived of pregnancy as an inevitability, a woman is deprived of her strongest reason not to have intercourse. Opposition to birth control is based on this same principle.

Right-wing women saw the cynicism of the Left in using abortion to make women sexually available, and they also saw the male Left abandon women who said no. They know that men do not have principles or political agendas not congruent with the sex they want. They know that abortion on strictly self-actualizing terms for women is an abomination to men—left-wing men and right-wing men and gray men and green men. They know that every woman has to make the best deal she can. They face reality and what they see is that women get fucked whether they want it or not; right-wing women get fucked by fewer men; abortion in the open takes away pregnancy as a social and sexual control over men; once a woman can terminate a pregnancy easily and openly and without risk of death, she is bereft of her best way of saying no—of refusing the intercourse the male wants to force her to accept. The consequences of pregnancy to him may stop him, as the consequences of pregnancy to her never will. The right-wing woman makes what she considers the best deal. Her deal promises that she has to be fucked only by him, not by all his buddies too; that he will pay for the kids; that she can live in his house on his wages; and she smiles and says she wants to be a mommy and play house. If in order to keep pregnancy as a weapon of survival she has to accept illegal abortion and risk death, she will do it—alone, in silence, isolated, the only reproach for her rebellion against actual pregnancy being death or maiming. In this mess of illegal abortion, she will have confirmed what she has been taught about her own nature as a woman and about all women. She deserves punishment; illegal abortion is punishment for sex. She feels shame: she may consider it the shame of sex but it is in part the shame that any human in captivity feels in being used—women being used in sex feel shame inseparable from sex. The shame will confirm that she deserves suffering; suffering in sex and birth and aborted birth is the curse of her sex; illegal abortion is deserved suffering. But illegal abortion also serves her because it puts abortion out of sight. No one has to be confronted with another woman making a choice, choosing not to be a mother. No one must face women openly with priorities other than marriage and conformity. No one must face a woman refusing to be bound by pregnancy. The women who rebel against their function must do it secretly, not causing grief, embarrassment, or confusion to other women isolated in their own reproductive quagmires, each on her own, each alone, each being a woman for all women in silence and in suffering and in solitude. With illegal abortion life or death is up to God: each time, one submits to the divine hand, divine finger on divine revolver pointed at the already bloody flesh of a woman, divine Russian roulette. It is a final, humiliated submission to the will of a superior Male who judges absolutely. Death is a judgment and so is life. Illegal abortion is an individual hell; one suffers, does penance: God decides; life is forgiveness. And no one need face it until it happens to her—until she is the one caught. This is the way in which women are moral idiots in this system: ignoring whatever has to do with other women, all women, until or unless it happens to oneself. Right-wing women also believe that a woman who refuses to bear a child deserves to die. Right-wing women are prepared to accept that judgment against themselves; and when they survive, they are guilty and prepared to pay—to martyr themselves for an act of will to which they had no right as women. There is no better measure of what forced sex does to women—how it destroys self-respect and the will to survive as a self-determining human being—than the opposition of right-wing women to legal abortion: to what they need to save themselves from being butchered. The training of a girl to accept her place in sex in marriage and the use of a woman in sex in marriage means the annihilating of any will toward self-determination or freedom; her personhood is so demeaned that it becomes easier to risk death or maiming than to say no to a man who will fuck you anyway, with the blessings of God and state, 'til death do you part.

4

Jews and Homosexuals

A minister from Oklahoma, dressed in a shiny brown polyester suit, hair greased down even shinier than the shiny suit, smile from ear to ear even shinier than the shiny hair, was picketing, leafleting, and preaching outside the Sam Houston Coliseum in Houston. He was full of love for the Lord, love for his neighbors, the love of Christ; it was sin he hated, especially when it was embodied in the filthy lesbians who had come to Houston to destroy the work of God. He kept preaching to the feminists converging on the Coliseum that nothing was as loathsome as homosexuality; but in women! to contemplate the abomination in women whom God commanded to obey their husbands as Christ was so repugnant to this minister that he predicted God might call down the walls of the Coliseum then and there. I approached him alone to talk as other women ignored him entirely. I asked him what he thought of the high-spirited, vital women going in: did they all seem evil and loathsome? could he tell which were lesbians and which were not? what kind of harm did lesbians do to other people? if lesbians did no one harm (for instance, did not murder, did not rape), why was he, a minister, called on to denounce lesbians? was not this particular sin, so singularly lacking in malice, better left to God to judge? why did lesbians provoke not only God's judgment but also the minister's wrath? He referred to these passages from Romans:*

*The translation quoted is the King James Version. However, the phrases

Professing themselves to be wise, they became fools,
And changed the glory of the uncorruptible God into an image made like to corruptible man, and to birds, and four-footed beasts, and creeping things.
Wherefore God also gave them up to uncleanness through the lusts of their own hearts, to dishonour their own bodies between themselves;
Who changed the truth of God into a lie, and worshipped and served the creature more than the Creator, who is blessed for ever. Amen.
*For this cause God gave them up unto vile affections: for even their women did change the natural use into that which is against nature;**
And likewise also the men, leaving the natural use of the woman, burned in their lust one toward another; men with men working that which is unseemly, and receiving in themselves that recompence of their error which was meet. (Italics mine)
And even as they did not like to retain God in *their* knowledge, God gave them over to a reprobate mind, to do those things which are not convenient;†
Being filled with all unrighteousness, fornication, wickedness, covetousness, maliciousness; full of envy, murder, debate,‡ deceit, malignity; whisperers,
Backbiters, haters of God, despiteful, proud, boasters, inventors of evil things, disobedient to parents,
Without understanding, convenant breakers, without natural affection, implacable, unmerciful:
Who knowing the judgment of God, that they which commit such things are worthy of death, not only do the same, but have pleasure in them that do them.§ (Italics mine)

Romans 1:22–32

---

indicated by a footnote reference are slightly different in the Revised Standard Version and are perhaps clearer in meaning, as shown in the following notes.

*Their women exchanged natural relations for unnatural, and men likewise gave up natural relations with women . . .

†To a base mind and to improper conduct.

‡Strife.

§Though they know God's decree that those who do such things deserve to die, they not only do them but approve those who practice them.

There is nothing like this in the Old Testament. According to Maimonides:

> Women are forbidden to engage in lesbian practices with one another, these being *the doings of the land of Egypt* (Lev. 18:3), against which we have been warned . . . Although such an act is forbidden, the perpetrators are not liable to a flogging, since there is no specific negative commandment prohibiting it, nor is actual intercourse of any kind involved here. Consequently, such women are not forbidden for the priesthood on account of harlotry, nor is a woman prohibited to her husband because of it, since this does not constitute harlotry. It behooves the court, however, to administer the flogging prescribed for disobedience, since they have performed a forbidden act. A man should be particularly strict with his wife in this matter, and should prevent women known to indulge in such practices from visiting her, and her from going to visit them.[1]

I asked the minister how Christians who value obedience to God's literal word justified such a radical reinterpretation of the Old Testament. The New Testament, he said, was concealed in the Old Testament; nothing in it was really new in the sense of being original; the New Testament made God's real meaning clear; the Jews had become blind to the spirit of the law—enter the Holy Spirit and the revealed word. I suggested that the anti-Jewish tone of some of the New Testament might be considered new and that it was possibly related to what I at least considered a new attitude toward lesbians: Jews and female homosexuals, politically united by damnation for the first time. In Romans, Jews are abandoned by God the Father; the covenant of manhood, sealed by circumcision, loses its meaning:

> For he is not a Jew, which is one outwardly; neither *is that* circumcision, which is outward in the flesh:
>
> But he *is* a Jew, which is one inwardly; and circumcision *is*

> *that* of the heart, in the spirit, *and* not in the letter . . .*
> Romans 2:28–29

The Gentile gets God's masculinity (a new God, God the Son) without an outward mark. The cutting of the penis no longer means masculinity; it begins to resemble castration. All the feminized creatures—Jews, unnatural women (lesbians), unnatural men (homosexuals)—are linked together in Romans and are promised God's "indignation and wrath" (Romans 2:8). The Jews who obey the law are replaced by the Christians who know the law not by learning it but by being it. The first Christian hit list of sinners is compiled: lesbians, male homosexuals, Jews.

Talk of the Jews animated the minister. He was married to a Jewish girl. He supported the state of Israel: see Amos, ninth chapter. The Jews were up on his pedestal. But the Jews, I insisted, did not abhor lesbians or forbid lesbian acts or damn or search out or ostracize lesbians: not by law or by actual practice. Christ, he said at some length and with no small amount of bitterness, had died because the Jews had overlooked a lot. The Jews had had some funny ideas until Paul came along.

But where, I asked him, did he get his sense of personal repugnance? Didn't I see how vile a sin it was, he asked, referring back to the New Testament, which condemned not only lesbians and all homosexuals but also those who accepted in others this most heinous of sins? And didn't I understand what lesbians and male homosexuals were by nature: filled with wickedness, covetousness, maliciousness, envy, murder, strife, deceit, malignity; backbiters, haters of God, inventors of evil things, without natural affection, unmerciful. Romans, it must be apparent, is not kind in its estimation of homosexuals, male or female. Any Christian who meets homosexuality in the pages of the New Testament for the first time

---

*Revised Standard Version: "real circumcision is a matter of the heart, spiritual and not literal."

is likely to fear homosexuals, hate homosexuals, and despise any liberal tolerance for that viciousness that God abhors. The New Testament damns those who tolerate homosexuality; and the New Testament does say that homosexuals "are worthy of death."

In the course of my conversation with the minister, a group of women had gathered around us. The weather was beautiful, the convention exciting, the women were high on goodwill and feminist dreams of sisterhood and solidarity. The women, it must be said, were nice and happy and enthusiastic and everyone was pretty from radiant smiles and high hopes. The minister's style was nice too—outgoing, sincere, warm, expansive, full of prejudiced conviction but without meanness. He did not want to hurt anyone. He hated sin, and especially he found lesbian sin loathsome; but it was a conviction pure in its detachment from individual human beings—he had never seen one. Many of the women listening giggled as he and I talked. But what about these women, I asked, or what about me? Are we all damned? Are we bad? Do you know which of us is lesbian? Are we all full of envy, murder, strife, deceit, malignity? Are we without natural affection or unmerciful? He looked up and around and his skin crawled. He reacted to the sight of us suddenly as frightened girls do to mice or bugs or spiders.

The women's movement, he said, was a communist conspiracy, an internal poison in America. The communists wanted abortion legalized in the United States in order to exterminate Americans and to damn us in God's eyes. The Russians invented abortion and they insidiously had the ideology of abortion planted in the United States by agents and dupes; and the liberals and the Jews spread it. And now the communists had new tactics—lesbians in the women's movement. It was a Russian plot to turn the United States into Sodom and Gomorrah so that God would hate the United States and destroy it and the Russians would win; and Marx, the anti-Christ, had been a Jew, and a lot of lesbians were Jews, he was no anti-Semite, he had married a Jewish girl but of course she had been baptized and had accepted Christ. The Bible—meaning the New Testament because the Old Testament had really become irrelevant since the New Testament fully revealed what had been concealed in the Old Testament—was the only hope for America's survival because it revealed God's will. A strong and righteous nation depends on fulfilling God's will. God's will is that wives obey their husbands, who are as Christ to them. Husbands must love their wives; wives must obey their husbands. The feminists in Houston (who were, in fact, entering the Coliseum almost two by two in a sacrilegious if unintentional parody of Noah's Ark) were part of the communist plan to spread lesbianism, destroy the family by destroying the wife's obedience to Christ through the agency of her husband: the feminists were going to destroy the United States by spreading evil. The minister's eyes were darting in all directions and he seemed visibly sick from the sudden recognition that the women around him and the woman he was talking to might actually be lesbians, and some certainly were: full of malignity, inventors of evil things. I asked him if I could talk with him again, some other time. He moved away, repelled, nervous, silent, the rich evangelical blather with which he had been fulminating when I first encountered him now stopped entirely. He had actually been near some real ones, unnatural, worthy of death.

Inside the Coliseum too there was a right-wing Christian presence. In Mississippi and Utah, official convention delegates not only embodied opposition to all women's rights, including the Equal Rights Amendment, but were linked with the Ku Klux Klan. The Utah delegation, in a press release, denied any association with the Klan and claimed that the sponsors of the conference "have sought to destroy our credibility by name-calling and trying to link us with extremist groups like the Ku-Klux Klan." The Utah delegation considered the whole conference a propaganda effort "carefully designed to quash the views of women opposing the

Equal Rights Amendment and reproductive freedom recommendations."[2] The National Commission on the Observance of International Women's Year (IWY) announced in September, two months before the conference, its decision to uphold the right of all elected delegates to participate in the convention unless election fraud could be proven. State elections were supposed to include in the official delegations "groups which work to advance the rights of women; and members of the general public, with special emphasis on the representation of low-income women, members of diverse racial, ethnic and religious groups, and women of all ages."[3] The true wrath of the IWY Commission was, in fact, for the racist composition of several of the delegations from right-wing states. Alabama was cited as a state "whose population is 26.2 per cent black, yet will be represented in Houston by 24 delegates, 22 of whom are white."[4] Mississippi stood out as the most vicious violator of the law's intent. The IWY Commission characterized Mississippi as "a state whose population is 36.8 per cent black, and yet will be represented in Houston by an all-white delegation, five of whom are men, whose election is alleged by local authorities to be the result of Klanlike activities." An individual who identified himself as Grand Dragon of the Realm of Mississippi, United Klans of America, Inc., Knights of the Ku Klux Klan, claimed: "We controlled the one [delegation] in Mississippi."[5]

I interviewed a man from the Mississippi delegation on the convention floor. Press access to the official elected delegates when the convention was in session was tightly controlled. The system of access strongly favored male reporters, since permanent floor passes were handed out to dailies, whose representatives were mostly male. The women's monthly magazines were low on the priority list of media coverage: and most of the reporters for those monthly women's journals were women. As a result, someone like myself, representing *Ms.*, had at most a half hour on the floor with the delegates at any single time, a very long wait for that half hour of access—and the prospect of being physically thrown out as soon as one's time was up. So when I raced in, I raced right over to the Mississippi delegation.

I asked several women to talk with me. They refused even to look at me. Whoever managed them disciplined them well. They were a wall of silence. Finally I approached a man sitting on an aisle. I said that I was from *Ms.* magazine and would like to ask him some questions. I was wearing overalls and a T-shirt, and a press pass with *Ms.* in large inked letters was hanging from my neck. The man laughed and turned to the woman next to him, whispered in her ear, she laughed and turned to the woman next to her and whispered in her ear, she laughed and turned to the woman next to her and whispered in her ear, and so on down the row of delegates. The man did not turn back to me until the identification had been passed to the end of the line. Some of the women had not laughed; they had gasped.

I asked the man why he was at the conference. He said that his wife had wanted him to be there to protect women's right to procreate and to have a family. I asked him if he was a member of the Klan. He claimed high office in the organization. He talked about the Klan's militant role in protecting women from all kinds. He himself was physically rather slight, not particularly tall, wore glasses; I suspected I was physically stronger than he was. Many times during the interview I realized that it would take a white sheet and all that that white sheet symbolized to hide this man's own physical vulnerability to attack. He himself was nondescript; the Klan was not. When I recognized the fear this man inspired in me, and measured that fear against his own physical presence, I felt ashamed: and yet I was still afraid of him.*

---

*Klan and Nazi groups threatened violence at the convention: we were promised bombings and beatings. Some women were in fact beaten up, others were physically threatened, and the possibility of being hurt was considered both real and immediate by all the conference participants with whom I talked.

He said that women needed the protection of men. He said that the Klan had sent men to the convention to protect their women-folk from the lesbians, who would assault them. He said that it was necessary to protect women's right to have families because that was the key to the stability of the nation. He said that homosexuality was a Jew sickness. He said that homosexuality was a lust that threatened to wipe out the family. He said that homosexual teachers should be found out and run out of any town they were in. They could all go to Jew New York. Trying to keep up my end of the conversation, I asked him why he was against homosexual teachers, especially if their homosexuality was private. He said that there was no such thing as private homosexuality, that if homosexuals were in schools, children would be corrupted and tainted and molested and taught to hate God and the family; homosexuality would claim the women and the children if they were exposed to it; its presence at all, even hidden, anywhere, would take people from family life and put them into sin. His description was almost voluptuous in that no one, in his estimation, would remain untouched.

Are you really saying, I asked slowly and clearly and loudly (so that the women delegates could continue to overhear the conversation), that if homosexuality were openly visible as a sexual possibility or if there were homosexual teachers in schools, everyone would choose to abandon heterosexuality and the family? Are you really saying, I asked carefully and clearly and slowly, that homosexuality is so attractive that no one would choose the heterosexual family over it? He stared at me, silent, a long time. I am afraid of violence and the Klan, and I was afraid of him. I repeated my questions. "You're a Jew, ain't ya," he said and turned away from me, stared straight ahead. All the women in the row who had been looking at me also turned away and stared straight ahead in utter silence. The only woman whose head had been otherwise engaged had not looked up except once: she had taken one hard stare at me in the beginning and had then turned back to her work: knitting blue baby booties, the Klan's own Madame Defarge; and I could imagine my name being transferred by the work of those hands from the press pass on my chest into that baby-blue wool. She sat next to the Klansman, and she knitted and knitted. Yes, I am a Jew, I said. I repeated my questions. He memorized my face, then stared straight ahead.

In my few remaining minutes on the floor, I implored the Mississippi women to talk to me. I went hurriedly from row to row, expecting somewhere to find one rebellious sign of interest or simple compassion. One woman dared to speak to me in whispers, but did not dare look at me; instead she looked down into her own lap, and the woman next to her got jittery and upset and kept telling her to "think again." She whispered that she was against the Equal Rights Amendment because girls would have to go to war. I said: we say we love our children but isn't it true that if we send our boys to war we can't love them very much? why are we willing to have them killed if we love them? At this point the marshals forced me physically to leave the floor. They did not ask or tell or say, "Time's up"; they pushed.*

In the face of the Klan and the marshals, I risked one more trip back to the Mississippi delegation. On the floor, delegates were milling around; it was a brief recess (but the same strict time limits applied for journalists). In the sheer confusion of the numbers and the noise, the discipline of the Mississippi delegation had relaxed slightly. A Mississippi woman explained to me that as a Christian woman she was in a superior position, and that this superior position was not to be traded for an equal position. I asked her if she really meant to say that boys were less valuable; and was that why we sacrificed them in wars—because we didn't think they were worth very much? She said that it was the nature of boys to guard

*The system of press access to the convention floor that favored male journalists over female was set up by a male "feminist." It was outrageously, unashamedly, and inexcusably sex-discriminatory.

and to protect, which included going to war and also taking care of their families. She was not prepared to say that boys were less valuable than girls, only that women were superior to men in Christianity, had a favored place based on and because of the male's role as protector. God, she said, wanted her husband to protect her. The Equal Rights Amendment would force her to take responsibility for decision making and for money. She did not want to take this responsibility because to do so would be against the will of God. She then said that she was equal spiritually in God's eyes but in no other way. I said that seemed to mean that in every other way she was inferior, not superior. She said that feminists want women and men to be the same but that God says they are different. The Equal Rights Amendment would permit homosexuality because men and women would no longer be as different as God wanted them to be. Being homosexual was a sin because women tried to be the same as men, and homosexuality confused the differences between men and women, those differences being the will of God. The recess ended, and with the return of order (delegates seated and under discipline again) no more talk between the Mississippi woman and myself was possible. The marshals approached; don't you fucking touch me, I said loudly, ending forever the possibility of further conversation with the Mississippi delegation; and I ran out fast so that the marshals fucking wouldn't touch me.

The Utah delegation had women supporters who attended the convention as observers, a nonvoting status. Most of the right-wing women did not care to attend the conference unless they were delegates; instead they attended Phyllis Schlafly's counterconvention in another part of town. I was interested in the Utah women because they had wanted to show themselves in an arena where they were a small and unpopular minority. They all wore similar black dresses, mourning I supposed for the unborn, mourning perhaps for us all, the feminists so ungodly who surrounded them. The Mississippi delegation had been a unit unto itself, not interacting at all with the world of people and ideas around them. My own evaluation was that indeed the Mississippi delegation had strong Klan participation and leadership; more generally, it was not only male-dominated but male-controlled, almost martially controlled. The Utah delegation with its supporters who dared to mingle with the enthusiastic feminists who numbered in the thousands acted with a different kind of conviction: the women were especially concerned with stopping abortion; they were passionate advocates of their values, tied to the Mormon Church, perhaps under direct orders, but nevertheless speaking for themselves with emotional conviction. A state legislator from Utah, an official delegate, was stern, forbidding, serious, and willing to exercise what power she had in the service of her beliefs: the Equal Rights Amendment legalizes abortion;* the Supreme Court, in saying that all women could have abortions, opened the door for the state to say that all women must have abortions; pro-ERA women are ignorant and malicious; she is a feminist and introduces legislation in behalf of women, but finds that pro-ERA feminists do not know what the interests of women are; the interests of women are in a strong home and strong laws protecting the family in which the man, not the state, protects the woman; also the federal government in following any kind of feminist program takes freedom from her directly as a state legislator, which she finds a violation of states' rights. Another Utah delegate said she attended the convention because she did not want her tax money to go to pay for abortion. I asked her about Viet Nam War tax resisters: they withheld taxes because they did not want their money to pay for the war; did she withhold taxes to keep her money from paying for abortion? Yes, she said. Then, as an afterthought, she said that actually she didn't pay any taxes at all. Did her husband pay them, I asked. She thought so.

During the ratification of the resolution supporting homosexual rights, I sat in the audience. There was yelling and cheering;

*See chapter 1, p. 33, for an explanation of this non sequitur.

balloons were let loose through the whole hall when the resolution was finally ratified after some debate. The scene was one of wild exhilaration: the thousands of delegates and observers were celebrating. In the highest balcony I spotted a group of Utah women, dressed in their black dresses all the same, slowly, grimly exiting. There were maybe ten of them; they had seen it through to the end; they were not happy. I raced to the high balcony to talk with them. It was deserted up there; all the noise was hundreds of feet below us; them and me.

They were somber. How did they feel about this, I asked. It was horrible, the end of everything, the death of the country, an affront to God; homosexuality was a sin that deserved death, and here women had voted for it, were clapping and cheering in behalf of it. They were mortified, ashamed of women, ashamed of the ignorance of women's libbers. They admitted to never having known any homosexuals; they admitted that churchgoing men in their own communities were sexually molesting their own daughters; they admitted that they were surrounded by men who went to church and were at the same time adulterers. I asked them why then they were afraid of homosexuals. One woman said, "If you had a child and he was playing out in the street and a car was coming you would move him out of the way, wouldn't you? Well, that's all we're trying to do—get homosexuality away from our children." I began to argue that the car coming down the street was more likely to be a heterosexual male neighbor, or even daddy, than a male homosexual or a lesbian. One woman stopped being nice. "You're a Jew," she said, "and probably a homosexual too." I found myself slowly being pushed farther and farther back against the balcony railing. I kept trying to turn myself around as we talked, to pretend that my position in relation to the railing and the fall of several hundred feet was not precarious; I kept talking with them, lowering the threshold of confrontation, searching my mind for pacifist strategies that would enable me to maneuver away from the railing by getting them to turn at least slightly toward it. They kept advancing, pushing me closer and closer to the railing until my back was arched over it. They kept talking about homosexuals and Jews. I kept saying pleasant things about how I respected their religious views; I kept asking them about their own lives and plans and ideas. They closed in around me. I was completely isolated up there, and I was getting panicky, they were getting moblike and intransigent, I kept trying to make myself human for them, they kept at transforming me into the embodiment of every homosexual Jew in the hall, the direct cause of their frustration and anger, they kept saying there was no middle ground and sin had to be wiped out and they hated sin; and I was deciding that I had better risk breaking through what had become a menacing gang, breaking away from the railing by pushing them as hard as I could, knowing that if I didn't make it they would start beating on me, when two dykes, one of whom I knew well, appeared there and just stood, watching. I made the religious women aware of the presence of the lesbian women, just standing, watching; and they moved away slightly, they moved reluctantly backward. I straightened up, moved away from that dreadful railing. I kept talking and slowly walked through the group of them, and the two lesbian feminists and I exited. I was shaking a lot. The woman I knew said quietly: we saw you up there and thought you might be in trouble, you just kept getting closer and closer to that railing, they were crowding you pretty bad, you shouldn't have been up there alone with them. She was right; but in common with so many other women I did not take the danger to myself seriously—a self-deprecating habit. Jew, lesbian, feminist: I knew the hatred was real, but I had not imagined these apparently docile women hating so much that with tiny steps they would become a gang: so full of unexamined hate that they would have pushed me over that railing "accidentally" in defense of Christianity, the family, and the happily heterosexual, churchgoing child molester down the block. In my own body, bent back over that railing, I knew the cold terror of being a homosexual Jew in a Christian country.

*

"Anti-Semitism," wrote Jean-Paul Sartre, "does not fall within the category of ideas protected by the right of free opinion. Indeed, it is something quite other than an idea. It is first of all a *passion*."[6] The great hatreds that suffuse history, pushing it forward to inevitable and repeated horror, are all first passions, not ideas. Hatred of blacks, hatred of Jews, and long-standing, intense, blood-drenched nationalist hatreds* are forms of race hatred. Hatred of women and hatred of homosexuals are forms of sex hatred. Race hatred and sex hatred are the erotic obsessions of human history: passions, not ideas. "If the Jew did not exist," Sartre wrote, "the anti-Semite would invent him."[7] The carrier of the passion needs the victim and so creates the victim; the victim is an occasion for indulging the passion. One passion touches on another, overlays it, burrows into it, enfolds it, is grafted onto it; the configurations of oppression emerge.

In patriarchal history, one passion is necessarily fundamental and unchanging: the hatred of women. The other passions molt. Racism is a continuous passion, but the race or races abused change over the face of the earth and over time. The United States is built on a hatred of blacks. In Western Europe, the Jew is the primary target. This does not stop the black from being hated by those who hate Jews first, or the Jew from being hated by those who hate blacks first. It means instead that one, and not the other, signifies for the dominant culture its bottom, its despised, its expendables. Homosexuality is elevated and honored in some societies, abhorred in others. In societies where hatred of homo-

---

*Noting the high opinion Amerikan slaveholders had of Irish laborers, English actress Fanny Kemble wrote in 1839: "How is it that it never occurs to these emphatical denouncers of the whole Negro race that the Irish at home are esteemed much as they esteem their slaves . . ." See *Journal of a Residence on a Georgian Plantation in 1838–1839* (New York: New American Library, 1975), p. 129.

sexuality has taken hold, fear of homosexuality is a terrifically powerful tool in the social manipulation and control of men: pitting groups of men—all of whom agree that they must be *men*, higher and better than women—against each other in the futile quest for unimpeachable masculinity. Hatred of homosexuality makes possible astonishing varieties of social blackmail and male-male conflict. In racism, the racially degraded male is sexually stereotyped in one of two ways. Either he is the rapist, the sexual animal with intense virility and a huge and potent member; or he is desexualized in the sense of being demasculinized—he is considered castrated (unmanned) or he is associated with demeaning (feminizing) and demeaned (not martial) homosexuality. It is the relationship of the dominant class to masculinity that determines whether males of the racially despised group are linked with rape or with castration/homosexuality. If the dominant group insists that the racially despised male is a rapist, it means that the dominant males are effeminate by contrast; it is they who are tinged with homosexuality in that they are less manly. They will climb the masculinity ladder by killing or maiming those whom they see as racially inferior but sexually superior. The Nazis transparently craved masculinity. It was the Jew who had stolen it from them by stealing the women they should have had. According to Hitler in *Mein Kampf:*

> With satanic joy in his face, the black-haired Jewish youth lurks in wait for the unsuspecting girl whom he defiles with his blood, thus stealing her from her people.[8]

German men unmanned by their own recent history (World War I) and a host of social and psychological inadequacies, as exemplified in their leader, found a savage redemption: the annihilation of a racial group of men perceived as being more male*—which, in this

---

*The racist perception of the Jewish woman "as a harlot, wild, promiscuous, the sensuous antithesis of the Aryan female, who was blond and

setting, means more animal, less human, not the human husband but the animal rapist. This annihilation was an act of mass cannibalism by which one group of men, lacking masculinity, got it from a mountain of corpses and from the actual killing as well.

In the United States, the black man was characterized as a rapist after the end of slavery. During slavery, his condition as chattel was seen to unman him entirely. His degradation was as a symbolically castrated man; a mule, a beast of burden. (His use as a stud to impregnate black women slaves to increase the slave wealth of the white master does not contradict this.) Vis-à-vis the white man, he was unmanned; and vis-à-vis the white woman he was unmanned.* Early in Reconstruction, May 1866, a fairly optimistic Frederick Douglass wrote that, though sometimes he feared a genocidal slaughter of blacks by whites, the movement of the former slaves "to industrial pursuits and the acquisition of wealth and education"[9] would lead finally to acceptance by whites. He recognized that even in success there was danger,

> for the white people do not easily tolerate the presence among them of a race more prosperous than themselves. The Negro as a poor ignorant creature does not contradict the race pride of the white race. He is more a source of amusement to that race than an object of resentment. Malignant resistance is augmented as he approaches the plane occupied by the white race,

---

pure" (see Andrea Dworkin, *Pornography: Men Possessing Women* [New York: Perigee Books, 1981], p. 147) also exacerbated the conviction that the racially superior men were not man enough: she provoked them endlessly with her savage eroticism, but they could not tame or satisfy her—they could not satisfy their craving for what they took her to be.

*The raping, impregnating, and whipping of black female slaves, women and girls, affirmed their gender: their slavery was an intensification of how men use women, not a contradiction of how women should be used in terms of sex. Slavery unmanned a man; it sexed a woman, made her even more absolutely available for sex and sadism. White male sexual domination of her, unrestrained use of her, made Southern white manhood supreme and irrefutable.

> and yet I think that that resistance will gradually yield to the pressure of wealth, education, and high character.[10]

By 1894, scores of black men had been murdered, lynched, beaten; mob violence against black men was frenzied and commonplace. "Not a breeze comes to us from the late rebellious states," Douglass wrote in "Why Is The Negro Lynched?" published in a pamphlet in 1894, "that is not tainted and freighted with Negro blood."[11] The white Southerners, deprived of their unmanned slaves, had found a justification for racist hatred: the black man—as part of his racial nature—raped white women. "It is a charge of recent origin," wrote Douglass rightly, "a charge never brought before; a charge never heard of in the time of slavery or in any other time in our history."[12] The end of slavery unmanned the white slaveowners. It was the former slaves who reminded them at every turn of that lost manhood, that lost power. It was gone, someone had taken it; they had been humiliated by the loss of the war and the loss of their slaves (those who had not owned slaves were still humiliated by the loss of them). The whites created the black rapist to reflect what the whites had in fact lost: the right to systematic rape of women across race lines. The whites created the black rapist to justify the persecution and killing of black men—and the literal castration of individuals to stand in for the symbolic castration of the whole group under them in slavery, the foundation of their sense of male power, the material basis of their male power. Rape has been traditionally viewed as a crime of theft: a woman stolen from a man to whom she rightfully belongs as wife or daughter. The black rapist was accused of a crime of theft, only what he stole was not the white woman; he stole the master's masculinity. The crime had nothing to do with women—it almost never does. The white men, unmanned, were accusing the black man of having raped them; the white woman was used as a figurehead, a buffer, a symbolic carrier of sex, a transmitter of sex man-to-man*—she almost always is.

Jewish males have experienced many turns of this homophobic screw. As the putative killers of Christ, it was hard for the "turn-the-other-cheek" Christians to take masculinity from them: killing God is a virile act. But the early Christians did just that. Jews and homosexuals are linked together in Romans in a propagandistic, highly evocative way. What has gone wrong? There are lesbians and male homosexuals, and the Jewish relationship to God through law is not enough. Lesbians are explicitly named to make the social consequences of sin clear: the women have become unnatural; they are no longer sexually submitting to men. The men are not just having sex with each other; they are unmanly enough to leave the women to each other. Naming lesbians provides a frame of reference in which one can gauge the loss of masculinity inherent in the unnatural acts of men. The unnatural acts of men are seen to lessen the polarization of the sexes. (In a society that admires male homosexuality, for instance, ancient Greece, these same acts are seen to heighten that polarization by glorifying maleness and so serve male supremacy.) So Paul, in Romans, establishes that homosexuals—lesbians named first—are full of malignity and worthy of death and then goes on to blame the failure of Jews and Jewish law for all that is most odious in the world—namely, homosexuality first:

---

*Strindberg wrote in his diary when his third wife left him: "It is as if, through her, I was entering into forbidden relationships with men . . . This torments me, for I have always had a horror of intimacy with my own sex; so much so that I have broken off friendly relations when the friendship offered became of a sickly nature, resembling love." (See August Strindberg, *Inferno and From an Occult Diary*, trans. Mary Sandbach [New York: Penguin Books, 1979], p. 314.) He also quotes Schopenhauer: "My thoughts are led through my woman to the sexual acts of an unknown man. In certain respects she makes a pervert of me, indirectly and against my will" (p. 310).

> And as Esaias said before, Except the Lord of Sabaoth had left us a seed, we had been as Sodoma, and been made like unto Gomorrha.
>
> What shall we say then? That the Gentiles, which followed not after righteousness, have attained to righteousness, even the righteousness which is of faith.
>
> But Israel, which followed after the law of righteousness, hath not attained to the law of righteousness.
>
> Romans 9:29–31

The Jew is even insidiously likened to the Greek, that pederast of universal fame: "For there is no difference between the Jew and the Greek: for the same Lord over all is rich unto all that call upon him" (Romans 10:12).

Then there is circumcision. According to Paul, it no longer signifies manly connection with God. Paul's denunciation of Jewish law virtually effeminizes not only the law—ineffectual against sin as it is—but the Jew, whose carnality could be restrained or governed by it. Paul's repudiation of Jewish law sounds almost like a sexual boast: "For we know that the law is spiritual: but I am carnal, sold under sin" (Romans 7:14). Anti-Semitism has been so versatile in so-called Christian societies because the Christians, nominal or passionate, could exploit the Jews both as killers of Christ (rapists*) or as overt or covert homosexuals (unmanly, wicked, deceitful, full of strife, malignity, unnatural; intellectuals tied to the abstract, ineffective law; smart as men who know the law are and also devious the way men who know the law are; faithless to God because they engaged in homosexual acts, because women castrated or effeminized them by being lesbian, because they socially tolerated homosexuality). Early on, Paul understood that his pacifist God nailed in exemplary masochistic sexual passion

*The sadism of this deicide establishes a basis for attributing to the Jews the most vile acts of cruelty, all tinged with sexual sadism: slaughter of infants to use their blood is a charge that, with rape, reappears cyclically.

to a cross had to offer converts masculinity: otherwise, Christ's suffering would not play in Peoria. The sexual brilliance of the passion could not hide the morbid femininity of the Jew who suffered it—willingly, as an act of human will. It was Paul's genius to link ineffective and effeminate Jewish law and Jews with unnatural homosexuals worthy of death. It was Paul's genius to exploit Christ as the prototypical Jew—he suffered like a female, it was his passion, an ecstasy of agonized penetration—and then to have the resurrection of Christ symbolize a new nature, a Christian nature: it dies, then rises. The son, born a Jew, was worthy of death—homosexual as Jews are, effeminate as Jews are, with their weak law and tenuous masculinity. The son resurrected triumphed over the father and over death. Those who were like him, Christians, shared in the victory, got closer to the real God (the one who won); got more masculine than that Jew who had died in unspeakable agony on the cross because the resurrected Christ was more masculine. The crucifixion without the resurrection would have left Jews and their God the repositories of patriarchal religious authority. The resurrection turned Jews from patriarchs into pansies, except when it was more useful to concentrate on them as the killers of Christ. The simple, cruel, rather monotonous God of the Jews could scarcely compete with the trebled divinity: The Father, The Son, The Holy Ghost—a father whose son superseded him in range of affect, emotion, and bravery, and whose Holy Ghost was purely and ideally phallic and all-penetrating. It was Paul, back on earth, who established the social ramifications of this religion of revelation rather than of law for the Jews who might be queer enough to cling to one god rather than his trebled usurper: like homosexuals, you are worthy of death.

*

The Old Testament does not contain the bloodlust against homosexuals and homosexuality found in the New Testament. There is no mention of lesbians at all. Lesbian acts are inferred to be among the "doings of Egypt" prohibited in Leviticus. No textual reference to Gomorrah suggests that it was destroyed because of lesbianism: this too has been inferred. It is not women who are commanded: "The nakedness of thy sister, the daughter of thy father, or daughter of thy mother, *whether she be* born at home, or born abroad, *even* their nakedness thou shalt not uncover" (Leviticus 18:9). All of the sexual prohibitions in Leviticus, including the prohibition against male homosexuality, are rules for effectively upholding the dominance of a real patriarch, the senior father in a tribe of fathers and sons. The controlling of male sexuality in the interests of male dominance—whom men can fuck, when, and how—is the essential in tribal societies in which authority is exclusively male. The rules in Leviticus are blueprints for minimizing intratribal sexual conflict among men. In chapter 18 of Leviticus, incest is broadly defined and prohibited; adultery, male homosexuality, intercourse with a menstruating woman, and intercourse with animals are also forbidden. In chapter 20 of Leviticus, death by stoning is the sentence "for every one that curseth his father or his mother" (Leviticus 20:9), for adulterers, for one who has intercourse with his father's wife or his daughter-in-law, for male homosexuality, for bestiality. Incest with one's sister and intercourse with a menstruating woman are not capital crimes: the punishment is being cut off from one's people. The heinous crime is not in the sexual act committed per se; it is certainly not in any abuse of women per se. The heinous crime is in committing a sexual act that will exacerbate male sexual conflict and provoke permanently damaging sexual antagonism in the tribe among men. For the Hebrews, sexual transgression that warranted death had the potential, if widely practiced, to cause the erosion of the power of men as a class by creating internecine sexual warfare within the class. The subordination of women was a means to male social cohesion. The regulation of that subordination through a regulation of male sexual behavior was straightforward and eminently practical: men were supposed to sacrifice some measure of pleasure to maintain power. Incest with one's sister did not incite male-male conflict so much as did intercourse with one's daughter-in-law or with the wife of one's father. Therefore, the punishment was not death by stoning. The prohibitions in Leviticus on sexual practices are without exception shrewd and pragmatic in these terms. All of the prohibitions further the aims of male dominance in the patriarchal tribe and contribute to the stability of male power. This is true too of the oft quoted prohibition of male homosexuality: "Thou shalt not lie with mankind, as with womankind: it *is* abomination" (Leviticus 18:22). This means simply that it is foul to do to other men what men habitually, proudly, manfully, do to women: use them as inanimate, empty, concave things; fuck them into submission; subordinate them through sex. The abomination is in the meaning of the act: in a male-supremacist system, men cannot simultaneously be used "as women" and stay powerful because they are men. The abomination is also, perhaps most of all, in the consequences of the act in a rigidly patriarchal tribal society: sexual rivalry among men meant trouble, feuds, war. The Jews were a tribe perpetually at war with others; they could not afford war among themselves.* And from the real beginning—once outside of Eden—the Jews reckoned with the anarchistic evil of fratricide: Cain and Abel, Jacob and Esau, Joseph and his brothers—all were tragic stories of brothers torn apart by jealous conflict over the blessing that showed they were the beloved, and these struggles to be the best-loved had huge historical consequences for the Jews. Actual carnal sex, the patriarchs recognized, would have made it worse, not better, intensified the conflict. Sexual acts among men threatened the social harmony on which the power of men depended, a social harmony made tenuous enough by the kind of sexual lust that male

*A more complex martial society, which the Hebrews became, could more easily socially tolerate homosexual liaisons, which the Hebrews apparently did. See discussion of David and Jonathan, p. 134.

dominance produces: the lust for forced sex. Directing that lust toward women, and trying to regulate which women, made the lust produced by male dominance work in behalf of male dominance, not against it so that it would collapse of its own sexual weight. In the Hebrew system, adultery and some other sexual transgressions of the familial pact were genuinely construed to be as bad as male homosexuality. There is no special repudiation of male homosexuality in the laws of Leviticus. There is no special punishment for it, though the punishment is death. There is no special characterization of the one who commits the act: he is not different in kind or degree from those who break other sexual prohibitions and are judged to deserve death by stoning.

The fact that the Hebrews attributed no special significance to the prohibition against male homosexuality in Leviticus and had no strictly sexual repugnance for the act is revealed and underscored by Maimonides' explication of the law, which will no doubt astonish modern readers:

> In the case of a man who lies with a male, or causes a male to have connection with him, once sexual contact has been initiated, the rule is as follows: If both are adults, they are punishable by stoning, as it is said, *Thou shalt not lie with a male* (Lev. 18:22), i.e. whether he is the active or the passive participant in the act. If he is a minor, aged nine years and one day, or older, the adult who has connection with him, is punishable by stoning, while the minor is exempt. *If the minor is nine years old, or less, both are exempt.* It behooves the court, however, to have the adult flogged for disobedience, inasmuch as he has lain with a male, even though with one less than nine years of age.[13] (Italics mine)

The Hebrews wanted the perpetuation of male dominance. A male child under nine did not have male status. Sex with that male child did not count as a homosexual act. Maimonides takes it on himself to remind the court that the child is male—though not male enough to warrant the real protection provided by capital punishment as a deterrent, which is what the death sentence was in the Hebrew system. The rules governing judgments of guilt were so strict in actual practice that it is unlikely that capital punishment could have been invoked for private, consensual sexual acts of any sort. It was the intrusion of sex into the larger society that concerned the Hebrews. A male child under nine, at any rate, did not warrant that protection because he was not yet part of the ruling class of men.

Similarly, the story of Sodom and Gomorrah shows that it is essential to male power (to the power of men as a class) to protect men from the sexual lust of other men—to protect men from forced sex by putting women in their place. No legal piety interferes with protecting men from homosexual assault by other men (in the story of Sodom, homosexual gang rape). The story of Sodom is meant to show that when the simple mechanical strategy of using women, not men, as targets for nonconsensual sex breaks down entirely, a patriarchal society will be destroyed. So God ordains; so the Old Testament describes: and it is an accurate assessment of the importance of keeping women the objects of forced sex so that men will not be subjected to it and need not fear it.

The story of Sodom and Gomorrah begins with a conversation between God and Abraham: God says that "[b]ecause the cry of Sodom and Gomorrah is great, and because their sin is very grievous; I will go down now, and see whether they have done altogether according to the cry of it, which is come unto me; and if not, I will know" (Genesis 18:20–21). Abraham asks God if he will destroy Sodom if there are fifty righteous men in the city. God promises that if there are fifty, he will spare the city. Abraham, after a few more interchanges, gets God to promise: "I will not destroy *it* for ten's sake" (Genesis 18:32). Two angels go to Sodom, where Lot bows down to them and offers them hospitality: safety in his home, washing of the feet, unleavened bread:

> But before they lay down, the men of the city, *even* the men of Sodom, compassed the house round, both old and young, all the people from every quarter:
>
> And they called unto Lot, and said unto him, Where *are* the men which came in to thee this night? bring them out unto us, that we may know them.
>
> And Lot went out at the door unto them, and shut the door after him.
>
> And said, I pray you, brethren, do not so wickedly.
>
> Behold now, I have two daughters which have not known man; let me, I pray you, bring them out unto you, and do ye to them as *is* good in your eyes: only unto these men do nothing; for therefore came they under the shadow of my roof.
>
> Genesis 19:4–8

The crowd, "both old and young, all the people from every quarter," attacked; the angels who appeared as men pulled Lot inside to save him, and "they smote the men that *were* at the door of the house with blindness, both small and great: so that they wearied themselves to find the door" (Genesis 19:11). The angels told Lot to leave Sodom because they were going to destroy it. Lot told his sons-in-law, but they did not believe him. In the morning, the angels told Lot to take his wife and two unmarried daughters; he lingered, the angels transported Lot and the women outside the city. God told Lot to go into the mountains and not to look back; Lot pleaded to be able to go to a nearby city; God said he would spare that city for Lot's sake: "Then the Lord rained upon Sodom and upon Gomorrah brimstone and fire from the Lord out of heaven; and he overthrew those cities, and all the plain, and all the inhabitants of the cities, and that which grew upon the ground" (Genesis 19:24–25). God remembered Lot, and spared him, and in the wave of destruction of cities, God sent Lot into the mountains, where Lot lived with his two daughters: "And the firstborn said unto the younger, Our father *is* old, and *there is* not a man in the earth to come in unto us after the manner of all the earth: Come, let us make our father drink wine, and we will lie with him, that we may preserve seed of our father" (Genesis 19:31–32). On successive nights, each had sex with her drunken father and both became pregnant. Both had sons, a blessing, and each of those sons became the father of a whole people, a blessing.

That the people of Sodom meant the strangers harm is clear. The nature of that harm is less clear. The demand of the mob to bring the strangers out "that we may know them" is sexual because the use of "know" usually is in biblical diction. The attempt of Lot to substitute his virgin daughters for the men suggests that the mob would have gang-raped the men. Whether the women in the mob were voyeurs or purveyors of other forms of violence is impossible to know: and yet the threat to the men does not seem to be only sexual; it seems to include sexual assault by men, beating, maiming, and murder. The mixed mob indicates the breakdown of male class power in the same way that the assault on the male visitors does: the rules that keep men exercising power as a class over women as a sexually and socially subject group have broken down absolutely; that *is* the destruction of the city. The destruction of Sodom is certainly not for breaking a sexual prohibition on homosexuality. The daughters who get their father drunk to have intercourse with him and bear his children also break laws: yet they are blessed. The lesson is not that the inferred homosexual assault is worse than the accomplished incest because one is homosexual and the other is heterosexual. Laws against incest come first in Leviticus and are repeated or invoked in other parts of the Old Testament. The lesson is that when men are not safe from other men—a safety that can only be achieved by keeping women segregated and for sex—the city will be wiped out. The daughters, in committing incest, broke the law in order to perpetuate patriarchal power: as a result of what they did, peoples, tribes, cities, were created. Whatever furthers male dominance, even when forbidden, will not destroy the city but build it. Sin, in the Old Testament, is first of all political. Law in the Old Testament is the regulation of society for the purposes of power, not morality. The Old Testament is a handbook on sexual politics: the rights of patriarchs and how to uphold them.

David perhaps also breaks a sexual prohibition. His love for Jonathan is indisputable, probably carnal, and goes beyond the abomination of lying with mankind as with womankind: "I am distressed for thee, my brother Jonathan: very pleasant hast thou been unto me: thy love to me was wonderful, passing the love of women" (II Samuel 1:26). David makes this declaration of love on learning of Jonathan's death in battle. Jonathan's father, Saul, also died, and he is remembered in the most heterosexual of frameworks: "Ye daughters of Israel, weep over Saul, who clothed you in scarlet, with *other* delights, who put ornaments of gold upon your apparel" (II Samuel 1:24). The passage on Jonathan follows the passage on Saul, so the contrast is very marked. And then there was a lot more war and David became king and time passed; but still, David's concern was with Jonathan: "Is there yet any that is left of the house of Saul, that I may shew him kindness for Jonathan's sake?" (II Samuel 9:1). David found that Jonathan had a son who was lame and serving another family. David restored all Saul's land to this son "for Jonathan thy father's sake" (II Samuel 9:7) and claimed Jonathan's son as his own: "he shall eat at my table, as one of the king's sons" (II Samuel 9:11). There is no sin, no condemnation, no wrath of God. Like the incest of Lot and his daughters, this union made Israel stronger, not weaker. The homosexual bond extended the loyalty and protection of King David to Jonathan's son, the grandson of Israel's first king, Saul. David, through his love of Jonathan, a love "passing the love of women," having survived Jonathan, might be seen as Saul's logical heir. Hebrew society had become more complex than in the early tribal days; Saul and David led armies; in a martial society, homosexuality is often seen to contribute to social cohesion among men. At least in this period, the Hebrews seem to have viewed it that way; with David and Jonathan in particular it worked that way; and Israel, its patriarchy intact (unlike that of Sodom), thrived. The

God of the Jews may not have been tolerant, but he was practical.

There is nothing in the Old Testament to justify the vilification of homosexuals or homosexuality that began with Paul and still manifests virulently in the fundamentalist Right in Amerika. It takes the magical claim that the New Testament is "concealed" in the Old to sustain the illusion of divine sanction for this special hatred of homosexuality. It is more than concealed; it is not there. Paul saw the power of the father in decline. The power of the son was taking its place. The Jews were confused and divided, and patriarchal power was not effectively being maintained by Jewish law. Paul worshiped male power; therefore Paul worshiped the son, was converted to the son's side when he saw the potential of that side for power. He was opportunistic, politically brilliant, and a master of propaganda. It was the shrewd Paul who finally undermined the law that had for centuries kept patriarchal power intact but now was failing, in decline. He scapegoated homosexuals as unnatural, deceitful, full of malignity, worthy of death, the source of intolerable evil; and then he blamed the Jews, and especially the law of the Jews, for the existence of homosexuality. "Therefore," Paul proclaimed in Romans 3:20, "by the deeds of the law there shall no flesh be justified in his sight: for by the law *is* the knowledge of sin." Paul introduced the hatred of homosexuality into the Judeo-Christian tradition, and he introduced the hatred of Jews into it too. In Christian countries, the two groups have suffered contempt, persecution, and death in each other's shadow ever since; they have been linked by demagogues seeking power through hate—demagogues like Paul; trying to pacify the likes of Paul, they have often enough repudiated and hated each other; and each group has hidden from the soldiers of Christ in its own way.

Democracies electing their sewage
till there is no clear thought about holiness
a dung flow from 1913

and, in this, their kikery functioned, Marx, Freud
and the american beaneries
Filth under filth . . .
Ezra Pound, "Canto 91"

The textual bases for what became the major anti-Semitic charges against the Jews are in the Gospels. Some Jews were money changers in the temple, tax collectors, liked money; some Jews plotted to have Christ killed; some Jews asked Christ tricky legalistic questions to try to expose him as a poseur or a heretic (claiming to be God violated Jewish law); it was a crowd of Jews—but not all the Jews—that demanded the crucifixion of Christ. Jews denied Christ and Jews believed in Christ. Most Jews may have been the enemy of this new God because they did not recognize him; but it was Paul who made all Jews into the enemy of all Christians. The acts against Christ came to represent, as Paul saw it, the Jewish character; the acts against Christ summed up the Jews. It is Paul who begins to build institutional Christianity by destroying the institutions of Judaism; and it is Paul who begins to build a distinctly Christian character by annihilating the character of the Jews. The roots of the continuing association of the Jews as a people with culture, social liberalism (tolerating sin), and intellectualism go back to Paul: he constructed the modern Jew in history.

Before the coming of Christ, the law was God's word. The law signified God's presence on earth and among his people. The law had a divine significance. The Jews did not consider the law social; for them, one obeyed because it was written—obedience was faith. The coming of Christ meant that God's will was embodied in a person: son of man. In Paul's interpretation, the law became a body of dogma that interfered with faith. It became cultural, not sacred. It was the legalism of the Jews, their intellection, their pedantry, that kept them in sin, kept them from recognizing the Christ: in practical terms, the law became the symbol of Jewish resistance to this personal God, this God whom Paul knew—unlike Abraham, Moses, or David. Paul could speak in behalf of this new God, and any adherence to law that challenged Paul's authority was wickedness. The law of the Jews, the intellect of the Jews, and the culture of the Jews in fact were the enemies of Paul's authority as one, simply, who knew Christ.

In undermining the authority of Jewish law, Paul over and over linked that law to sin, especially to homosexuality. It was the social tolerance of the Jews for homosexuality in private that proved the corruption of Jewish law. It was the lack of masculinity implicit in this tolerance that lost the Jews physical circumcision as their mark of supreme manhood; spiritual circumcision, the kind that would not tolerate homosexuality, became the proof of manhood.

Paul named the Jews the enemy of Christ, of Christianity, and of Paul. He emphasized the Jewish character, which he invented: legalistic, intellectual, socially tolerant of sin, intellectually arrogant in putting law over revelation and faith, lost to Christ through intellection and abstraction and legalism and social liberalism, having a false relationship to God (no longer God's people). Paul was not talking about some Jews who did this and some Jews who did that; Paul was talking about *the* Jews.

It was especially important for Paul, in getting power, to change the perception of what Jewish law was and how it functioned. Turning something holy, from God, into something cultural, the work of a group of corrupt men, is to turn the absolute into the relative. Anything cultural can be changed or abandoned or manipulated. The people whose law begins to represent culture, not divinity, are more imperiled than they were because their status depends on the status of culture in general in any given society: the infamous "Whenever I hear the word 'culture' I reach for my gun" denotes how low the status of culture can be with obvious consequences to those who represent it. Also, unless the law is made concrete because people obey it, it is abstract: and the abstraction of Jewish law became, in Paul's rhetoric, a major synonym for sin; in a sense, concentrating on the abstraction of the law literally turned intellection (more abstraction) into sin. What was not faith in Christ was Jewish stuff: abstract laws, tolerance of sin, law and writing and thinking as cultural diversions from the true faith. What does it mean that Paul especially concentrates on the sin of homosexuality in relation to the Jews and their law: the homosexual Greeks were at the pinnacle of culture five centuries before the birth of Christ—reading, writing, and ideas were their domain; Paul passed the mantle of high culture to the Jews after the demise of Greek culture—law substituted for both dialogue and tragedy. Culture, through Paul's agency, came to mean both homosexuals (the Greek heritage) and Jews (the law as a basis for culture). For hundreds of centuries, believing Christians have committed mass murders, pogroms, vast persecutions, crafted and enforced systems of civil and religious law so vicious and discriminatory that Jews have been prohibited from owning land, denied citizenship and all manner of civil rights, and even been defined as subhuman: sexual intercourse with them has been regarded as a form of bestiality. In at least two genocides of indescribable cruelty, both Jews and homosexuals were searched for, found, and killed: the Inquisition and the Holocaust.

The suffering of the Jews, the seemingly endless attempt to purge the Jew from history and from society by driving him out or exterminating him, has not made the Jews good. Jews remain human, to the astonishment of everyone, including Jews. But even more shocking to Christians is the undeniable fact that persecution has not made Jews into Christians. As one liberal Christian leader said on Sunday-morning television: we thought the Jews would wither away; we have to face the fact that the Jews are still with us and that even after the Holocaust there are still Jews who cling to their identity as Jews; those of us who thought that conversion was the answer to the Jewish problem have to face the fact that we were wrong; we are going to have accept the fact that these are God's people in a very special sense—they cannot be wiped out, as recent history has shown, as our attempts to convert them have shown.

Not being Christian in a world that hates the Jew, the homosexual, the castrated male, haunts the post-Holocaust Jew: he has seen the future and it is annihilation. Especially the contemporary Jew is fighting for his masculinity. In the camps Jewish men were castrated: some, only some. The castration was literal for individuals; two thirds of the world's Jewry was exterminated, which castrates the people as a whole rather effectively. Nothing threatens the Jewish male now more than a perception of him as being deficient in masculinity. For this reason, Israel is a militarist nation: no one will ever again accuse the Jews of being soft. For this reason, Amerikan Jewish writers are apostles of machismo and pimp masculinity. And for this reason, there is a growing segment of the Amerikan Jewish population that is part of the Christian evangelical Right.

First, there is the trade-off. On television, a rabbi and a priest were talking. The priest said: we feel about abortion the way you feel about Israel. I think we can talk, said the rabbi. It is in the interests of male Jews (the power structure) to increase the population of Jews. The trade-off—abortion for Israel—is in the interests of Jews both for the sake of Israel and for the sake of rebuilding a Jewish population in the easiest way—through male domination.

Second, there is the effort to dissociate the Jewish men from any perception of femininity, being less masculine. Israel, of course, makes Jews more male: owning land, controlling a state, having a nation, having an army, having borders to defend and to transgress. In associating with the Christian Right, there is a repudiation of homosexuality, liberal social tolerance of it (still blamed on Jews), a strong move against women (reestablishing male dominance), and in general making an alliance with the rulers—with the

Christians who run a Christian country.

Third, there is the fact that suffering has not made Jews good, which means that there are greedy Jews who think that power means safety and also who take pleasure in power. The Christian Right offers Jews not only a means of dissociation from homosexuality but also real dominance over women, if the social order the Christians want is effectively legislated.

Fourth, there is the fact that suffering has not made Jews good, which means that there are Jews who hate homosexuals, women, blacks, children, reading, writing, air, trees, and everything else the Christian Right seems to hate.

Fifth, the right-wing emphasis on the importance of property offers Jews a way of changing the history of Jews with respect to property—whether the property is Israel or land or housing or factories or farms. The protection of property suggests to Jews that they will not be driven off what they own.

Sixth, religious conservatism has its analogue in social conservatism, in that both particularly uphold the rights of men to ownership of women and children. Right-wing Jews who are religiously orthodox see the secular pluralism of Western society in general and the United States in particular as taking Jews away from Judaism: this, despite the emphasis that Judaism puts on learning, makes them hostile to secular learning, secular intellectuals, secular Jews, any education that is not strictly and explicitly Jewish. This brings them into a harmony of values with Christians who do not like Jews because Jews represent learning: the right-wing Jews are under the illusion that they and the Christian Right dislike the same Jews for similar reasons.

Seventh, strangely enough it is in this quasi-religious coalition with the Christian Right that right-wing Jews seek to find the assimilation that has always been the hope of Jews. We feel the same way you do, they say; we have the same values you have, the same ideals, the same goals, and we are doing our share. It has been brilliant strategy on the part of the Christian Right in the United States to welcome the participation of Jews, to support the state of Israel, and to use pedestal anti-Semitism: rather than being ground under stomping boots, Jews loyal in their right-wing values are being lifted up onto a pedestal—where the footing is always precarious, as women know. Believing they can fit in—assimilate—these Jews are turning to the one group of people—the fundamentalists—who will never forget that "the Jews killed Christ." Anything not to be that castrate, that homosexual; there is more dignity in the killing of Christ than in the concentration camps when the measure is masculinity.

In the contemporary world, Jews have an extra burden as creators of culture: Freud and Marx were Jews. The ideas of both are repugnant to the Christian Right. Freud, right or wrong, made sex a central social issue. Marx brought half the world to revolution. It is Marx that the United States government and the Christian Right are fighting; armies are raised and missiles are built to do it. It is Freud who asked why the family works the way it does and suggested that the family was a sexual unit. The intellectual Jew Freud had ideas that undermined what the Christian Right regards as the cornerstone of Amerikan life: the family. The real question, of course, was not about the family as such but about the paterfamilias: who is daddy having sex with and why? Freud refused to ask that question finally; but perhaps it would not have ever been asked, or no one would be asking it now, if Freud had not dissected the sexual underbelly of the family with his formidable intellect.

Right-wing Jews have a special stake in repudiating the ideas of both Freud and Marx. Ideas are sissifying, and Jews need masculinity. The ideas of these two Jewish intellectuals are dangerous: dangerous because right-wing Christianity hates them, therefore dangerous to Jews who do not want to be hated. Jews are cultural radicals and political revolutionaries by contamination. It's the damn Jews, a Klan member will say; and even he will mean Freud and Marx.* Ideas, however potent, do not serve to masculinize Jews. Ideas only make Jews more Jewish: more effeminate as intellectuals.

In the end, Jewish men join up with the Christian Right because they want domination over women and children, which is the social program of the Right; and because they want to be the opposite of homosexual, whatever that is.

> Everything in woman is a riddle, and everything in woman hath one solution—it is called pregnancy.
> Nietzsche, *Thus Spake Zarathustra*

Within the frame of male domination, there is good reason for women to adhere to conservative or right-wing or orthodox Judaism or conservative or right-wing or fundamentalist or orthodox Christianity; and within the frame of male domination, there is good reason for women to hate homosexuality, both male and female.

---

*Charles Darwin, whose ideas are as radical and as central to the contemporary epoch as are Freud's and Marx's, was not a Jew, but never mind. Lyndon LaRouche, the leader of a neo-Nazi movement that is getting powerful in the United States, claims that "the Zionist evil" is one of the "key arms of the British intelligence body which is behind the operation to destroy America" and that the Anti-Defamation League is "literally the Gestapo of the British secret intelligence" in the United States. In the propaganda of Lyndon LaRouche, who has been behind such diverse groups as the U.S. Labor Party, the Fusion Energy Foundation, the National Democratic Policy Committee, and the National Anti-Drug Coalition, "British" is virtually a synonym for "Jewish." (See "Lyndon LaRouche's Goon Squads," Alan Crawford, *Inquiry*, February 15, 1982, pp. 8–10.) "Creationism" (God created the world in seven days, there was no evolution) is a main tenet of the orthodox (not neo-Nazi) Right; the ideas of Darwin are as despised as the ideas of Freud and Marx.

Women are interchangeable as sex objects; women are slightly less disposable as mothers. The only dignity and value women get is as mothers: it is a compromised dignity and a low value, but it is all that is offered to women as women. Having children is the best thing women can do to get respect and be assured a place. The fact that having children does not get women respect or a place is almost beside the point: poor women don't get respect and live in dung heaps; black women don't get respect and are jailed in decimated ghettos; just plain pregnant women don't get respect and the place they have is a dangerous one—pregnancy is now considered a *cause* of battery (stress on the male, don't you know): in perhaps 25 percent of families in which battery occurs, it is a pregnant woman who has been battered. In fact, having children may mean both increased violence and increased dependence; it may significantly worsen the economic circumstances of a woman or a family; it may hurt a woman's health or jeopardize her in a host of other ways; but having children is the one social contribution credited to women—it is the bedrock of women's social worth. Despite all the happy smiling public mommies, the private mommies have grim private recognitions. One perception is particularly chilling: without the children, I am not worth much. The recognition is actually more dramatic than that, much more chilling: without the children, I am not. Right-wing Judaism and right-wing Christianity both guarantee that women will continue to have a place outside history but inside the home: through childbearing. Without that, women know they have nothing. Homosexuality for women means having nothing; it means extinction. Well, who's going to have the babies? men ask when faced with women surgeons and politicians—as if the question had an intrinsic logic; or as if ending war were not logically a part of having "enough" people. "All this talk, for and against and about babies," wrote Charlotte Perkins Gilman, "is by men. One would think the men bore the babies, nursed the babies, reared the babies. . . . The women bear and rear the children. The men kill them. Then they say: 'We are running short of children—make some more.'"[14] The extinction women fear is not this extinction men conjure up: who will make the babies so that we can fight our wars? It is the extinction of women: women's function and with it women's worth. Men have one reason for keeping women alive: to bear babies. The sex of domination leads to death: it is the killing of body and will—conquest, possession, annihilation; sex, violence, death—that is pure sex; and it is the slow annihilation of the woman's will that is eros, and the slow annihilation of her body that is eros; her violation is sex, whether it ends in her aesthetic disappearance into oblivion or her body bludgeoned in a newspaper photograph or the living husk used and discarded as sexual garbage. Annihilation is sexy, and sex tends toward it; women are the preferred victims of record. Only having children moderates men's sexual usage of women: use them up and throw them away, fuck them to death, killing them softly. If women are not needed to run the country or write the books or make the music or to farm or engineer or dig coal or fix plumbing or cure the sick or play basketball, what are women needed for? If the absence of women from all these areas, from all areas, is not perceived as loss, emptiness, poverty, what are women for? Right-wing women have faced the answer. Women are for fucking and having children. Fucking gets you dead, unless you have children too. Homosexuality—its rise in public visibility, attempts to socially legitimize or protect it, a sense that it is attractive and on the move and winning not only acceptance but practitioners—makes women expendable: the one thing women can do and be valued for will no longer be valued, cannot be counted on to be that bedrock of women's worth. This is true of both lesbianism and male homosexuality, in that both negate women's reproductive value to men; but male homosexuality is especially terrifying because it suggests a world without women altogether—a world in which women are extinct. "[I]n sorrow thou shalt bring forth children," God cursed Adam's woman (Genesis 3:16)—she is referred to as "the woman" until she and Adam are expelled from Eden and Adam names her

Eve "because she was the mother of all living" (Genesis 3:20). On expulsion from Eden man knew sex leading to death; and woman knew childbearing in sorrow and pain, on which her well-being, such as it is, still depends. The sorrow was apparently avoided altogether by Phyllis Schlafly, who waxes euphoric on having children: "None of those measures of career success [traveling to "exciting faraway places," having authority over others, winning, or earning a fortune] can compare with the thrill, the satisfaction, and the fun of having and caring for babies, and watching them respond and grow under a mother's loving care. More babies multiply a woman's joy."[15] The thrill, the endlessly multiplying joy, was not in God's original intention; and indeed, it is unlikely that Schlafly has outwilled him. In the sorrow of having children there is the recognition that one's humanity is reduced to this, and on this one's survival depends. Being a woman is this, or it is unspeakably worse than this. Homosexuality brings up for women the barrenness of not even having this. A woman has committed her life to bringing forth children in order to have a life of dignity and worth; she has found the one way in which she is absolutely necessary; and then, that is gone as an absolute. It must be an absolute, because there are women who stake their lives on it as an absolute; it is certainly what women have had to count on. Everything that women have to gain from homosexuality—and women have a great deal to gain from it: less forced penetration of themselves, for instance—is obliterated by the fear of losing what value women have, a fear conjured up by homosexuality in women whose own right to life is in having children. Despite all the happy talk of the total women, there is a fierce anxiety there: if men did not need babies, and women to have them, these bright wives would be shivering on street corners like the other fast fucks. Her womb is her wealth; her use in childbearing is his strongest tie to her; she holds his [sic] children, actual and potential, hostage, for her own sake. It is not rational to hate homosexuals because they force one to experience a terror of extinction: the cold chill of being useless, unnecessary, expendable. But passions are distinguished by their illogic: one can describe them and find an interior logic in them up to a point—then there is a sensational leap into hate, dazzling, crazed, obsessional. Homophobia, like anti-Semitism, is not an idea; it is a passion. For women, hatred of homosexuals—despised because they are associated with women—is more than self-defeating; it is almost breathtakingly suicidal, encouraging as it does the continuing hatred of anything or anyone associated with women. But the perception that having children is the only edge women have on survival at the hands of men is right; it is an acute perception, grounded in an accurate reading of what women are for and how women are used by men in this sexual system. Without reproduction, women as a class have nothing. In sorrow or not, bearing babies is what women can do that men need—really need, no handjob can substitute here; and homosexuality makes women afraid, irrationally, passionately afraid, of extinction: of being unnecessary as a class, as women, to men who destroy whatever they do not need and whose impulses toward women are murderous anyway.

5

The Coming Gynocide

> Rich as you are
>
> Death will finish
> you: afterwards no
> one will remember
>
> or want you; . . .
> Sappho

In *A Room of One's Own*, first read as a paper in 1928, the prescient Virginia Woolf called the attention of the women in her audience to a statement by a popular British journalist of the time who warned "that when children cease to be altogether desirable, women cease to be altogether necessary."[1] The woman who is deviant because she has no children, as Woolf was even in her avant-garde set, is often aware of how tenuous her existence is: it is a courtesy extended to her—letting her go on—despite the fact that she is not earning her womanly keep in the womanly way. She knows how little the world at large needs her or values her for anything else she does even when she is exceptional; and if she understands how systematic and relentless the valuation of her kind is, she also knows that at the heart of the male system there is a profound contempt for anything in women that is individual, that is independent of the class definition or function, that cannot finally be perceived and justified as incidental to motherhood.

Had anyone thought seriously about how women "cease to be altogether necessary," they might have thought in terms of population control: there are too many people; governments decide to feed all the people, which provides a certain incentive for finding ways to see that there are less people; this is presented to the people as a humanistic program to increase the quality of life for a smaller, less burdensome, less troubled population; the women who were giving birth to the teeming masses are not altogether necessary anymore. There is lots of liberal hope and goodwill. The Right has reason to be pleased too, since society operates largely according to its conception of value: poor, black, Hispanic, and immigrant populations would inevitably be the targets of state-run population-control programs; the teeming masses, so messy, so poor, so dark, would disappear, or significantly diminish in numbers, taking with them the poverty for which their color seems responsible. Get rid of those dirty beggars in India. Get rid of the bastards those black women on welfare keep producing. Get rid of the Jews too, the old and sick, the Gypsies, the homosexuals, the political dissidents—as the Nazis did, often in the name of creating a better-quality population. But the Nazis did not just kill to get rid of the population garbage. They had a program of breeding. Himmler developed a plan for a Women's Academy of Wisdom and Culture: it would give a degree called "Exalted Woman." Birth control advertising was forbidden; birth control clinics were shut down; abortions were forbidden and the Nazis were fierce enforcers of antiabortion laws; all so that Aryan women would breed. In 1934, the Nazis established the Mother Service Department. Its purpose was to educate women over eighteen to fulfill the duties of womanhood Nazi-style. "The program of our Nationalist Socialist woman's movement contains really only one single point," said Hitler in 1934. "This point is the child that must come into being and that must thrive."[2] Fiancées of S.S. men had to take the training offered by the Mother Service Department. Pure German women were encouraged to bear the children of S.S. men and were supported by the Nazi state. Himmler established homes for these women. No abortion, no birth control, no careers other than motherhood for the racially pure; imprisonment, rape, sometimes sterilization, and death for the others. The racially privileged woman is not free; the conditions of her survival are predetermined; she may get rewards for meeting them but outside of them she has no chance. While the racially inferior women are being used one way, the racially superior women are being used in what appears to be an opposite way: but it is not. These are two sides of the same coin. The two sides travel together, materially inseparable and yet unalterably divided. Neither side, in this case, has a life outside totalitarian womanhood. In such a society, the racially privileged woman has the best deal; but she is not free. Freedom is something different from the best deal—even for women.

State-run population programs always have the racist tinge and are sometimes explicitly and murderously racist. Population-control programs run by any state or state-controlled agency or beholden to any male interest or clique are very different from the ideology and practice of reproductive freedom. Reproductive freedom has as its basic premise the notion that every individual woman must control her own reproductive destiny. She has a right to be protected from state intrusion and from male intrusion: she has a right to determine her own reproductive life. Abortion on demand, for instance, is at the will of the pregnant woman; sterilization of poor women is usually at the will of the male doctor who represents his race and class and is often paid by the state or acts in accordance with the interests of the state. Sterilization abuse in the United States has been practiced primarily on very poor black and Hispanic women. Contraceptives are tested on the women in Puerto Rico, which has the virtue of being a U.S. colony as well as having a brown-skinned population. Contraceptive drugs known to be highly toxic are tested systematically on women in the Third World with that astonishingly familiar misogynist justification—"They want it." The evidence of this collective will is that the women line up for injections of such drugs. It is frequently not mentioned that a chicken or other food is payment for taking the shot, and the women are starving and so are their children. Those who have seen institutionalized programs of population control as a humane and sensible solution to some aspects of mass poverty have been unable to face the problem intrinsic to these programs: the poor are often also not white, and the enthusiasm of state planners for population control is often based on this fact. Children of these women long ago ceased to be altogether desirable; and these women long ago ceased to be altogether necessary.

The marginality of these masses of women because of race has obscured how much their expendability has to do with being women. "Made in South America Where Life Is Cheap" read the advertisements for the pornographic film *Snuff*, which purported to show the torture, maiming, and murder of a woman for the purposes of sexual entertainment: the removing of the woman's uterus from her slit abdomen was the sexual act to which the man in the film who was doing the cutting supposedly climaxed. Life is cheap for both women and men wherever life is cheap, and life is cheap wherever people are poor. But for women, life is in the uterus; and the well-being of women—economic, social, sexual—depends on what the value of the uterus is, how it will be used and by whom, whether or not it will be protected and why. Whatever her race or class—however much she is privileged or hated for one or both—a woman is reducible to her uterus. This is the essence of her political condition as a woman. If she is childless, she is not worth much to anyone; if her children are less than desirable, she is less than necessary. On a global scale, racist population programs already exist that provide the means and the ideological justifications for making masses of women extinct because their children are not wanted. The United States, a young, virile imperialist power compared to its European precursors, has pioneered this kind of reproductive imperialism. The United States was the perfect nation to do so, since the programs depend so much on science and technology (the nation's pride) and also on a most distinctive recognition of precisely how expendable women are as women, simply because they are women. Obsessed with sex as a nation, the United States knows the strategic importance of the uterus, abroad and at home.

Inside the United States, gynocidal polices are increasingly discernible. The old, the poor, the hungry, the drugged, the mentally ill, the prostituted, those institutionalized in wretchedly inhumane nursing homes and mental hospitals, are overwhelmingly women. In a sense, the United States is in the forefront of developing a postindustrial, post-Nazi social policy based on the expendability of any group in which women predominate and are not valued for reproduction (or potential reproduction in the case of children). Public policy in the United States increasingly promises to protect middle-class or rich white women owned in marriage who reproduce and to punish all other women. The Family Protection Act—a labyrinthian piece of federal legislation designed to give police-state protection to the male-headed, male-dominated, female-submissive family—and the Human Life Amendment, which would give a fertilized egg legal rights adult women are still without, would be the most significant and effective bludgeoning instruments of this public policy if passed. Along with already actual cutbacks in Social Security, Medicaid, and food programs, these laws are intended to keep select women having babies and to destroy women who are too old to reproduce, too poor or too black or brown to be valued for reproducing, or too queer to pass. This, in conjunction with the flourishing pornography industry in which women are sexually consumed and then shit out and left to collect flies, suggests that women will have to conform slavishly to right-wing moral codes to survive; and that, too poor or too old, a woman's politics or philosophy however traditionally moral will not make her life a whit more valuable. The use the state wants to make of a woman's uterus already largely determines—and will more effectively determine in the future—whether she is fed or starved, genuinely sheltered or housed in squalor, taken care of or left in misery to pass cold, hungry, neglected days.

The association of women with old age and poverty predates the contemporary Amerikan situation, in which women are the bulk of both the old and the poor. In 1867, Jean Martin Charcot, known primarily for his work with the institutionalized insane, did a systematic study of old age. The population he studied was old women in a public hospital in Paris—female, old, poor, urban. Since that time, many psychological and sociological generalizations about the old have been framed as if the population under discussion were male, even when it was exclusively female as in Charcot's study. Many observations about the old were made by professional men about poor women. As if to signal both the symbolic and actual relationship between old age and women, the first person in the United States to receive a Social Security check after the passage of the Social Security Act in 1935 was a woman, Ida M. Fuller. Now in the United States, when there is no doubt whatsoever that the old are primarily female, that the poor are primarily female, that those on welfare are primarily female, that those in nursing homes are primarily female, that those in mental institutions are primarily female, there is still no recognition that the condition of poverty is significantly related to the condition of women; or that the status of old people, for instance, is what it is because the bulk of the old are women. "Indeed," writes one writer on old age, "relatively recent trends in the aging of America may have changed the status of older Americans. It is conceivable, for instance, that the elderly have become a much larger burden to society since World War I. After all, women, very old persons, and those 'stuck' in deteriorating locations now constitute a greater proportion of the aged population than ever before."[3] Women, very old persons, and those "stuck" in deteriorating locations: women, women, and women. "After all," women, women, and women "now constitute a greater proportion of the aged population than ever before"—the status of the old has changed, gone down;

they are more of a burden; "after all," they are women. In 1930, there were more men over sixty-five than women; by 1940, there were more women. In 1970, there were 100 women to 72 men over sixty-five. In 1990, for every 100 women there will "only" be 68 men (as the experts put it). The situation is getting worse: because the more women there are, the fewer men, the worse the situation gets. Old women do not have babies; they have outlived their husbands; there is no reason to value them. They live in poverty because the society that has no use for them has sentenced them to death. Their tenacity in holding on to life is held against them. Cuts in Social Security and food programs for the old directly issue from the willingness of the U.S. government to watch useless females go hungry, live in viciously degrading poverty, and die in squalor. On the television news, social workers tell us several times a week that old people are going hungry: "they have just enough food to keep them alive," one said, "but they never eat enough to stop them from being hungry." Then we see the interviews with old people, the cafeterias where old people who can walk go to get their one meal of the day. They are mostly women. They say they are hungry. We can observe, if we care to, that they are female and hungry.

Within this population of the old, there are the people in nursing homes. "There are more than 17,000 nursing homes in the United States—as opposed to roughly 7,000 general hospitals—and their aggregate revenues exceed $12 billion a year," writes Bruce C. Vladeck in *Unloving Care: The Nursing Home Tragedy*. "They have been described as 'Houses of Death,' 'concentration camps,' 'warehouses for the dying.' It is a documented fact that nursing home residents tend to deteriorate, physically and psychologically, after being placed in what are presumably therapeutic institutions. The overuse of potent medications in nursing homes is a scandal in itself. Thousands of facilities in every state of the nation fail to meet minimal government standards of sanitation, staffing, or patient care. The best governmental estimate is that roughly half the nation's nursing homes are 'substandard.'"[4] In 1978, according to Vladeck, there were still nursing homes "with green meat and maggots in the kitchen, narcotics in unlocked cabinets, and disconnected sprinklers in nonfire-resistant structures."[5] Over 72 percent of the nursing home population is female. Women in nursing homes are generally widows or never married, white, poorer than most of their peers (70 percent having incomes under $3000 a year consisting mainly of Social Security benefits), and have several chronic diseases. According to *The New York Times* (October 14, 1979), the average age of the person in such an institution is 82 and 50 percent have no family, get no visitors, and are supported by government money. Conditions are most terrible in nursing homes supported by government funding of patient care: nursing homes for the destitute, for those on Medicaid. The policy of the United States government is that old people must become paupers:* spend any money of their own that they have, after which the government takes over; the paupers are unable to defend themselves

---

*See "Loose Laws Make Care of Aged Costly," by Gertrude Dubrovsky, *The New York Times*, October 21, 1979. In a subsection called "How the Programs Work," Dubrovsky explains:

"As of April 1977, the last period for which such figures were available, a nursing-home patient under Medicaid could not have an income greater than $533.39 a month. However, should this same person want to remain at home and receive community-based health-related services, his monthly income must be less than $200.

"Thus, Medicaid laws are biased in favor of institutional care.

"Morever, Medicaid imposes strict personal-asset limits of $1,500 for a single person or $2,500 for a couple.

"To be accepted by a nursing home under Medicaid, a person must sell his home, liquidate his assets and turn them over to Medicaid as a gift, in which case he stays on Medicaid.

"Or, he may give the funds directly to the nursing home as a private payment until the money falls below the allowable level. When that happens, the patient reapplies for Medicaid, but may be put on a waiting list."

against the conditions in the homes in which they are kept. Once paupers, they must accept confinement on the state's terms because they have no money and nowhere to go. The state's terms all too frequently are neglect, degradation, filth, and not infrequently outright sadism.

The nursing home population is markedly white. Blacks die younger than whites in the United States—perhaps the result of systematic racism, which means inadequate health care, shelter, and money over a lifetime. Blacks alone comprise a full 11.8 percent of the U.S. population and yet only 9 percent of the old are people of color, including Asians, Native Americans, and Hispanics. Nationally, so-called nonwhites (including blacks) comprise only 5 percent of the nursing home population. In New Jersey, for instance, according to *The New York Times* (October 21, 1979), out of 8,683 beds in eighty nursing homes, blacks occupied 532 and Hispanics or "others" occupied 38 (6.5 percent). It seems that blacks especially are left to suffer the diseases of old age on their own and to die on their own; and that whites are institutionally maintained in appalling conditions—kept alive but barely. If this is true, the social function of nursing homes becomes clearer: out of sight, out of mind. Blacks are already invisible in ghettos—young, middle-aged, old. Black women have been socially segregated and marginalized all their lives. Perceptions of their suffering are easily avoided by an already callous white-supremacist populace, the so-called mainstream. It is white women who have become poor and extraneous with old age; they are taken from mainstream communities where they are useless and dumped in nursing homes. It is important to keep them away from those eager, young, middle-class white women who might be demoralized at what is in store for them once they cease to be useful. Kept in institutions until they die as a punishment for having lived so long, for having outlived their sex-appropriate work, old white women find themselves drugged (6.1 prescriptions for an average patient, more than half the patients given drugs like Thorazine and Mellaril); sick from neglect with bedsores, urinary, eye, and ear infections; left lying in their own filth, tied into so-called geriatric chairs or tied into bed; sometimes not fed, not given heat, not given any nursing care; sometimes left in burning baths (from which there have been drownings); sometimes beaten and left with broken bones. Even in old age, a woman had better have a man to protect her. She has earned no place in society on her own. With a man, she will most likely not end up in a prison for the female old. She has more social value if she has a man, no matter how old she is—and she will also have more money. After a lifetime of systematic economic discrimination—no pay for housekeeping, lower pay for salaried work, lower Social Security benefits, often with no rights to her husband's pension or other benefits even after decades of marriage if he has left her—a woman alone is virtually resourceless. The euphemistically named "displaced homemaker" foreshadows the old woman who is put away.

The drugging of the predominantly female nursing home population continues in old age a pattern established with awful frequency among women: women get 60 to 80 percent of the prescriptions for mood-altering drugs (60 percent of the prescriptions for barbiturates, 67 percent for tranquilizers, and 80 percent for amphetamines). Women are prescribed more than twice the drugs that men are for the same psychological conditions. One study of women in Utah, cited by Muriel Nellis in *The Female Fix*, "showed that 69 percent of women over the age of thirty-four who were not employed outside the home and who were members in good standing of the Mormon Church use minor tranquilizers."[6] Such women are considered a high-risk group for addiction by the time they are forty-five or fifty.

The dimensions of female drug addiction and dependency are staggering. In 1977, 36 million women used tranquilizers; 16 million, sleeping pills; 12 million, amphetamines; and nearly 12 million women got prescriptions for these drugs from doctors for the first time. As Nellis, who cites these figures,* makes clear:

> Those numbers do not include whole classes of prescribed pain killers, all of which are mood altering and addictive. Nor do they include the billions of doses dispensed to patients directly, without a prescription, in doctors' offices, in military, public, or private hospitals, and in clinics or nursing homes.[7]

According to the Food and Drug Administration, between 1977 and 1980 Valium was the most prescribed drug in the United States.

At best it can be said that the woman's lot in life, the female role, necessitates a lot of medical intervention in the form of mood-altering drugs. At worst it must be said that these drugs are prescribed to women because they are women—and because the doctors are largely men. The male doctor's perception of the female patient, conditioned by his belief in his own difference from her and superiority to her, is that she is very emotional, very upset, irrational, has no sense of proportion, cannot discern what is trivial and what is important. She has no credibility as an observer of her own condition or even as one who can report subjective sensations or feelings with any integrity or acuity. She is overwrought not because of any objective condition in her life but because she is a woman and women get emotional and overwrought simply because that is how women are. Doctors have prescribed tranquilizers to women for menstrual cramps, which have a physiological cause; for battery—the battered woman is handed a prescription and sent home to the batterer; for pregnancy—a woman is chemically helped to accept an unwanted pregnancy; for many

*Testimony in 1978 by the acting director of the National Institute on Drug Abuse before the House Select Committee on Narcotics Abuse and Control.

physiologically rooted diseases that the doctor does not care to investigate (but he would examine a man carefully, not give a tranquilizer); and for physiological and psychological conditions that result from stress caused by environmental, political, social, or economic factors. When a man and a woman go to doctors complaining of the same symptoms, she is dismissed or handed a tranquilizer and he is examined and given tests. *Hysteria* means suffering of the womb. Since antiquity it has denoted biological womanhood. Freud is credited by some sentimentalists as a feminist because he insisted that men could be genuinely hysterical too. He was the first to assert that hysteria could manifest in someone without a womb. This was very liberal and rebellious, and Freud's was a lone voice. Medical opinion was that hysteria as a pathology was exclusively limited to women because women had wombs and because women were obviously hysterical. Despite Freud's apostasy and its subsequent acceptance in psychoanalytic theory, hysteria is still associated with the female. She does not have reason or intellect; she has emotion. She starts with a lot of emotion by virtue of being female; when she gets more emotion than is socially acceptable, or when emotion begins to interfere with the exercise of her female functions or the performance of her female duties, then she is sedated or tranquilized. Female complaints to male doctors are perceived as emotional excrescences; and indeed, women learn as girls that either they convince through emotional display or they do not convince at all, so that women do tend to persuade by force of feeling and do learn early to compensate for the almost certain knowledge that they will not be believed because they are not credible no matter how accurate, restrained, or logical they are. The solution to female emotional excess, whether expressed by the woman—appropriately by her lights—or hallucinated by the male doctor, is keeping women calm or numb or asleep with drugs. The dulling of the female mind is neither feared nor noticed; nor is the loss of vitality or independence. The female is valued for how she looks—sometimes droopy eyelids are quite in fashion—and for domestic, sex, and reproductive work, none of which requires that she be alert. She is given drugs because nothing is lost when she is drugged, except what is regarded as the too thick edge of her emotional life. She is given drugs because she is not much valued; she takes the drugs because she is not much valued; she stays on the drugs because she is not much valued; the doctors keep prescribing the drugs because she is not much valued; the effects of addiction or dependency on her are not much noted because she is not much valued. These are prescription drugs, regarded as appropriate medications for women. The junkie, for the most part, is left to the violent life of the streets; the woman addicted to prescribed drugs has already been tamed and is kept tamed by the drugs. The drugs are prescribed to these huge numbers of women each and every year because their usage not only supports but significantly upholds social policy with respect to women: their effects reinforce women in traditional female roles, postures, and passivity; they dull women's perceptions of and responses to an environment and predetermined social status that are demeaning, aggravating, and enraging; they quiet women down. The use of these drugs to numb these masses of women shows only how little women are worth—to the doctors who do the prescribing, to the women themselves, to the society that depends on this mass drugging of women to help in keeping women as a class quiescent and women as individuals invisible or aberrant. Thirty-six million women can be tranquilized in a year and the nation does not notice it, does not miss their energy, creativity, wit, intellect, passion, commitment—so much are these women worth, so important is their contribution, so indelible is their individuality, so essential is their vigor.

In addition to being too emotional, women can be too fat. In fact, it is hard not to be; and it is sometimes pointed out that Amerikan standards of beauty dictate a leanness closer to the skeletal depravity of concentration camp victims than to any other socially recognized physiognomy. Most amphetamines are prescribed as diet pills, although women use them to propel themselves through the normal routine of a day. Depression is commonplace among women because housework is boring, sex is boring, cooking is boring, children are boring, and the woman resents being bored but cannot change it. Depression is commonplace among women because women are often angry at the conditions of their lives, at what they must do because they are women, at the way they are treated because they are women; and depression truly is anger turned inward. Depression is commonplace among women because a woman's life is often a series of dead ends, joy in which is the measure of femininity. A decade or two ago, doctors prescribed amphetamines with a reckless abandon. Now they are more cautious, and not only because amphetamines wreak havoc on the human body: amphetamines lead women away from femininity toward aggression, social dysphoria, and a paranoia that threatens the women's compliance as a sexual partner; tranquilizers and sleeping pills interfere much less with the female life as it should be lived, no matter how serious the addiction. Doctors justify the use of amphetamines—by those 12 million women users in one year, for instance—in terms of getting women thinner. Women get the drug by saying they want or need to be thinner no matter how thin they are; or doctors prescribe the drug without explanation as to its qualities and effects—especially they make no reference to its addictive nature and to the high it produces. The woman knows her value is in becoming what the man wants to have; she has no sense of self outside his evaluation of what she should be. Male doctors essentially share the same male values; and women accept their authority as men, not just as doctors. The woman's body is evaluated according to a sexual aesthetic, not according to a medical ethic. Amphetamines prescribed by a doctor reinforce the misogynist rule that a woman's only wealth is her body as an object; and that any act of self-destruction—like taking amphetamines—is both justified and sexually enhancing if it makes her what men want. Doctors accept and sometimes encourage this logic; doctors often subscribe to it and pass it on to women. If women are not thin, what are they? This is not a standard that can be applied to a respected or self-respecting individual or to a respected or self-respecting group; it is applied ruthlessly to women and it is not applied to men.

But the doctors know that women use amphetamines not just to get thinner but also to stay awake in the course of brutally soporific days; to push away paralyzing bouts of depression that come from the quality of the woman's life—her accurate perception of it; to get the energy to put one foot in front of another in a life she hates but feels powerless to change. So that even the use of amphetamines—with effects that are apparently opposite to those of tranquilizers and sedatives—keeps the woman in her life as it is and as a male-dominated society wants it to be; it keeps her functioning in the domestic sphere, whether exclusively or not; it keeps her going through the habits of being female; it keeps her executing the routines of a life that dissatisfies her profoundly. And the social imperative is to keep her there, no matter what the cost to her as an individual. So the doctors write the prescriptions. Prescribed amphetamines keep the woman conforming when she was ready to stop dead in her tracks, keep her female when she would rather be genuinely inert and inanimate, keep her doing what she could not bring herself to do without them.

These drugs—amphetamines, tranquilizers, sedatives—are agents of social control; an elite male group does the controlling; women are the class controlled. The willingness of the doctors—male medical professionals—to use these drugs on women systematically and the perceptions of women that lead them to do so are evidence of the expendability of women, the essential worthlessness of women when measured against a human standard as opposed to a standard of female function. One does not dump drugs on society's best and brightest; nor is a drug habit encouraged in those who have work to do, a future with some promise, and a right to dignity and self-esteem. Through the use of drugs, the doctors are doing their part in the social control of women. They have shown themselves willing—even eager sometimes—to go further. Decades ago clitoridectomies were all the rage as doctors did their surgical bit to control sexual delinquency in women. Now, after being out of fashion for a few short years, the doctors are trying to bring psychosurgery back into style. In a violent society, they say, it is more than useful; it is necessary. The ideal patient for lobotomy is considered to be a black female. Her violence, apparently, is simply in being a black female. She is ideal for the operation because afterward she can still perform the functions for which she is best suited: she can be female in all the conventional ways, and she can still clean other people's houses.

Surgeons, however, need step in only where welfare programs have already failed to provide a pool of cheap black female labor. In *Regulating the Poor: The Functions of Public Welfare*,* Frances Fox Piven and Richard A. Cloward show that black women have been given less money than white women in welfare payments and as a result have had to do menial work to achieve the barest subsistence; or have been kept off the welfare rolls altogether by administrators who have manipulated regulations to exclude blacks, in keeping with the racist policies of local or state governments. This pattern of discrimination was particularly evident in the South, but it was also found in other regions of the country:

> There are many mechanisms by which Southern welfare departments deny or reduce payments to blacks, thus keeping them in the marginal labor market. The "employable mother" rule [that a mother must work if the welfare agency determines

*An important book that analyzes the economic value of racism under capitalism but sadly fails to address the exploitation of women as such; as a result, the social and sexual controls on the welfare population are understood superficially; the ubiquitous and almost self-renewing nature of the controls is not taken seriously enough—it is not recognized that as long as the sexual oppression is intact, the controls will keep appearing, even if reform seems to have eliminated them.

> that there is appropriate work for her] . . . has been applied discriminatorily against black women: when field hands are needed, Southern welfare officials assume that a black woman is employable, but not a white woman.[8]

These machinations of the welfare system are commonplace and pervasive. A great effort has been made—contrary to public perceptions—to keep black women off the welfare rolls, to make them even more marginal and often even poorer than those on welfare. The specifics can change—for instance, which women must work, when, and why—but the kind of control the welfare system seeks to exercise over poor women does not change. The first "employable mother" rule was invoked in Louisiana in 1943; Georgia adopted the same kind of regulation in 1952; in 1968 a federal court in Atlanta struck down Georgia's "employable mother" rule, which was widely considered to have negated the force of that rule in the states where it existed; and yet in 1967 Congress had required states to make mothers on welfare report for work or work training—a law erratically enforced and therefore subject to the same abuses as the old "employable mother" regulation. The kind of control welfare exercises over poor women does not change because the population welfare is designed to control does not change: female.

The question of suitable employment is raised persistently within the welfare system: what is to be expected of women with children? should they work or stay home? what kind of work are they offered or forced to take? is that work entirely determined by prejudgments as to their nature—what can and should be expected of them because they are female, female and black, female and white, female and poor, female and unmarried? In New York City, women on welfare say that they have been strongly encouraged by welfare workers to turn to prostitution, the threat being that the individual woman may in the future be denied welfare benefits because the caseworker knows the woman could be making big bucks on the street; or in emergencies, women on welfare are told to raise the money they need by turning a trick or two. In Nevada, where prostitution is legal, women on welfare have been forced off welfare because they refused to accept the suitable employment of prostitution; once it is a legal, state-regulated job, there is no basis for refusing it. Prostitution has long been considered suitable employment for poor women whether it is legal or not. This is particularly cynical in the welfare system, given the fact that women on welfare have been subjected to "fornication checks"—questioned about their sexual relations at length, questioned as to the identity of the fathers of so-called illegitimate children, questioned as to their own sexual habits, activities, and partners—and have been denied welfare if living with a man or if a man spends any time in the domicile or if having a sexual relationship with a man. Their homes could be inspected anytime: searches were common after midnight, when the welfare workers expected to find the contraband man; the courts put a stop to late searches but daytime searches are still legal. Beds, closets, and clothes were inspected to see if any remnant of a male presence could be found. Sometimes criminal charges of fornication were actually brought against the mothers of illegitimate children; the purpose was to keep them from getting welfare. For instance, in one typical case, a New Jersey woman was convicted of fornication and given a suspended sentence; she was forced to name the father, who went to prison. Welfare workers were allowed to interrogate children concerning the social and sexual habits of their mothers. Women on welfare have even been required to tell when they menstruate. Women on welfare have had no rights to sexual privacy; and in this context, turning them toward prostitution goes right along with refusing to allow them private, intimate, self-determined sexual relations. Prostitution is the ultimate loss of sexual privacy. Gains made in the courts in the 1960s to restore rights of privacy to these women are being nullified by new welfare policies and regulations designed to control the same population in the same old ways—practices that reappear in new guises but are built on the same old attitudes and impinge on the welfare population in the same old and cruel ways. The state is a jealous lover, except when it pimps.

Aid to Families with Dependent Children (AFDC) is the largest federal welfare program: this is welfare for women and their dependent children. As of 1977, 52.6 percent of the recipients were white, 43 percent were black, and 4.4 percent were designated as "American Indian and other." Welfare fundamentally articulates the state's valuation of women as women; the condition of women determines the philosophical bases and practical strategies of the welfare system;* the racist structure of class provides a framework in which women can be isolated, punished, and destroyed as women. In the welfare system, racism increases the jeopardy for black women in particular in a multiplicity of ways. But the degradation built into the welfare system in general and AFDC in particular originates in social attitudes toward women: in sexual contempt for women; in paternalistic assumptions about women; in moral codes exclusively applied to women; in notions of immorality that have no currency except when applied to women. Women not on welfare are cruelly hurt by these same endemic woman-hating attitudes; but women on welfare have nothing between them and a police-state exercise of authority and power over them in which and by which they are degraded because they are women and the state is the real head of the household. AFDC controls women who have no husbands to keep them in line; it caretakes women, keeps them always hungry and dependent and desperate and accessible; it keeps them watching their children go

*This is not to suggest that welfare does not have devastating consequences for black men. It is to suggest that the whole system, including its impact on black men, is ultimately comprehensible only when we understand to what extent the feminizing of the oppressed is part of public policy and therefore fundamentally related to the degradation of women as a class.

hungry and underclothed and uneducated; it tells them exactly what they are worth to their lord and master, the state, in dollars and cents. In 1979 they were worth $111 per month in Alabama, $144 per month in Arkansas, $335 per month in Connecticut, $162 per month in Florida, and so on. In Hawaii they were worth most: $389 per month. In Mississippi they were worth least: $84 per month. In New York State, with the largest welfare budget, they were worth $370 per month. These were average payments per month per family (for the woman and her dependent children).

Suitable employment standards, for instance, in whatever form they appear, are used to degrade women: to punish women for being poor by enclosing them in a terrible trap—they have children to raise and the only work they are offered will not feed their children, it is degrading work, it is a dead end, it is meaningless, it is intrinsically exploitative; and women with husbands who have some money or good jobs or steady jobs are being pressured to stay home and be *good* mothers. How is the mother in the welfare population supposed to be a good mother? The answer is always the same: she is not supposed to have had the children to begin with, and she is not supposed to have any more, and her suffering is no more than she deserves. The welfare system combines the imperatives of sex and money: get a man to marry and support you or we will punish you and yours until you wish you were all dead. The welfare system also combines the imperatives of morality and money: your shameless bad ways got you knocked up, girl; now you be good or we are going to do you in. Even when the issue is suitable employment, it is always in the air: you wouldn't be here if you hadn't done wrong; so where we send you is where you go and what we tell you to do is what you do—because you deserve it because you are bad.

So, in addition to suitable employment, the welfare system has been—and will continue to be—preoccupied with what are called "suitable homes" and with what can be called "suitable morality," something of a redundancy. Most AFDC programs were established by 1940; by 1942 over half the states had "suitable homes" laws. These laws demanded that women meet certain social and sexual standards in order to qualify for welfare benefits: illegitimate children, for instance, would make a home not suitable; any infraction of conventional social behavior for women might do the same; any overt or noticeable sex life might do the same. The women could keep the children—the homes were suitable enough for that—but were not entitled to any money from the chaste government. As Piven and Cloward make very clear, this meant that the women had to work doing whatever menial labor they could find; they simply had no recourse. But it also meant that the state had become the instrument of God: welfare's mission, from the beginning, was to punish women for having had sex outside of marriage, for having had children outside of marriage, for having had children at all—for being women. With righteousness on its side, the welfare program and those who made and executed its policies punished women through starvation for having "unsuitable homes," that is, illegitimate children.

Mothers and their dependent children are purged en masse from the welfare rolls whenever a state government decides its purity is being sullied because it gives money to immoral women. A typical purge, for instance, took place in Florida in 1959. Seven thousand families with over 30,000 children were deprived of benefits because of the suitable home law. According to a report for the then Department of Health, Education, and Welfare, these families met all the eligibility requirements for welfare but were denied benefits "where one or more of the children was illegitimate . . . or where the welfare worker reported that the mother's past or present conduct of her sex life was not acceptable when examined in the light of the spirit of the law."[9] Other states, including Northern states, have done the same. By virtue of being illegitimate, the children are being reared in unsuitable homes; therefore, they can starve. This is a fine exercise in state morality. The benefit to the state is concrete: the women must do the cheapest labor; in economic terms, welfare is a refined instrument of state power and of capitalism. In what looks like chaos, it accomplishes a serious goal—creating and maintaining a pool of degraded labor, cheaper than dirt. In terms of its other function, it is not so refined an instrument yet. It is supposed to keep these women from having children; it is supposed to discourage them, punish them, force them to have fewer children. It is supposed to use the twin weapons of money and hunger—reinforced by fear of suffering and death—to stop these women from reproducing. Sterilization has a legislative history in the United States: in 1915 thirteen states had mandatory sterilization laws (for "degenerates"); and by 1932 twenty-seven states had laws mandating sterilization for various kinds of social misfits. As Linda Gordon said in *Woman's Body, Woman's Right:* "The sterilization campaign tended to identify economic dependence with hereditary feeble-mindedness or worse."[10] It has been proposed over and over again: if these women are going to keep having these bastards, after the second or third or fourth, we have the right to stop them, sterilize them—for their own good and because we are paying the bills. Sterilization has been practiced on poor women piecemeal. So far there is no judicial carte blanche that extends the power of the state explicitly to the tying of tubes because a woman is on welfare. But when doctors sterilize Medicaid women, they know they are acting in concert with the best interests of the government that administers welfare; and the government does not hesitate to pay the doctor for his good deed. So far, the strategies of the state in stopping women on welfare from having children have been crude. The government has tried to police their sexual relations, enforce chastity, keep men out of their homes, punish them for having illegitimate children, starve them and their children: state policy is one of absolute, cruel, murderous paternalism.

Welfare policy has usually been interpreted in terms of its impact on black men. From the state (police) side, the effort is to keep a shiftless man from living off the welfare benefits of a woman; to keep men from defrauding welfare by using benefits intended for women and children; to get black families back into the patriarchal mode, that is, headed by males, for reasons of traditional morality or economics; to force black men to marry black women and be legally responsible for the children. From the antiracist side, welfare policy has been seen as a blanket effort to destroy black men or the black family, which, when headed by a woman, is seen as inherently degraded. The absent black male is the political focus and priority. But neither side penetrates to the real meaning of welfare policy because both sides keep their eye on the man as the significant figure in the drama. The state, obviously, does not intend any economic dignity for that man or that same state would not promote black male unemployment in its economic policies and create a situation, through welfare, in which husbands are forced to abandon women and children so as to be sure they do not starve. From the antiracist perspective, the efforts of welfare have been deeper and far more malevolent than can be realized if its impact on men is seen as primary, because the effort has been to stop or significantly diminish reproduction through social control of women. The notion that the state has acted to promote the conventional male-dominated family (by persecution of unmarried mothers, for instance) is only superficially viable. If that were its real interest, other state policies would support that same goal. Instead, welfare policy has directly concerned itself with controlling women. The most intrusive and degrading regulations back from the beginning of welfare all have to do with women as women: all have to do with a gender-specific regulation of motherhood and sex. These policies all articulate the reproductive worth of women on welfare to the state, and that value is almost entirely negative.*

The causes of the need for welfare (from the human, not the state, point of view) are in the systematic economic discrimination against women, with black women suffering the most stark eco-

---

*The one positive value is that the women and their progeny are cheap labor, as discussed previously in this chapter.

nomic deprivation, and in the systematic sexual degradation of women. Welfare is the barest maintenance for those who, being female and poor, would otherwise slowly die. Those kicked off the welfare rolls in the endless quest for those who are poor but pure get jobs where they are paid *less* than welfare provides; and welfare provides shit. They work, keeping those upholders of the Protestant work ethic happy, and go hungry at the same time. The poverty of women is appalling. As of December 1981, the Bureau of Labor Statistics reported that unemployment for females who headed households was nearly twice that of males who headed households: 10.6 percent for the women; 5.8 percent for the men. Gay Talese, who wrote about the sex industry, found it meaningful in terms of sexual liberation that the women in massage parlors giving him handjobs were college graduates and *even* Ph.D.'s. It is meaningful—but in terms of what women have to do to earn money, even with college educations and advanced degrees. The welfare system that seeks to control women, and ultimately to destroy expendable women (black and poor white women, Hispanics, the females of any marginal groups), can count on the continuing poverty of these women as women; they are never going to do better because they are women and there are no social means to enable them to do better, except marriage upward. The poverty of these millions of women is assured; and so is the state's continued access to them; and so too is their continuing sexual humiliation by state intrusion, the welfare agencies being thus far the major enforcement arm of state policy. Since reproductive containment (at best) has been the goal of welfare, there will be continued state intrusion into the reproductive lives of poor women—with the endemic racism of the United States putting black women consistently at the highest risk. The intrusion will be under the guise of morality, as it has always been, a morality applied exclusively to women, a morality that no right-wing senator or congressman would ever think of using the state to apply to men. It will also be disguised—by those more secular—as concern for the black family: controlling the sexual promiscuity of the woman, reinstating the black man in the master's bedroom, such as it is on his block. Under the surface, there will be a different truth: the state, through the welfare system as a whole, wants to control the fertility of the woman and will not ever let the black man come in out of the cold. The state regulates the sexual use of nonwelfare women for the benefit of men as a class, and it attempts to control the fertility of nonwelfare women in cooperation with the men whose interests it represents: the men who are lovers, fathers, husbands, rapists, and police all at the same time. But the state directly *owns* the sexuality of women on welfare—at least from its point of view it does—and it wants to own their fertility outright too. Sometimes the state explicitly exercises the ownership it has in enforcing so-called moral standards for a subject group of women: sometimes it punishes women for having had children against its will. The slow starving and degrading of these women is not yet widely viewed as genocidal; genocide is not articulated as state policy. That is because the political and legal tools available to welfare in its pursuit of reproductive control of poor women have been crude. But illegal abortion, which looms large on the horizon in the form of the monstrous Human Life Amendment, and forced sterilization, practiced sporadically so far but lurking for decades as what the government really wants to do, will make a genocidal policy practical, effective, and frankly inevitable. When abortion is illegal, black women, Hispanic women, and poor women get slaughtered.* Allowing the government to regulate the uterus—as in the Human Life Amendment—will directly preface an overt policy of forced sterilization. Forced sterilization cannot be explicit state policy until a measure like the Human Life Amendment is adopted: until abortion is absolutely reckoned murder legally and is punished as murder, so that the state is empowered literally to investigate the woman's womb, her menses, her discharges. Once every fertilized egg must be

---

*See chapter 3, "Abortion," pp. 98–99.

brought to term, what are we to do with all those poor, promiscuous, dumb sluts who keep having bastards? After all, doesn't the government have the right to force such women to stop having babies? isn't the government paying for them? aren't those women immoral, fucking around and having babies for the money? If every fertilized egg is going to be brought to term—under penalty of a murder charge for failing to discharge that obligation—isn't it best just to insist that women taking government money have their tubes tied? And doesn't this combination of illegal abortion—prohibited in a way never existing before, prohibited from conception—and forced sterilization finally meet the not-so-hidden agenda of welfare: doesn't it finally provide the state with a way to control—absolutely and effectively—the fertility of poor women? Enough poor women can be kept having enough babies to provide whatever cheap labor is essential; but the rest are expendable.

And what is going to happen to women, these women and all women, when the tools of reproductive control of women are no longer technologically (medically) crude? when the technology catches up with the political and legal leap into the Orwellian future? What is going to happen to women when life can be made in the laboratory and men can control reproduction not just socially but also biologically with real efficiency?

The value of a female life is determined by its reproductive value. What will happen to all the women who are not altogether necessary because *their* children in particular are not altogether desirable? The old women starving in poverty are starving because their reproductive lives are over and they are worth nothing. The old women incarcerated in cruel nursing homes are there because their reproductive lives are over and they are worth nothing. The women who are too poor or too black or brown and who have too many children are starved and threatened and degraded and slowly killed through state-sponsored neglect *because* they are having children, because they reproduce too much, because the value put on their reproducing is negative and characterized by annihilating disregard. The women who are kept in line now, millions upon millions of them each year, through the judicious application of mood-altering drugs, are kept chemically happy, calm, tranquil, or energetic so that they will hang in there, have and raise the children and keep house for their husbands even though their lives fill them with distress and addiction is what keeps them conforming. They too are part of a throwaway population of females: because their own well-being is viciously subordinated to a predetermined standard of what a woman is and what a woman does and what a woman needs to be a woman (she needs to keep doing female things, whether she wants to or not). What are the lives of all these women worth? Is there anything in the way they are viewed or valued that upholds their human dignity as individuals? They already matter very little. They are treated with cruelty or callous indifference. They have already been thrown away. It is public policy to throw them away. What is going to happen to women when reproduction—the only capacity that women have that men really need (Portnoy's piece of liver can substitute for the rest in hard times)—is no longer the exclusive province of the class women? What is going to happen to women who have only one argument for the importance of their existence—that their reproductive capacities are worth a little something (shelter, food, solace, minimal respect)—when men can make babies?

> And yet, there is a solitude which each and every one of us has always carried with him, more inaccessible than the ice-cold mountains, more profound than the midnight sea; the solitude of self. Our inner being which we call ourself, no eye nor touch of man or angel has ever pierced. It is more hidden than the caves of the gnome; the sacred adytum of the oracle; the hidden chamber of Eleusinian mystery, for to it only omniscience is permitted to enter.

> Such is individual life. Who, I ask you, can take, dare take on himself the rights, the duties, the responsibilities of another human soul?
>
> Elizabeth Cady Stanton, speech, January 18, 1892

> There is no thing named love in the world. Women are dinks. Women are villains. They are creatures akin to Communists and yellow-skinned people and hippies. We march off to learn about hand-to-hand combat. Blynton grins and teases and hollers out his nursery rhyme: "If ya wanta live, ya gotta be ag-ile, mo-bile, and hos-tile." We chant the words: ag-ile, mo-bile, hos-tile. We make it all rhyme.
>
> Tim O'Brien, *If I Die in a Combat Zone*

There are two models that essentially describe how women are socially controlled and sexually used: the brothel model and the farming model.

The brothel model relates to prostitution, narrowly defined; women collected together for the purposes of sex with men; women whose function is explicitly nonreproductive, almost antireproductive; sex animals in heat or pretending, showing themselves for sex, prancing around or posed for sex.

The farming model relates to motherhood, women as a class planted with the male seed and harvested; women used for the fruit they bear, like trees; women who run the gamut from prized cows to mangy dogs, from highbred horses to sad beasts of burden.

These two poles of the female condition are only superficially and conceptually distinct and opposite. Men say the two are poles to begin with, distinct and opposite. That male conceit is registered and repeated until it is easier to repeat the concept by rote than to see the reality. But the concept is only accurate (descriptive) from a male point of view—that is, if one accepts the male definitions of both the acts involved and the women involved. In the course of women's lives, and therefore from a woman-based perspective, the two conditions overlap and intersect, each reinforcing the efficacy of the other. Any woman can be both a prostitute and a mother, a prostitute and a wife (a potential mother), or one then the other in either order; and any woman can be subject to the imperatives of both the brothel and the farming models of female usage. On a grand scale, more women become mothers, fewer prostitutes.

In general, the euphemisms of religion and romantic love keep women from ever recognizing the farming model as having to do directly and personally with them. Modern women do not think of themselves as cows, nor as land that the man seeds; but male-headed marriage incorporates both these vivid traditions of female definition; and the laws have been built on these same images and ideas of what women are for; and the real history of women has had as its center the actual use of women as cows and as land. The way women are treated, valued, and used has remarkably little in common with how women perceive themselves. The legend says that vampires cannot see themselves in mirrors, but in this case the vampires' victims cannot see themselves: what would stare back—the cow, the land, the uterus, the crop, the plowing, the planting, the harvest, being put out to pasture, going dry—would annihilate the delusion of individuality that keeps most women going. The laws that made women chattel derived from an analogy between women and cows that hundreds of centuries of men found apt, and the sexual slur was apparently a neutral observation infused with the spleen of the moment—she's a cow. The idea that the male plants and the woman is planted in originates in antiquity, and Marcuse among others has reiterated the idea that woman is the land in more modern times. The farming model is not discussed as such, even among feminists. It too clearly reveals the hopeless impersonality, degradation, and futility implicit in women's subordinate position.

The brothel model is more familiar, partly because the situation of prostitutes is held up to all women as warning, threat, inevitable doom and damnation, the hellish punishment of girls gone wrong: punishment for being women involved in sex without the protection of marriage and the purpose of reproduction; punishment for being bad or rebellious or sexually precocious; punishment for being female without the cleansing sacraments.

In the brothel model, the woman is acknowledged to be for sex without reference to reproduction. She will still have babies perhaps, but no one owes her anything: not the father, not the state, not the pimp, not the john, no one. Some women on the Left accept the male leftist view that this is a giant step for womankind: that this separation of sex and reproduction is in fact a form of freedom—freedom from domestic constraint and domestic submission, freedom from an intrinsically totalitarian association of sex with reproduction. They do not recognize that in the brothel model sex is dissociated from reproduction so that the sex can be sold, so that sex (not babies) is what is produced, so that an intrinsically totalitarian association is forged between sex and money expressed lucidly in the selling of the woman as a sexual commodity. In the brothel model, the woman is considered to be sexually free even by those who think prostitution is bad or wrong; sexual freedom is when women do the things men think are sexy; the more women do these things, the more sexually free they are. Whatever the conditions of the woman's life, there is no perception that prostitution is by its nature antithetical to freedom. Sometimes the prostitute is construed to be economically liberated. In selling sex, money passes through her hands: more money than the housewife or the secretary will have in hand on any given night. The brothel model particularly fosters these obfuscations of the female condition because the women are entirely interchangeable; perceived in terms of function they are entirely interchangeable; even among themselves, any one could step out of her own life into the life of the next woman and not notice the difference. Nothing that happens in the brothel is seen or has to be seen or recognized or remembered or reckoned with: these women live outside of history and what happens to them happens behind closed doors and in a place constructed to control the kind of women in it. They live entirely on male terms. Whatever happens to them is appropriate on those male terms because of what they do and what they are, all of which is expressed in where they are. The impersonality of the brothel as a working place is precisely congruent with the impersonality of their sexual function; men romanticize the place and the function for themselves, to themselves, for their own sakes, men among men; but even men are not so dense as to try to romanticize prostitution to the prostitute.

In the brothel model, the women are held to a strictly sexual standard of behavior and accountability: they sell themselves for sex, not to make babies. They do what men want them to do for money that men pay them and that then they usually turn over to a man. Women are defined strictly with reference to sex and they are defined unfailingly without reference to personality or individuality or human potential; they are used without reference to anything but sex orifices and sex class and sex scenes. In the brothel model, several women belong to one man or in some cases are supervised by an older woman who is herself accountable to a rich man or men. The job of the women is to bring in—to a man or to a house—a certain amount of money by servicing a certain number of men. They sell parts of their bodies—vagina, rectum, mouth; and they also sell acts—what they say and what they do. In sex, they absorb, endure, or get indifferent toward an enormous amount of male aggression, hostility, and contempt. Men have few restraints in expressing to prostitutes—during sex or in any sexual scenario—their real attitudes toward women as a class; they have no reason to feel constrained, since the woman is there to be a woman, period—to be inferior, subservient, and used. She is there because the man wants a woman, someone exactly of her class, someone who is her sex function, not human but an it, a cunt: she is there for that reason, not for anything human in her. Her function is limited, specialized, sex-specific, and intensely and intrinsically dehumanizing.

It is essential to recognize how genuinely accepted both the brothel model and prostitution are in the social structure, and how this disposition of women is simply accepted as inevitable because they are women. However evil prostitution is held to be, however righteous or religious men are said to be, the brothel model does more than endure; it thrives. However marginal the women are said to be, they form the sex nucleus of a sex industry that is in no sense marginal. The brothel model thrives because men accept it and all that is part of it as proper treatment for sexual women: women who are sexual in male terms, women who get fucked by many men, women who get fucked outside the protective custody of a traditional father or husband. The staying power of both the brothel as an institution and prostitution as a practice comes from the efficacy of both for regulating the sexual use of women and the disposition of sexually exploitable women. Think of what it means. The brothel is most often something like a prison—women cannot come and go freely. Women are displayed, used, and treated like sexual things or sexual animals, all penned up. The brothel exists usually with the tacit or overt protection of police and politicians; the brothel is used by the rich and powerful as well as by all other kinds of men; the brothel is the kind of place men like to have women in, confined in, locked in, penned in, shut in; the brothel suggests a wealth of women available to the man, it means he is rich in having so many women in one place for him, it means he chooses absolutely and his will is done by whomever he chooses. Prostitution is the way women are used in the brothel model; it is what women are shut in for, penned in for. The street corner merely extends the brothel beyond the walls of a building into the cold and rain. Pimps run several prostitutes; and usually some or all live together, whether business is done in the domicile or not. This is a version of the brothel: a kind of public harem. The brothel model can simply be imposed on a neighborhood, which then becomes a ghetto for prostitutes. In some cities with good reputations for socially advanced ideas, women sit in windows, posing for potential customers. This is widely regarded as a humane and civilized way of conducting the business of prostitution. The brothel, in such cities, is considered a nice place, good for the girls. It is the acceptance of the brothel model as an appropriate way of treating some women, these women, sexed women, prostituted women, used women, degraded women, public women, any women, that has unyielding and unchanging social significance for all women. Once a prostituted woman exists, she can be shut up in a house where men come to find and use women like her, to use her because she is a woman. It is naughty to force her to prostitute herself, though women and girls are mainly forced into prostitution; but once prostituted—by whatever means—she is for sex and the brothel is her proper abode and the use made of her there is proper; it is a woman's place, and this is accepted by the religious and irreligious, police and outlaws, users and abstainers. A pimp's women are referred to as his "stable," but the analogy with horses is misleading. Horses are treated better, being more valuable. Prostitutes get treated like women; no analogy fits. For men this way of life would be seen clearly as a deprivation of human freedom; for women it is appropriate to what they are—women. These women are not missed; in fulfilling this sexual function, it is not thought that *they* are wasted. There is a difference between female garbage and human waste. In the United States, there are hundreds of thousands of these women; in the world, millions upon millions. The brothel model keeps these women locked in for sex, and both the devout and the sexually liberated think that is the way it should be. Both think this is a sexy way for women to live. The women are disposed of, used for what they are seen to be, used as their sex, their class-defined essence and function, the sex work to which some percentage of the sex class must be dedicated.

This use of women is thought to be not only an inevitable and appropriate use of women but one that always was and always will be.

The defenses of the brothel model applied to women are entrenched. In his study of prostitution, first published in 1857, William Acton articulated what has come to be accepted as a moderate, sensible point of view:

> It seems to me vain to shut our eyes to the fact that prostitution must always exist. Regret it as we may, we cannot but admit that a woman if so disposed may make profit of her own person, and that the State has no right to prevent her. It has a right, however, in my opinion, to insist that she shall not, in trafficking with her person, became a medium of communicating disease, and that, as she has given herself up to an occupation dangerous to herself and others, she must, in her own interest and that of the community, submit to supervision.[11]

The state creates the conditions in which the woman is prostituted, sanctions force against her to effect her prostitution by systematically ignoring it, creates the economic conditions that mandate her prostitution, fixes her social place so that her sex is a commodity; and then, prostitution is seen to exist because the woman wills it and the political question is whether or not the state should interfere with this expression of her will. What is seen as the eternal dimension of prostitution—why it must always exist—is that the will of women to prostitute themselves will always exist. This means, simply, that men accept that the conditions that create prostitution are acceptable, fixed, and appropriate because prostitution is a proper use of women, one congruent with what women are. The harm done is when she carries disease. Wherever prostitution is legal and regulated, it is usually to control disease, to protect men from disease; the woman is the instrument by which harm comes to the man.

It is the social and economic construction of the woman's will that is the issue: both in that feminists assert that this will is constructed outside the individual and in that apologists for the sexual exploitation of women—again both religious and irreligious—insist that the will is interior, individual, an individual assertion of a female sexual nature.

The notion of female will always articulated in discussions of prostitution (and currently pornography) also is central in a new area of discourse on what women are for: surrogate motherhood. A man, married to an infertile woman or on his own, wants a baby; he buys the egg and the use of the womb of a surrogate mother—a woman who will accept the introjection of his sperm through artificial insemination, gestate and give birth to what is contractually established as his child. In vitro fertilization—in which the egg is extracted from a woman surgically, fertilized in a petri dish, then vaginally introjected into the female—expands the possibilities of surrogate motherhood. The uterus is exempt from the immune response. Scientists already are able to remove the egg of one woman, fertilize it outside her body, then introduce it into a second woman's uterus, where it will gestate.* They have not done so, but there is no technological barrier to doing so. These two reproductive technologies—artificial insemination and in vitro fertilization—enable women to sell their wombs within the terms of the brothel model. Motherhood is becoming a new branch of female prostitution with the help of scientists who want access to the womb for experimentation and for power. A doctor can be the agent of fertilization; he can dominate and control conception and

*According to Gena Corea, an expert in these technologies and their effects on women, "men are hoping to fertilize an egg *inside* a woman's body (in vivo), flush it out and then transfer that embryo to another woman. *That* has not yet been done." Letter to the author, February 12, 1982. The pure sadism of this seems outstanding.

reproduction. Women can sell reproductive capacities the same way old-time prostitutes sold sexual ones but without the stigma of whoring because there is no penile intrusion. It is the womb, not the vagina, that is being bought; this is not sex, it is reproduction. The arguments as to the social and moral appropriateness of this new kind of sale simply reiterate the view of female will found in discussions of prostitution: does the state have a right to interfere with this exercise of individual female will (in selling use of the womb)? if a woman wants to sell the use of her womb in an explicit commercial transaction, what right has the state to deny her this proper exercise of femininity in the marketplace? Again, the state has constructed the social, economic, and political situation in which the sale of some sexual or reproductive capacity is necessary to the survival of women; and yet the selling is seen to be an act of individual will—the only kind of assertion of individual will in women that is vigorously defended as a matter of course by most of those who pontificate on female freedom. The state denies women a host of other possibilities, from education to jobs to equal rights before the law to sexual self-determination in marriage; but it is state intrusion into her selling of sex or a sex-class–specific capacity that provokes a defense of her will, her right, her individual self—defined strictly in terms of the will to sell what is appropriate for females to sell.

This individual woman is a fiction—as is her will—since individuality is precisely what women are denied when they are defined and used as a sex class. As long as issues of female sexual and reproductive destiny are posed as if they are resolved by individuals as individuals, there is no way to confront the actual conditions that perpetuate the sexual exploitation of women. Women by definition are condemned to a predetermined status, role, and function. In terms of prostitution, Josephine Butler, a nineteenth-century crusader against prostitution, explained the obvious implications of its sex-based nature:

> My principle has always been to let individuals alone, not to pursue them with any outward punishment, nor drive them *out of any place* so long as they behave decently, but to attack *organized prostitution*, that is when a third party, activated by the desire of making money, sets up a house in which women are sold to men.[12]

This is the opposite of what the state does when prostitution is illegal: the state harasses and persecutes individual prostitutes and leaves the institutions and the powerful who profit from them alone. It does this because it is accepted that prostitution expresses the will of the prostitute, and that therefore punishing her is the proper expression of hostility toward prostitution. It is precisely this notion of individual responsibility (when in fact there is only a class-determined behavior) that perpetuates prostitution and protects the profits and power of those who sell women to men. Feminists, unlike the state, go after the institutions and the powerful, not the individual women, because feminists recognize above all that the prostitute is created by material conditions outside herself.* In the new prostitution of reproduction, which is just beginning to unfold, the third party that will develop the female population for sale will be the scientist or doctor. He is a new kind of pimp, but he is not a new enemy of women. The formidable institutions of scientific research institutes and medical hospitals will be the new houses out of which women are sold to men: the use of their wombs for money.

---

*This does not mean that prostitution is reinvented in every generation only through material conditions. The colonialization of women is both external and internal, as Kate Millett made clear in *Sexual Politics*. Sexual exploitation and abuse create in women a psychological submission to self-denigration; in *The Prostitution Papers* Millett went so far as to describe this submission as "a kind of psychological addiction to self-denigration." (See *The Prostitution Papers* [New York: Avon, 1973], p. 96.)

Before the advent of any reproductive technologies, the farming model used to be very distinct from the brothel model. Even though the woman was not human—the land—or was less than human—a cow—farming had the symbolic overtones of old-fashioned agrarian romance: plowing the land was loving it, feeding the cow was tending it. In the farming model, the woman was owned privately; she was the homestead, not a public thoroughfare. One farmer worked her. The land was valued because it produced a valuable crop; and in keeping with the mystique of the model itself, sometimes the land was real pretty, special, richly endowed; a man could love it. The cow was valued because of what she produced: calves, milk; sometimes she took a prize. There was nothing actually idyllic in this. As many as one quarter of all acts of battery may be against pregnant women; and women die from pregnancy even without the intervention of a male fist. But farming implied a relationship of some substance between the farmer and what was his: and it is grander being the earth, being nature, even being a cow, than being a cunt with no redeeming mythology. Motherhood ensconced a woman in the continuing life of a man: how he used her was going to have consequences for him. Since she was his, her state of being reflected on him; and therefore he had a social and psychological stake in her welfare as well as an economic one. Because the man farmed the woman over a period of years, they developed a personal relationship, at least from her point of view: one limited by his notions of her sex and her kind; one strained because she could never rise to the human if it meant abandoning the female; but it was her best chance to be known, to be regarded with some tenderness or compassion meant for her, one particular woman. Nevertheless, the archaic meaning of the verb *to husband* is "to plow for the purpose of growing crops." There is not a lot of room for tenderness or compassion in that. Still, it is no wonder that women hang on possessively to any generic associations of women as such or "the female" with the land, nature, earth, the environment, even though those culturally sanctioned associations posit a female nature that is not fully human and perpetuate a hard and mean tradition of exploitation: there is some splendor and some honor in the association. The association has a deep resonance for men too, though not the same sentimental meaning: they after all did the plowing. The cultural and sexual intersection of women and earth is potent for men when they bomb "her," strip-mine "her," scorch "her," torch "her," denude "her," defoliate "her," pollute "her," despoil "her," rape "her," plunder "her," overcome, manipulate, dominate, conquer, or destroy "her." The significance of the farming model is both wide and deep. It has been the major way of using women—as mothers to produce children; metaphorically speaking, men have used the earth as if it were female, a huge fertile female that—one way or another—they will fuck to death. There are limits to how much the land can endure and produce, plowed so much, respected so little.

Both the farming model and the brothel model dispose of women as women: they are paradigms for the mass use of a whole class; in both there is no humanity for women. The brothel model has been efficient. It uses the women in it until they are used up. Men get sex from them with a graceful economy of means: effective force; hunger, degradation, drugs; rare escape. The woman is easily reduced to what she sells. Women under the yoke of the brothel model do not organize political movements; they do not rebel collectively; the yoke is too heavy. Quite simply, a percentage of the class women is given over to the brothel model; whatever its laws, societies accept this disposition of a significant number of females for sex service. Once within that model, these women are controlled and used; what men want from them they get; their bodies go where their sex is wanted; there is an absolute equation between what they are and what they provide, between their physical bodies and their function, between their sex and their work. There is no wasted energy here: a prostituted female serves her purpose absolutely. The farming model has always been relatively inefficient. It is sloppier. Picking a woman who lives in the home with the man on a continuing basis is harder. Picking a woman who can and will have children is harder. There is more leeway for her attitudes to interfere. She has ways of saying no or subverting male sexual and reproductive intentions. The brothel model simply requires that the women under it be women: it does not matter who they are or what they are like or where they come from or what they think; they get worn down fast by being used the same way and being reduced to the same common denominator; nothing is necessary except that they be female. The farming model requires the constant application of force (explicit or implicit, usually a nice combination), incentive, reward; and a lot of plain luck with respect to fertility and reproductive vigor. When a man wants sons, as most do, the inefficiency inherent in the model is particularly emphasized: no matter how many babies she has, there is no certainty that any of them will be male. And, for all the coercion of the farming model, the women subject to it have organized politically, have found ways to seize the time between babies and domestic chores—here and there, now and then—to foment some rebellion. The very fact that such women have been involved in movements, especially feminist movements, argues for the inefficiency of the farming model. The farming model has haphazard success: there are too many factors besides the efficacy of the fuck that can interfere with the harvesting of the crop. The quality of the crop cannot really be predetermined either. Men, recognizing the inefficiency of the farming model, have simply imposed it on all women not prostituted so as not to miss a chance: they use social and economic sanctions to punish women who try to live outside it, especially so-called spinsters and lesbians. To anticipate and counterbalance the failures, the losses, the tremendous element of chance, the bad breaks, the power of men as a class has been exercised to keep all women not prostitutes reproducing under the explicit domination of a husband. This has been the best way men have had to control reproduction, to appropriate the uteruses of women in order to have children, to keep the women subject to the reproductive will of the men. The use of women by men in this reproductive tyranny has been presented as what women are for: a proper use of females, the best actualization of their human potential because, after all, they are women.

Reproductive technology is now changing the terms on which men control reproduction. The social control of women who reproduce—the sloppy, messy kind of control—is being replaced by medical control much more precise, much closer to the efficiency of the brothel model. This change-over—applying the brothel model to reproduction—is just beginning. It is beyond the scope of this book to explore or explain all the new technological intrusions into conception, gestation, and birth,* except to say that reproduction will become the kind of commodity that sex is now. Artificial insemination, in vitro fertilization, sex selection, genetic engineering, fetal monitoring, artificial wombs that keep the fetus alive outside the mother's body, fetal surgery, embryo transplants, and eventual cloning (some experts predict that human cloning will be accomplished within twenty-five years; however long it takes, it will be done)—all these reproductive intrusions make the womb the province of the doctor, not the woman; all make the womb extractable from the woman as a whole person in the same way the vagina (or sex) is now; some make the womb extraneous altogether or eventually extraneous; all make reproduction controllable by men on a scale heretofore unimaginable. The issue is not the particular innovation itself—whether it is intrinsically good or bad; the issue is how it will be used in a system in which women are sexual and reproductive commodities already, exploited, with lives that are worthless when not serving a specific sexual or reproduc-

---

* See Gena Corea, *The Mother Machine* (forthcoming, 1984). This book will explain the reproductive technologies, the experiments being done on women and animals to develop the technologies, and the view of women central to both the experimentation and the technologies.

tive purpose. For instance, cesarean sections saved women's lives when used in orthodox medical emergencies; but now doctors use them because they give doctors dominion over labor, because they involve cutting into the female body—a male pleasure—and so that the natural process of birth can be circumvented for the social convenience of the doctor. Cesarean sections are now used to express endemic male contempt for women. So it will be with reproductive technology or other medically sophisticated intrusions into reproduction. The ideology of male control of reproduction will stay what it is; the hatred of women will stay what it is; what will change will be the means of expressing both the ideology and the hatred. The means will give conception, gestation, and birth over to men—eventually, the whole process of the creation of life will be in their hands. The new means will enable men—at last—really to have women for sex and women for reproduction, both controlled with sadistic precision by men.

And there will be a new kind of holocaust, as unimaginable now as the Nazi one was before it happened: something no one believes "mankind" capable of. Using now available or soon to be available reproductive technology in conjunction with racist programs of forced sterilization, men finally will have the means to create and control the kind of women they want: the kind of women they have always wanted. To paraphrase Ernst Lubitsch's Ninotchka when she is defending Stalin's purges, there will be fewer but better women. There will be domestics, sex prostitutes, and reproductive prostitutes. Is there any reason to think that this projected future does not reflect the commonly accepted devaluation of women with which we live with relative complacency? Look again at what we have done—are doing now—to the old, those in nursing homes, the drugged, the prostituted, those on welfare, and to those bastions of female worth, wives and mothers, whose rape the law protects, whose battery the society invites, whose uteruses the state wants.

*

> We come after. We know now that a man can read Goethe or Rilke in the evening, that he can play Bach and Schubert, and go to his day's work at Auschwitz in the morning.
>
> George Steiner, *Language and Silence*

> Yet the enigma of woman's nature (if she has, that is, a nature, and is not merely a person altogether equal, hoof to human hoof, with man), the enigma, if it exists, is that women respond to him, of course they do, it is the simple knowledge of the street that murderers are even sexier than athletes. Something in a woman wishes to be killed went the old wisdom before Women's Liberation wiped that out, something in a woman wishes to be killed, and it is obvious what does—she would like to lose the weakest part of herself, have it ploughed under, ground under, kneaded, tortured, squashed, sliced, banished, and finally immolated.
>
> Norman Mailer, *Genius and Lust*

Not wanting to die, and knowing the sadism of men, knowing what men can do in the name of sex, in the fuck, for the sake of pleasure, for the sake of power, knowing torture, having been able to predict all the prisons from her place in the bedroom and the brothel, knowing how callous men are to those less than themselves, knowing the fist, bondage, the farming fuck and the brothel fuck, seeing the indifference of men to human freedom, seeing the enthusiasm of men for diminishing others through physical domination, seeing the invisibility of women to men, seeing the absolute disregard of humanity in women by men, seeing the disdain of men for women's lives, and not wanting to die—*and not wanting to die*—women propose two very different solutions for themselves in relation to men and this man's world.

The first honors the sexual and reproductive imperatives of men. This is the right-wing solution, though those who pursue it are—in terms of male-defined politics—all along the political spectrum from far Right to far Left. In this solution, women accept the definition of their sex class, and within the terms of that definition fight for crumbs of self-respect and social, economic, and creative worth. Socialist movements and revolutions are predicated on an acceptance of this sex-class definition, as are right-wing movements and counterinsurgencies. The far-Right expression of this solution is usually highly religious, and it is the religious idiom that makes it distinguishable from other expressions of what is essentially the same accommodation to male power. Specifically, the sex-class accommodation is seen as a function of religious orthodoxy: in accommodating, women are faithful to a divine father; women accept traditional religious descriptions of women, female sexuality, and female nature; women accept the duties of sexual and reproductive submission to men. The far-Right solution translates the presumed biological destiny of women into a politics of orthodox religion: even in a secular republic, far-Right women live in a theocracy. Religion shrouds women in real as well as magical grace in that the sex-class functions of women are formally honored, carefully spelled out, and exploited within clear and prescribed boundaries.

The second solution is offered by feminists. It proposes, in the words of Elizabeth Cady Stanton, "the individuality of each human soul . . . In discussing the rights of woman, we are to consider, first, what belongs to her as an individual, in a world of her own, the arbiter of her own destiny . . ."[13] This is simply a recognition of the human condition, in which women are included. It is also the precondition for the realization of Marx's greatest ethical idea: from each according to her ability, to each according to her need. It is the imposition of the sex-class definition of women on women—by any means necessary—that devastates the human capacities of women, making them men's subordinates, making them "women." Feminists have a vision of women, even women, as individual human beings; and this vision annihilates the system of gender polarity in which men are superior and powerful. This is not a bourgeois notion of individuality; it is not a self-indulgent notion of individuality; it is the recognition that every human being lives a separate life in a separate body and dies alone. In proposing "the individuality of each human soul," feminists propose that women are not their sex; nor their sex plus some other little thing—a liberal additive of personality, for instance; but that each life—including each woman's life—must be a person's own, not predetermined before her birth by totalitarian ideas about her nature and her function, not subject to guardianship by some more powerful class, not determined in the aggregate but worked out by herself, for herself. Frankly, no one much knows what feminists mean; the idea of women not defined by sex and reproduction is anathema or baffling. It is the simplest revolutionary idea ever conceived, and the most despised.

In the face of advancing reproductive technology, there will be even fewer women who dare claim their right to human life, human dignity, and human struggle as unique and necessary individuals, fewer and fewer women who will fight against the categorical disposition of women. Instead, more and more women will see protection for themselves as women in religious and devotional ideologies that formally honor the special sanctity of motherhood. This is the only claim that women can make under the sex-class system to a sacred nature; and religion is the best way to make that claim—the best available way. Against the secular power of male scientists women will try to pit the political power of misogynist males in religion. Women will try to use male theology and religious tradition wherever and however it sanctifies the mother giving birth. Women will hide behind theology; women will hide behind orthodox religious men; women will use conservative religious ideas against the science that will make women less necessary than they have ever been.

The power of the reproductive scientists will be advanced, however, precisely through the political and legislative initiatives of the theocrats: prohibiting abortion and then mandating forced sterilization will establish absolute state control of the uterus. The clash between reproductive scientists and male theocrats in terms of absolute values—especially the orthodox formulation of what constitutes the family—only appears to be irresolvable. When these two schools of unconditional male power over women have to negotiate public policy to the mutual benefit of both, the men of theology, with that remarkable resourcefulness that allowed for the burning of the witches, will find great virtue in any program in which fertilized eggs truly do supersede women in importance. They will also enjoy having both sex and reproduction on their own terms: being God in the concrete rather than worshiping him in the abstract. They will also enjoy—for its own sake—the extraordinary control they will have over women: more than Leviticus gives; more than Christ mandates; more than men have ever had, though no doubt still less than men deserve. Women will argue like the true believers they are for that old-time religion, but male theocrats will discover that God intended men to be the sole creators of life all along: did not God himself create Adam without female help and is not baptism the religious equivalent of being born of a male God? This is not farfetched for those who justify the subordination of women to men on the ground that God is a boy.

Ironically, cruelly, so typical of history ineluctably moving on, Right to Life groups are the only organized political opposition to reproductive technology, especially in vitro fertilization,* and are also the agents of its ascendancy in engineering legislation that would give the uterus and the fertilized egg to the state to protect and control. Even in giving the state the right to define when life begins, which Right to Life groups insist on doing, Right to Life

*Each fertilized egg in a petri dish is regarded as a human life; each time one is thrown away or "dies," murder has been done.

groups are taking that power from religion and transforming it into a police power of the state. For the sake of religion, they are taking from religion its moral authority to demand obedience from the faithful and turning that authority over to a soulless state apparatus incapable of moral discernment. They are taking from God what no atheist would dare and giving to Caesar what he has never dared claim for himself. The women in Right to Life groups want to protect not fertilized eggs but motherhood and their own worth as women in God's eyes as well as man's. They will learn the cruelest lesson of history: "Every decent End consumes itself. You kill yourself trying to reach it, and by the time you get there it's been turned inside out."[14] The words were written by Soviet dissident Abram Tertz (Andrei Sinyavsky), but every passionate political activist of conscience—whatever the "decent End"—has had occasion to say them, in trouble and in grief. What one means to do goes wrong, it becomes what one abhors. Right to Life women will see it too late: they will stay mesmerized by the small tributes men pay to the idea—not the reality—of women as mothers. The power the Right to Life women are fighting so hard to put into the hands of the state will eventually and inevitably be used (1) to redefine when life begins and what life is so that the male becomes its sole creator and (2) to determine and enforce which women reproduce, when, and how. The women not needed will have no claim to civil dignity or civil protection. The reason for female submission finally will be very simple and overwhelmingly clear: for women submission will be a matter of life or death, with the right of appeal to the sacredness of women as mothers no longer in the vocabulary of male supremacy.

When women cease to be altogether necessary, politically dissident women become altogether unnecessary. Once women are biologically expendable on a grand scale, political women need no longer be tolerated on any scale. Politically dissident women are considered unnecessary now: this is the mood toward feminists and other women who rebel; someday it will be policy, not a mood.

The criteria for politically dissident women—troublemakers—will be extended to include any women not domestics, sex prostitutes, or reproductive prostitutes. The religiously orthodox women will find themselves characterized as politically dissident women one day too: there they will be, advocating and upholding old laws, customs, and ideas that are no longer in the best interests of men. They will be demanding more than men want them to have and there will be no concessions from men: because men will be able to control reproduction without the mass complicity of women. Reduced to its simplest elements, the old misogyny was expressed by the ancient Greek Hipponax of Ephesus: "The two days in a woman's life a man can best enjoy are when he marries her and when he carries her dead body to the grave."[15] In the misogyny of the future—in the coming gynocide—he will have one day he can best enjoy: "when he carries her dead body to the grave." We come after, as George Steiner wrote; and we are women. We know what men can do.

6

Antifeminism

> some men
>
> would rather see us dead than imagine
> what we think of them/
> if we measure our silence by our pain
> how could the words
> any word
> ever catch up
> what is it we could call equal
>
> Ntozake Shange, "Slow Drag," from *Some Men*

Feminism is a much-hated political philosophy. This is true all along the male-defined, recognizable political spectrum from far Right to far Left. Feminism is hated because women are hated. Antifeminism is a direct expression of misogyny; it is the political defense of woman hating. This is because feminism is the liberation movement of women. Antifeminism, in any of its political colorations, holds that the social and sexual condition of women essentially (one way or another) embodies the nature of women, that the way women are treated in sex and in society is congruent with what women are, that the fundamental relationship between men and women—in sex, in reproduction, in social hierarchy—is both necessary and inevitable. Antifeminism defends the conviction that the male abuse of women, especially in sex, has an implicit logic, one that no program of social justice can or should eliminate; that because the male use of women originates in the distinct and opposite natures of each which converge in what is called "sex," women are not abused when used as women—but merely used for what they are by men as men. It is admitted that there are excesses of male sadism—committed by deranged individuals, for instance—but in general the massive degradation of women is not seen to violate the nature of women as such. For instance, a man's nature would be violated if anyone forcibly penetrated his body. A woman's nature is not violated by the same event, even though she may have been hurt. A man's nature would not provoke anyone to forcibly penetrate his body. A woman's nature does provoke such penetration—and even injury is no proof that she did not want the penetration or even the injury itself, since it is her nature as a woman to desire being forcibly penetrated and forcibly hurt. Conservatively estimated, in the United States a woman is raped every three minutes, and in each and every rape the woman's nature is at issue first and foremost, not the man's act. Certainly there is no social or legal recognition that rape is an act of political terrorism.

Antifeminism can accommodate reform: a recognition that some forms of discrimination against women are unfair to women or that some kinds of injustice to women are not warranted (or entirely warranted) by the nature of women. But underneath the apparent civility, there are facile, arrogant assumptions: that the remedies are easy, the problems frivolous; that the harm done to women is not substantial nor is it significant in any real way; and that the subordination of women to men is not in and of itself an egregious wrong. This assessment is maintained in the face of proved atrocities and the obvious intractability of the oppression.

Antifeminism is always an expression of hating women: it is way past time to say so, to make the equation, to insist on its truth. Antifeminism throws women to the wolves; it says "later" or "never" to those suffering cruel and systematic deprivations of liberty; it tells women that when their lives are at stake, there is no urgency toward either justice or decency; it scolds women for wanting freedom. It is right to see woman hating, sex hatred, passionate contempt, in every effort to subvert or stop an improvement in the status of women on any front, whether radical or reform. It is right to see contempt for women in any effort to subvert or stop any move on the part of women toward economic or sexual independence, toward civil or legal equality, toward self-determination. Antifeminism is the politics of contempt for women as a class. This is true when the antifeminism is expressed in opposition to the Equal Rights Amendment or to the right to abortion on demand or to procedures against sexual harassment or to shelters for battered women or to reforms in rape laws. This is true whether the opposition is from the Heritage Foundation, the Moral Majority, the Eagle Forum, the American Civil Liberties Union, the Communist Party, the Democrats, or the Republicans. The same antifeminist contempt for women is expressed in resistance to affirmative action or in defenses of pornography or in the acceptance of prostitution as an institution of female sex labor. If one sees that women are being systematically exploited and abused, then the defense of anything, the acceptance of anything, that promotes or continues that exploitation or abuse expresses a hatred of women, a contempt for their freedom and dignity; and an effort to impede legislative, social, or economic initiatives that would improve the status of women, however radical or reformist those measures are, is an expression of that same contempt. One simply cannot be both for and against the exploitation of women: for it when it brings pleasure, against it in the abstract; for it when it brings profit, against it in principle; for it when no one is looking, against it when someone who might notice is around. If one sees how exploited women are—the systematic nature of the exploitation, the sexual base of the exploitation—then there is no political or ethical justification for doing one whit less than everything—using every resource—to stop that exploitation. Antifeminism has been the cover for outright bigotry and it has been the vehicle of outright bigotry. Antifeminism has been a credible cover and an effective vehicle because the hatred of women is not politically anathema on either the Right or the Left. Antifeminism is manifest wherever the subordination of women is actively perpetuated or enhanced or defended or passively accepted, because the devaluation of women is implicit in all these stances. Woman hating and antifeminism, however aggressive or restrained the expression, are empirical synonyms, inseparable, often indistinguishable, often interchangeable; and any acceptance of the exploitation of women in any area, for any reason, in any style, is both, means both, and promotes both.

Antifeminism breaks down into contempt for particular kinds of women—as men envision the kinds of women there are. There is a spectrum of insult. Lesbians, intellectuals, and uppity women are hated for their presumption, their arrogance, their masculine ambition. Prudes, spinsters, and celibates may not want to be like men but they seem able to live without them; so they are treated with contempt and disdain. Sluts, "nymphos," and tarts are hated because they are cheap, not expensive, and because they are their sex raw or sex itself. These epithets (often in ruder form) directed against a woman are intended to malign her own relationship to her own gender or to sexuality as men define and enforce it. The epithets are situational: chosen and applied not to show what she is in her essential self but to intimidate her in a particular situation. For instance, if she does not want sex, she may be called a prude or a dyke, and after she has had sex, she may be called—by the very same observer—a slut. Expressing ideas a man does not like, she may be a slut or a dyke or a prude—depending on how any given man assesses her vulnerability to insult or depending on the man's own obsessional interest in prudes or sluts or dykes. Antifeminism is in the reduction of a woman to perceptions of her sexuality or relation to men or male sexuality; and antifeminism is in the ascribing of a specific masculine integrity to acts usually reserved for men—acts like making love with women or writing books or walking down the street without apology or speaking with authority. Ideas and acts uphold the potency and cultural vigor of these epithets, which reflect real values—how women are disdained, why, what women do wrong and get punished for. The breaking down of women into the insults used to describe women, the use of these insults to describe or intimidate or discredit, granting validity to these critiques of a female's posture, pose, stance, attitude, or act, are all expressions of both antifeminism and woman hating. When a woman expresses an opinion—about anything—and the response is to undermine perceptions of or question her sexuality, sexual identity, femininity, relations with men, the response can be identified without further analysis as implicitly antifeminist and woman-hating. It can and should be exposed as such. Antifeminism as a strategy for subverting what credibility women can muster runs the gamut from subtle innuendoes to overt hostility, all of which is designed to remind the woman herself and those listening to her that she is, after all, only a woman—and a defective one at that. The woman hating implicit in the antifeminism is designed to humiliate the woman so that she feels the humiliation and so that those listening can see her being humiliated and feeling it. Raising and manipulating antagonistic feelings toward a woman because she is a woman, using her sex and sexuality, reminding her and those around her of what she *is* and what she *is for*, are the same as raising and manipulating racist antagonisms against a black in a white-supremacist context. The response to the underlining of her sex so as to impugn her credibility should not rest on whether or not one agrees with the woman about whatever issue; the response should be a response to the antifeminism and misogyny being used against her. It is way past time to recognize, to say, to confront, the fact that women are isolated and destroyed by the ways in which epithets discredit them. The epithets are symbolic reminders of what she is reduced to, not human, woman, that lower thing; the epithets are accusations that remind the accused of her place as a woman and some alleged violation of its boundaries. Women fear epithets because they are warnings, threats, proof that a woman has made a wrong step in her relationship to the world around her, proof that a man or men have noticed her and are angry with her. Women fear these epithets because women fear the anger of men. That anger is the substance of both antifeminism and misogyny. The epithet is a weapon, whether hurled or delivered in a sulky or measured tone. The epithet is inevitably an act of hostility used in a spirit of vengeance. Calling a woman a name temporarily brands her; it molds social perceptions of her in a way that upholds her social inferiority; it frequently comes before the fist or before the fuck, and so women learn to associate it with uses of themselves that they abhor, hostile uses of themselves; and it frequently comes as he hits, as he fucks. The epithet degrades a woman by degrading her sex, sexuality, and personal integrity; it expresses a serious, not a frivolous, hatred—the hatred of women, a serious hatred with serious consequences to those against whom it is directed. Epithets as sex-based insults are like machine-gun rounds, fired off, bringing down whatever gets hit—anything female around. The hints of these sex-based insults, shadowed references to them, evocations of them, are used with persistence and skill in the public devaluing of women—in hating women and in the politics of contempt for women, in common discourse and in cultural discourse. Every time this use of a lexicon of hatred passes unremarked, every time the hate is expressed and there is no visible rebellion, no discernible resistance, some part of the woman to whom it happens dies and some part of any woman who watches dies too. Each time the use of such an epithet or its evocation passes without retaliation, something in women dies. Each time slut, dyke, prude, is used to keep women intimidated and each time its use is not repudiated (the repudiation cannot rest on whether or not the accusation is in any sense accurate, only in its use), antifeminism has stepped on another female life and crushed some part of it; woman hating has humiliated and hurt another woman or a woman again. Each time an honorable word—like lesbian—is used as a weapon of insult, or some honorable act—like a woman having sex because she wants to with a lover or lovers of her choice—is used as a weapon of insult, or some honorable choice—like being celibate—is used as a weapon of insult, the women who are and who do and who choose are irrevocably hurt and diminished. The answer is not as simple as losing one's fear of the words themselves (whether they apply or not), because any woman would be a fool not to be afraid of what is behind the words. Behind the words is the man who uses them and the power of his whole class over the woman against whom they are used. Each time contempt is expressed for the dyke, the prude, the slut, hatred is being expressed toward all women. Whether the insults are accepted in society, tolerated, encouraged, the main stuff of humor, or merely passively acquiesced in, the devaluing of women is perpetuated, the intimidation of women is furthered. Each time the insults are paraded or whispered—used against a woman as insult—the insults gain in potency from use, acceptance, and repetition; and any woman, however much she is or is not what the insult conveys, is more liable to manipulation, distortion, extortion, slander, and harassment; and antifeminism and woman hating are that much more entrenched. Woman hating is the passion; antifeminism is its ideological defense; in the sex-based insult passion and ideology are united in an act of denigration and intimidation. The tolerance for sex-based insult and its effectiveness in discrediting women are measures of the virulence of antifeminism and woman hating: how pervasive they are, how persuasive they are, how deeply rooted they are, what chance women stand against them. In our society, sex-based insult is the coin of the realm. Women live defensively, not just against rape but against the language of the rapist—the language of what a woman is called in intimacy and in public, loud and soft.

Antifeminism is also articulated through social models, of which there are three of continuing major importance: the separate-but-equal model; the woman-superior model; and the trusty, familiar male-dominant model.

The use of the separate-but-equal model is particularly cynical in the United States, where that model applied to race was the foundation for systematic racial segregation enforced by police power. Equality was always a chimera or a lie; separation was real. The model held that social institutions could be reasonably and fairly constructed on the basis of biology, for instance, race or skin color. What made separation necessary—the presumed inferiority of one of the biologically defined groups—made equality impossible. The idea of separation and the institutions of separation derived from a social inequality of such astonishing magnitude and crass cruelty that separation in idea or practice essentially denied that blacks had a human nature in common with whites or any common human standing. The separate-but-equal model itself originates in the conviction that men and women could not stand on common human ground. The model originates in the effort to justify the subordination of women to men (and in the justification to perpetuate that subordination) by positing male and female natures so biologically different as to require social separation, socially antithetical paths, social life bifurcated by sex so that there are two cultures, one male, one female, coexisting in the same society. The separate-but-equal model applied to sex predated the variation of the model applied to race. With respect to sex, the separate-but-equal model held that women and men were destined by biology for different social spheres. The spheres were separate but equal, which made the men and women separate but equal. The sphere of the woman was the home; the sphere of the man was the world. These were separate-but-equal domains. The woman was supposed to bear and raise the children; the man was supposed to impregnate her and support them. These were separate-but-equal duties. The woman had female capacities—she was intuitive, emotional, tender, charming (in women a capacity to arouse or entrap, not an attribute). The man had male capacities—he was logical, reasoning, strong, powerful (as a capacity and relative to the woman). These were separate-but-equal capacities. The woman was supposed to do domestic labor, the precise nature of which was determined by her husband's social class. The man was supposed to labor in the world for money, power, recognition, according to his social class. This was separate-but-equal labor.

Sex segregation in practice is necessarily different from race segregation: women are everywhere, in almost every home, in most beds, as intimate as it is possible to be with those who want to keep them separate. Given the nearly universal intimacy women have with men, it is astonishing to recognize how successful sex-segregation bolstered by the separate-but-equal model has been and continues to be. Women have invaded the male sphere of the marketplace, only to be segregated in female job ghettos. In jobs, duties, responsibilities, physical, moral, and intellectual capacities, division of labor within the home, the ethic and practice that still obtains is sex segregation. The separate-but-equal model applied to men and women continues to be effective because it is seen to correspond to biology accurately and fairly. The model has credibility because the sexual subordination of women to men is seen to be in the nature of things and a logical premise of social organization—a biological reality that is properly reiterated in social institutions, civil prerogatives, and sex-segregated obligations. The model is perceived as fair because in it men and women are kept biologically separate (discrete), socially separate (discrete), and they are declared equal because each is doing *equally* what is appropriate to their sex. Separation is seen to be the only real vehicle of equality for women. The notion is that women competing with men, not limited to a female sphere, could never achieve social or economic or sexual equality because of their nature—which in all of these areas would simply be inferior to male nature; females are inferior, however, only because they have left the female sphere, which in itself is equal, not inferior; females are only inferior to men in a male sphere, where they do not belong. Equality is guaranteed by setting up separate spheres according to sex and simply insisting that the spheres are equal. This amounts to a kind of metaphysical paternalism: constructing a social model in which women need not experience their inferiority as a burden but instead are assigned such social value as women that their inferiority is of equal social worth to the superiority of men. The separate spheres are declared equal with no reference to the material conditions of the persons in the spheres and this is the sense in which women have equality with men under this model. There need not be equality of rights, for instance; indeed, it is counterindicated. Since the sexes are not the same, they should not be treated the same, and something is wrong when a common standard is applied to both. In this social model, separation by sex class is viewed as the only basis for equality; sex segregation is the institutional expression of this egalitarian ethic, its program in fact. With sex as with race, separation is a fact; equality is a chimera or a lie.

The woman-superior model of antifeminism is found in two apparently opposing realms: the spiritual and the sexual. In the spiritual realm, the woman is superior to the male by definition; he worships her because she is good; her sex makes her moral or gives her the responsibility for a morality that is sex-specific. Being female, she is higher, by nature closer to some abstract conception of good. She is credited with a moral sensibility that men are hard put to match (but then, they are not expected to try): she is ethereal, she floats, her moral nature lifts her up, she gravitates toward that which is pure, chaste, and tasteful. She has an instinctive, sex-based knowledge of what is good and right. Her moral sensibility is unfailingly benign, always an influence toward the good. Her sex-class business includes the business of being virtuous—a strange assignment by sex, since the Latin root of the word *virtue* means "strength" or "manliness," which perhaps shows the futility of the project for her. This goodness of her sex is essentially based on a presumed chastity, a necessary chastity—of behavior but also of appetite. She, as a woman, is not supposed to know sexual desire. Men lust. As one who by her nature does not lust, she is the opposite of man: he is carnal; she is good. There is no notion of female morality or of a woman's being good in the world that is not based largely on chastity as a moral value. The great female tragedies are stories of sexual falls. The tragic flaw in a female hero—Hardy's Tess or Tolstoy's Anna Karenina—is sexual desire. All the drama of a female life, in great or in banal works, basically replicates the biblical fall. Seduction (or rape) means knowledge, which is sexual desire; sexual desire means descent into sin and inevitable punishment. As a cultural symbol, the good female is innocent: innocent of sex, innocent of knowledge—chaste in both ways. Historically, ignorance has been a form of grace for the good woman; education was denied women to keep them morally good. The elevation of a woman requires that she have this innocence, this purity, this chastity: she must not know the world, which men embody. The worship of a woman or a female religious symbol is often the unmediated worship of chastity. The virgin is the great religious symbol of female good, the female who is by nature (in her body) good, who embodies the good. The awe and honor accorded the chaste female by men are frequently pointed to to show that men do not hate or degrade women, that men worship, adore, and admire women. The morally superior nature of women is honored mostly in the abstract, and women are worshiped mostly in the abstract. The worship is worship of a symbol—a symbol manipulated to justify the uses to which fallen women are put. The morally good woman is put on a pedestal—a small, precarious, raised stage, often mined, on which she stands for as long as she can—until she falls off or jumps or it goes boom.

In the secular world, women are also credited with having a sense of good that is intrinsically female, a sense of good that men do not have. This is a frequent feature of contemporary environmentalist or antimilitarist movements. Women are seen to have an inborn commitment to both clean air and peace, a moral nature that abhors pollution and murder. Being good or moral is viewed as a particular biological capacity of women and as a result women are the natural guardians of morality: a moral vanguard as it were. Organizers use this appeal to women all the time. Motherhood is especially invoked as biological proof that women have a special relationship to life, a special sensitivity to its meaning, a special, intuitive knowledge of what is right. Any political group can appropriate the special moral sensibility of women to its own ends: most groups do, usually in place of offering substantive relief to women with respect to sexism in the group itself. Women all along the male-defined political spectrum give special credence to this view of a female biological nature that is morally good.

However this premise about a biologically based morality is used, the woman-superior model of antifeminism is operating to keep women down, not up, in the crude world of actual human interchange. To stay worshiped, the woman must stay a symbol and she must stay good. She cannot become merely a human in the muck of life, morally flawed and morally struggling, committing acts that have complex, difficult, unpredictable consequences. She must not walk the same streets men do or do the same things or have the same responsibilities. Precisely because she is good, she is unfit to do the same things, unfit to make the same decisions, unfit to resolve the same dilemmas, unfit to undertake the same responsibilities, unfit to exercise the same rights. Her nature is different—this time better but still absolutely different—and therefore her role must be different. The worshiping attitude, the spiritual elevation of women that men invoke whenever they suggest that women are finer than they, proposes that women are what men can never be: chaste, good. In fact men are what women can never be: real moral agents, the bearers of real moral authority and responsibility. Women are not kept from this moral agency by biology, but by a male social system that puts women above or below simple human choice in morally demanding situations. The spiritual superiority of women in this model of ludicrous homage isolates women from the human acts that create meaning, the human choices that create both ethics and history. It separates women out from the chaos and triumph of human responsibility by giving women a two-dimensional morality, a stagnant morality, one in which what is right and good is predetermined, sex-determined, biologically determined. The worship of women, devotion to that in woman which raises man, respect for some moral sensibility allegedly inborn only in women, is the seductive antifeminism, the one that entrances women who have seen through the other kinds. Being worshiped (for most women) is preferable to being defiled, and being looked up to is better than being walked on. It is hard for women to refuse the worship of what otherwise is despised: being female. Woman's special moral nature has sometimes been used to plead her case: being moral, she will be able to upgrade the morality of the nation if she has the rights of citizenship, the tone of the marketplace if she is employed, the quality of the church if she officiates, the humanism of government if she is in it; being moral, she will be on the side of good. It has also been argued, more loudly and more often, that her moral nature must not be contaminated by vulgar responsibilities; that she has a special moral role to play in making the nation and the world good—she must be in her person the example of good that will civilize and educate men and make the nation moral. One cannot do what men do—not in government, not in the family, not even in religion, not anywhere—and be an example of good. "It is the task of the Positive Woman," wrote Phyllis Schlafly, "to keep America good."[1] Women keep Amerika good by being good. Many women who hate Schlafly's politics would agree that women have a special moral responsibility "to keep America good." They have a different political program of good in mind and a different conception of women's rights, but their conception of a biologically determined morality in which women are better than men is not different. Antifeminism allows for this sentimentality, encourages and exploits this self-indulgence; liberation does not. As Frederick Douglass wrote over a century ago: "We advocate women's rights, not because she is an angel, but because she is a woman, having the same wants, and being exposed to the same evils as man."[2]

The woman-superior model of antifeminism also takes a sexual form, one that is purely pornographic. The central conceit of woman-hating sex, sex as conquest and possession, dominance and submission, is that the woman has real power: she is only the apparent victim; she is only seemingly powerless. Her power is in her capacity to provoke erection or lust. Men suffer arousal passively—against their will or regardless of their will. They then act on what a woman, or any sex object, has provoked. She provokes what she wants. When a man has an erection and commits a sexual act because of it or in response to it, he is acting in response to a provocation by a woman, whose nature and intent are well met by his act. In pornography, the male sexual values that inform and permeate rape and other forced sex acts are articulated without apology. The genre insists that sex is conquest, that the woman who resists wants to be forced, hurt, brutalized; that the woman who wants sex gets pleasure from being used like a thing, from pain and humiliation. The genre insists that rape, battery, physical torture, bondage, capture, and imprisonment are things done to women because women provoke them the same way that women provoke erection: by being there, by being female. Provoking these acts is the power women have over men; women get men to do these things, to perform these sex acts. In the world men seem to exercise power, but all of that comes to nothing in the face of the lust provoked by a woman. Whatever he does to her, she is still more powerful than he is because he wants her, he needs her, he is being driven by a desire for her. In the sexual woman-superior model, power is articulated as being intrinsically female because power is redefined beyond reason, beyond coherence: as if power is in the corpse that draws the vultures. This pornographic conception of female power is fundamental to the antifeminism of sexual-liberation movements in which unlimited sexual use of women by men is defined as freedom for both: she wants it; he responds; voilà! the revolution. It is also fundamental to the antifeminism of the legal system with respect to sexual crimes like rape, battery, and sexual abuse of children, especially girls. The female is still seen as the provocation for what might be a legitimate sex act, depending on just how provocative she was. Her will is regarded as probably implicit in the use the male made of her. The female is seen to have power over the man—and responsibility for what he has done to her—because he wanted her so bad: she has provoked whatever desire motivated him to act. His desire is what gives her power. Her power is in her sexual nature, her existence as a woman to which he responds—not in her behavior. For this reason, rape inquiries search her behavior to find the truth about her nature. If her nature is finally seen to warrant his act, he is not responsible for it—she is. This is the power of women in pornographic sex. The apologies for this sexual system that claim that women are powerful because women are desired—in fact, that go so far as to insist that women are sex-dominant and sex-controlling—uphold this phantasmagoric female power, keeping women in real life powerless. The antifeminism is directly implicit in the pornographic conceptions of female power, female nature, and female freedom. Her power is in being used, her nature is to be used, and her freedom is in being used. Or, her power is in provoking men to hurt her, her nature is to provoke men to hurt her, and her freedom is in provoking pain. Or, her power is in making men force her to do what she does not want to do, her nature is to make men force her to do what she does not want to do, and her freedom is in being forced to do what she does not want to do. These principles of antifeminism effectively confound both power and freedom: the response in most women is to want neither. A woman's individual nature is more than confounded: it is frequently annihilated.

The male-dominant model of antifeminism is virtually everywhere. Its woman-hating dimensions have been discussed brilliantly in many feminist texts; here the focus will be on how it functions to stop a liberation movement. Religion and biology are the great roots of the metaphysical idea that men are superior to women because they are. Whether male dominance is described as a kind of perpetual biological pillaging or the will of a merely wrathful God, the hostility in male dominance is what is most consistently justified by the idea of male dominance. Keeping women a subject people is hostile. The genius of the male-dominant model of antifeminism is the transmogrification of this hostility into what passes for love. When one group conquers another, the act of conquest is clearly hostile; when a man conquers a woman, it is to express romantic or sexual love. Invasion is an act of hostility, unless the male is invading the female, in which case "violation" is used to mean love. Beating someone up is an act of hostility, unless a man is beating a woman whom he loves: women, it is said, consider beating proof of love and demand or provoke this proof. When a man tyrannizes a people, he is hostile to their rights and freedom; when a man tyrannizes a woman, he is well within the bounds of his role as husband or lover. When a group deemed inferior is targeted for violence in propaganda, that propaganda is unarguably hostile; when men target women for sexual violence in pornography, the material, the targeting, and the violence are considered expressions of sexual love. Mass terrorization of one group by another is hostile, unless women are terrorized by men raping, in which case each rape must be examined for signs of love. Confining a group, restricting them, depriving them of rights because they were born into one class and not another are hostile acts, unless women are being confined, restricted, and deprived of rights by the men who love them so that they will be what men can love. There is hostility in the world, which one recognizes as historical and social cruelty; and then there is the love of man for woman. The acts may be the same but they are so very different, because what is done to women is measured by an absolutely unique standard: is it sexy? Women are taken to be sex, so if it—whatever it is—is done to a woman, it is likely to be sexy. If it is sexy, it comes under the aegis of love. Hostility is defined in the dictionary as "antagonism." Love is seen to be a grand antagonism; so is a great sexual passion, while the everyday fucks are little antagonisms oft repeated. The torturer is just a real obsessed lover when the victim is a woman, especially a woman whom he knows intimately. Rape is just another kind of love; and nothing—no law, no political movement, no higher consciousness—has yet made rape less sexy for those who see love in male dominance. Chains are sexy when women wear them, prisons are sexy when women are in them, pain is sexy when women hurt, and love includes all this and more. Beat up a man for speaking his mind and there is a human-rights violation—hunt him or capture him or terrorize him and his human rights have been violated; do the same to a woman and the violation is sexy. Nothing that falls within the purview of the love of man for woman qualifies as a violation of human rights; instead, violation becomes a synonym for sex, part of the vocabulary of love. The love of the superior for the inferior must by its nature be fairly horrific, fairly terrifying, grossly distorted. When men love women, every hostile act demonstrates that love, every brutality is a sign of it; and every complaint that a woman makes against the hostility of male dominance is taken to be a complaint against love, a refusal to be a real woman, that is, to suffer male hostility as an ecstasy, to suffer love.

The male-dominant model of antifeminism also proposes that freedom is inimical to the situation of women because women must always bargain. Since men are dominant, aggressive, controlling, powerful because of God or nature, the weak women must always have something to trade to get the protection of these strong men. Either the woman is too weak to care for herself or she is too weak to fend off men; in either case, she needs a male protector. If she needs a male protector, she must not only bargain to get him; she must continuously bargain to keep him or to keep him from abusing the power he has over her. This compromises any possibility of self-determination for her. The dependence of women on men, the inability of women to have and to manifest a self-sustaining and self-determined integrity, and the fundamental definition of a woman as a whore by nature are all established as being implicit in the biological relationship between men and women: implicit and unalterable. This feature of the male-dominant model is unique to it. Neither the separate-but-equal model nor the woman-superior model puts women in a metaphysically defined, biologically determined relationship of prostitution to men. (Perhaps this virtue of the male-dominant model accounts for its ubiquity.) The bargain women must make because men are biologically dominant is pointed to whenever a woman achieves. The bargain is searched for—what did she sell to whom to enable her to do whatever she did? The necessity for bargaining is used to stop rebellion. The bargain necessitated by his greater aggression, strength, and power is the principal reason for refuting the possibility of her claim to independence in this model of antifeminism. He is dominant; she must submit. Submission in the face of greater strength, greater aggression, greater power, is unavoidable. She is simply not strong enough to be on her own—especially not if he wants her because she is not strong enough or aggressive enough to stop him from taking her. So each woman has to make a deal with at least one of the strong ones for protection; and the deal she makes, being based on her inferiority, originating in it, acknowledges the truth and inevitability of that inferiority. In needing to bargain because she is too weak not to, she proves that antifeminism—the repudiation of her freedom—is grounded in simple biological necessity, biological common sense, biological realism.

Because the male is presumed dominant by natural right or divine will, he is supposed to have an exclusive authority in the realm of public power. The antifeminism predicated on natural male dominance also maintains that men naturally dominate government, politics, economics, culture, state and military policy—that men naturally assert their dominance by running all social and political institutions. The token woman here and there in no way interferes with the effectiveness of virtually all-male clubs of power in erasing any hope of real authority or influence for women. One woman on the Supreme Court, one woman in the Senate, a woman prime minister, an occasional woman head of state, are not so much role models as rebukes to economically demoralized women who are supposed to accept the tokens as what they too could have been if only they themselves had been different—better, smarter, richer, prettier, not such schlemiels. Token women must go out of their way not to offend the male sense of femininity, but by their visibility they inevitably do so. As a result, the token women give out the correct line on femininity and at the same time bear the brunt of the critical perception that obviously they are not at home being fucked. The woman who is not a token is mostly condescended to by the token, a condescension that she feels not only acutely but often, since the token is always pointed out to her as proof that her own situation does not result from an exclusionary social system. Every all-male or nearly all-male group—profession, institution, business, club, or power clique—is a concrete embodiment of antifeminism. By its existence it upholds and proclaims the dominance of men over women. By its existence it reinforces the social inferiority of women to men, perpetuates the political subordination of women to men, mandates the economic dependence of women on men, and endlessly revitalizes the sexual submission of women to men. The all-male clique of power communicates the antifeminism of male dominance everywhere it operates, all the time, without exception. The power of men to make decisions and determine policy, to create culture and to control the institutions of culture, is simultaneously held to be the logical outcome of male dominance and proof of its existence. Every institution that is structurally male-dominant is also ideologically male-dominant; or its structure would change. Every group that is structurally male-dominant functions as concrete resistance, material resistance, to the liberation of women: it prohibits the exodus of women from the obligations and disadvantages, not to mention the cruelties, of inferiority. Any area that is virtually all male is hostile to women, to political rights, economic parity, and sexual self-determination for women. The verbal support of men in all-male institutions, groups, or cliques of power for mild feminist reform has no value in the world of real, substantive change for women: it is the all-male structure itself that must be subverted and destroyed. Male dominance and the antifeminism that defends it can only be repudiated by being ended; those who construct it by literally being the bricks of which it is built cannot change it by merely disputing it. The antifeminism in exclusively male enclaves is not made humane through gestures; it is immune to modification through diplomatic goodwill. As long as a road is closed to women, it is closed to women; and that means that women cannot take that road, however nicely the men on it suggest they would not mind. The road is not only a road to power or independence or equity; it is often the only road away from tremendous abuse. The antifeminism in an all-male institution cannot be mitigated by attitude; nor can male dominance—always the meaning of an all-male enclave—ever accept that women are not inferior to men. The token woman carries the stigma of inferiority with her, however much she tries to dissociate herself from the other women of her sex class. In trying to stay singular, not one of them, she grants the inferiority of her sex class, an inferiority for which she is always compensating and from which she is never free. If the inferiority were not reckoned universally true, she of all women would not have to defend herself against the stigma of it; nor would her own complicity in the antifeminism of the institution (through dissociation with lesser women) be a perpetual condition of her quasi acceptance. Male dominance in society always means that out of public sight, in the private, ahistorical world of men with women, men are sexually dominating women. The antifeminism in the all-male rulership of society always means that in the intimate world of men with women, men are politically suppressing women.

The three social models of antifeminism—the separate-but-equal model, the woman-superior model, and the male-dominant model—are not inimical to one another. They mix and match with perfect ease, since logic and consistency are not prerequisites for keeping women down: no one need prove his case to justify the subordination of women; no one need meet a rigorous standard of intellectual, political, or moral accountability. Most people, whatever their political convictions, seem to believe parts of each model, the pieces adding up to a whole view. Fragmented philosophical and ideological justifications for the subordination of women exist in a material context in which women are subordinated to men: the subordination is self-justifying, since power subordinates and power justifies; power both serves and consoles itself. Separate-but-equal, woman-superior, and male-dominant antifeminism can even be used sequentially as one whole argument for the practice of male supremacy: men and women have different capacities and different areas of responsibility according to sex but their functions and attributes are of equal importance; women are morally superior to men (a different capacity, a different area of responsibility), except when they provoke lust, in which case they have real power over men; the biological dominance of men over women is (a) counterbalanced by the real sexual power of women over men (in which case each has separate-but-equal powers) or (b) proved in that women are too good to be as aggressive and as rudely dominant as men or (c) naturally fair and naturally reasonable because natural submission is the natural complement to natural dominance (and dominance and submission are separate-but-equal spheres, submission marking the woman as morally superior unless the submission is sexually provocative, in which case her sex gives her different-but-equal power). Either this is true or it is not. Either the arguments of antifeminism, one by one or the whole lot, are true or they are not. Either there are separate-but-equal spheres or there are not. Either women are morally better than men or they are not. Either women have sexual power over men simply by being women or they do not; either provoking lust is power or it is not. Either men are dominant by nature or will of God or they are not. Antifeminism says all this is true; feminism says it is not. The so-called feminism that says some of it is true and some of it is not cannot combat antifeminism because it has incorporated it. Antifeminism proposes two standards for rights and responsibilities: two standards determined strictly by and applied strictly to sex. Feminism as the liberation movement of women proposes one absolute standard of human dignity, indivisible by sex. In this sense, feminism does propose—as antifeminists accuse—that men and women be treated the same. Feminism is a radical stance against double standards in rights and responsibilities, and feminism is a revolutionary advocacy of a single standard of human freedom.

To achieve a single standard of human freedom and one absolute standard of human dignity, the sex-class system has to be dismembered. The reason is pragmatic, not philosophical: nothing less will work. However much everyone wants to do less, less will not free women. Liberal men and women ask, Why can't we just be ourselves, all human beings, begin now and not dwell in past injustices, wouldn't that subvert the sex-class system, change it from the inside out? The answer is no. The sex-class system has a structure; it has deep roots in religion and culture; it is fundamental to the economy; sexuality is its creature; to be "just human beings" in it, women have to hide what happens to them as women because they are women—happenings like forced sex and forced reproduction, happenings that continue as long as the sex-class system operates. The liberation of women requires facing the real condition of women in order to change it. "We're all just people" is a stance that prohibits recognition of the systematic cruelties visited on women because of sex oppression.

Feminism as a liberation movement, then, demands a revolutionary single standard of what humans have a right to, and also demands that the current sexual bifurcation of rights never be let out of sight. Antifeminism does the opposite: it insists that there is a double standard of what humans have a right to—a male standard and a female standard; and it insists at the same time that we are all just human beings, right now, as things stand, within this sex-class system, so that no special attention should be paid to social phenomena on account of sex. With respect to rape, for instance, the feminist starts out with a single standard of freedom and dignity: everyone, women as well as men, should have a right to the integrity of their own body. Feminists then focus on and analyze the sex-class reality of rape: men rape, women are raped; even in those statistically rare cases where boys or men are raped, men are the rapists. Antifeminists start out with a double standard: men conquer, possess, dominate, men take women; women are conquered, possessed, dominated, and taken. Antifeminists then insist that rape is a crime like any other, like mugging or homicide or burglary: they deny its sex-specific, sex-class nature and the political meaning undeniably implicit in the sexual construction of the crime. Feminists are accused of denying the common humanity of men and women because feminists refuse to fudge on the sex issue of who does what to whom, how often, and why. Antifeminists refuse to acknowledge that the sex-class system repudiates the humanity of women by keeping women systematically subject to exploitation and violence as a condition of sex. In analyzing the sex-class system, feminists are accused of inventing or perpetuating it. Calling attention to it, we are told, insults women by suggesting that they are victims (stupid enough to allow themselves to be victimized). Feminists are accused of being the agents of degradation by postulating that such degradation exists. This is a little like considering abolitionists responsible for slavery, but all is fair when love is war. In ignoring the political significance of the sex-class system except to defend it when it is under attack, antifeminists suggest that "we're all in this together," all us human beings, different-but-together, a formulation that depends on lack of clarity for its persuasiveness. Indisputably, we're all in rape together, some of us to great disadvantage. Feminism especially requires a rigorous analysis of sex class, one that is ongoing, stubborn, persistent, unsentimental, disciplined, not placated by fatuous invocations of a common humanity that in fact the sex-class system itself suppresses. The sex-class system cannot be undone when those whom it exploits and humiliates are unable to face it for what it is, for what it takes from them, for what it does to them. Feminism requires precisely what misogyny destroys in women: unimpeachable bravery in confronting male power. Despite the impossibility of it, there is such bravery: there are such women, in some periods millions upon millions of them. If male supremacy survives every effort of women to overthrow it, it will not be because of biology or God; nor will it be because of the force and power of men per se. It will be because the will to liberation was contaminated, undermined, rendered ineffectual and meaningless, by antifeminism: by specious concepts of equality based on an evasion of what the sex-class system really is. The refusal to recognize the intrinsic despotism of the sex-class system means that that despotism is inevitably incorporated into reform models of that same system: in this, antifeminism triumphs over the will to liberation. The refusal to recognize the unique abuses inherent in sex labor (treating sex labor as if it were sex-neutral, as if it were not intrinsically part of sex oppression and inseparable from it) is a function of antifeminism; the acceptance of sex labor as appropriate labor for women marks the triumph of antifeminism over the will to liberation. The sentimental acceptance of a double standard of human rights, responsibilities, and freedom is also the triumph of antifeminism over the will to liberation; no sexual dichotomy is compatible with real liberation. And, most important, the refusal to demand (with no compromise being possible) one absolute standard of human dignity is the greatest triumph of antifeminism over the will to liberation. Without that one absolute standard, liberation is mush; feminism is frivolous and utterly self-indulgent. Without that one absolute standard as the keystone of revolutionary justice, feminism has no claim to being a liberation movement; it has no revolutionary stance, goal, or potential; it has no basis for a radical reconstruction of society; it has no criteria for action or organization; it has no moral necessity; it has no inescapable claim on the conscience of "mankind"; it has no philosophical seriousness; it has no authentic stature as a human-rights movement; it has nothing to teach. Also, without that one absolute standard, feminism has no chance whatsoever of actually liberating women or destroying the sex-class system. Refusing to base itself on a principle of universal human dignity, or compromising, retreating from that principle, feminism becomes that which exists to stop it: antifeminism. No liberation movement can accept the degradation of those whom it seeks to liberate by accepting a different definition of dignity for them and stay a movement for their freedom at the same time. (Apologists for pornography: take note.) A universal standard of human dignity is the only principle that completely repudiates sex-class exploitation and also propels all of us into a future where the fundamental political question is the quality of life for all human beings. Are women being subordinated to men? There is insufficient dignity in that. Are men being prostituted too? What is human dignity?

Two elements constitute the discipline of feminism: political, ideological, and strategic confrontation with the sex-class system—with sex hierarchy and sex segregation—and a single standard of human dignity. Abandon either element and the sex-class system is unbreachable, indestructible; feminism loses its rigor, the toughness of its visionary heart; women get swallowed up not only by misogyny but also by antifeminism—facile excuses for exploiting women, metaphysical justifications for abusing women, and shoddy apologies for ignoring the political imperatives of women.

One other discipline is essential both to the practice of feminism and to its theoretical integrity: the firm, unsentimental, continuous recognition that women are a class having a common condition. This is not some psychological process of identification with women because women are wonderful; nor is it the insupportable assertion that there are no substantive, treacherous differences among women. This is not a liberal mandate to ignore what is cruel, despicable, or stupid in women, nor is it a mandate to ignore dangerous political ideas or allegiances of women. This does not mean women first, women best, women only. It does mean that the fate of every individual woman—no matter what her politics, character, values, qualities—is tied to the fate of all women whether she likes it or not. On one level, it means that every woman's fate is tied to the fate of women she dislikes personally. On another level, it means that every woman's fate is tied to the fate of women whom she politically and morally abhors. For instance, it means that rape jeopardizes communist and fascist women, liberal, conservative, Democratic, or Republican women, racist women and black women, Nazi women and Jewish women, homophobic women and homosexual women. The crimes committed against women because they are women articulate the condition of women. The eradication of these crimes, the transformation of the condition of women, is the purpose of feminism: which means that feminism requires a most rigorous definition of what those crimes are so as to determine what that condition is. This definition cannot be compromised by a selective representation of the sex class based on sentimentality or wishful thinking. This definition cannot exclude prudes or sluts or dykes or mothers or virgins because one does not want to be associated with them. To be a feminist means recognizing that one is associated with all women not as an act of choice but as a matter of fact. The sex-class system creates the fact. When that system is broken, there will be no such fact. Feminists do not create this common condition by making alliances: feminists recognize this common condition because it exists as an intrinsic part of sex oppression. The fundamental knowledge that women are a class having a common condition—that the fate of one woman is tied substantively to the fate of all women—toughens feminist theory and practice. That fundamental knowledge is an almost unbearable test of seriousness. There is no real feminism that does not have at its heart the tempering discipline of sex-class consciousness: knowing that women share a common condition as a class, like it or not.

What is that common condition? Subordinate to men, sexually colonized in a sexual system of dominance and submission, denied rights on the basis of sex, historically chattel, generally considered biologically inferior, confined to sex and reproduction: this is the general description of the social environment in which all women live. But what is the real map of that environment? Which crimes create the topography? Drawing 1 shows the basic condition of

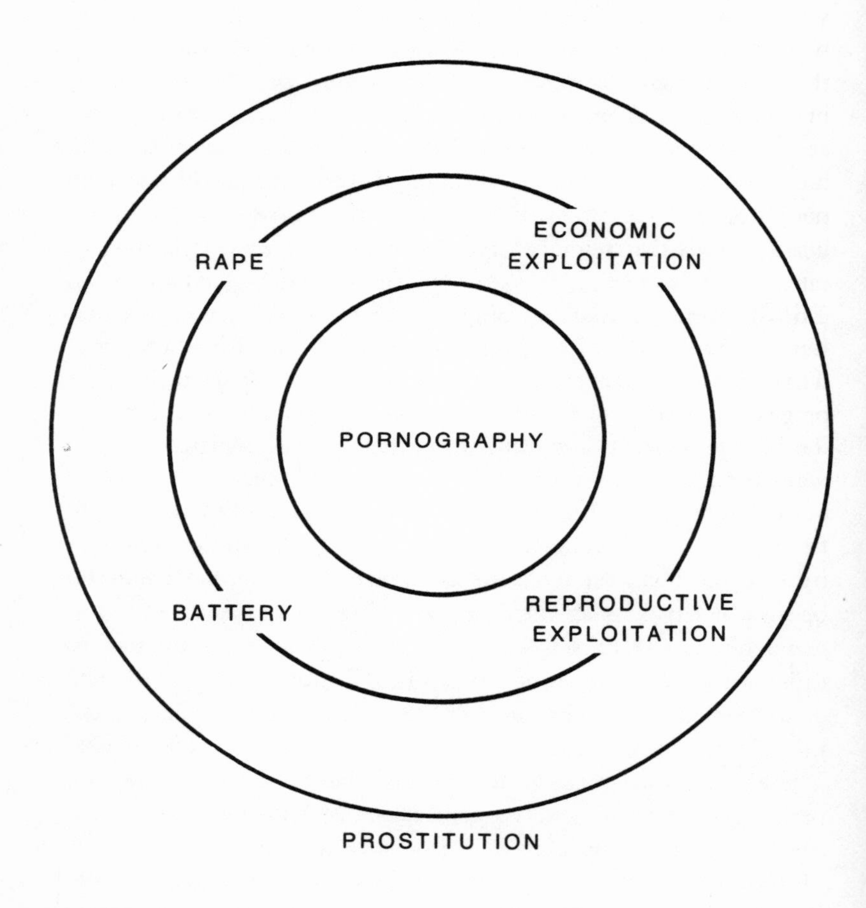

DRAWING 1. THE CONDITION OF WOMEN

women, a lateral view of the female bottom of sex hierarchy. Rape, battery, economic exploitation, and reproductive exploitation are the basic crimes committed against women in the sex-class system in which they are devalued because they are women. The crimes are points on a circle because it is a closed system, from nowhere to nowhere. These specific crimes are each committed against huge percentages of the female population at any given time. Rape, for instance, consists not only of police-blotter rape but also marital rape, incestuous abuse of girls, any sex that is coerced. Battery is estimated to have happened to 50 percent of married women in the United States alone. All housewives are economically exploited; all working women are. Reproductive exploitation includes forced pregnancy and forced sterilization. There are few female lives not touched by one, two, or three of these crimes and significantly determined by all of them. At the heart of the female condition is pornography: it is the ideology that is the source of all the rest; it truly defines what women are in this system—and how women are treated issues from what women *are*. Pornography is not a metaphor for what women are; it is what women are in theory and in practice. Prostitution is the outer wall, symbolically the mirror reflection of the pornography, metaphorically built out of brick, concrete, stone, to keep women in—in the sex class. Prostitution is the all-encompassing condition, the body trapped in barter, the body imprisoned as commodity. With respect to the circle of crimes—rape, battery, reproductive exploitation, economic exploitation—the crimes can be placed anywhere in the circle in any order. They are the crimes of the sex-class system against women; they are the crimes that keep women women in an immovable system of sex hierarchy. They are crimes committed against women as women. Economic exploitation is a specific of women's condition; it is not a sex-neutral political category into which the experience of women sometimes falls. Women are segregated in job ghettos as women; the lower pay of women is systematic; the sale of sex is a fundamental dimension of economic exploitation, whether in prostitution, marriage, or in the marketplace; when women move in large numbers into high-status jobs (male jobs), the jobs lose status (become female jobs); doing the same or comparable jobs as men, women get paid less. Economic exploitation is a key crime against women but it is not the same economic exploitation that men experience. The construction of causality among the crimes or even the establishment of sequentiality (in which order the crimes appeared in history or prehistory) is ultimately irrelevant. It does not matter whether rape came first and caused the systematic economic degradation of women, or whether economic exploitation created conditions in which the production of children got the value it now has, or whether men batter because of jealousy over women's reproductive capacity, or whether the etiology of rape is in the superior physical strength of men to women discovered in acts of battery that later became sanctioned and systematic. One can follow the circle around in either direction (see drawing 2) and construct marvelous theories of causality or sequentiality, most of which are plausible and interesting; and one can try to prioritize the political importance of the crimes. But what must matter now is the condition of women now: these crimes are now its features, its characteristic events, its experiential absolutes, its inescapable attacks on women as women. These crimes are real, systematic, and define the condition of women. The relationships between them do not matter so much as the fact that they are facts: equal, essential, basic facts. Seen in this light, prohibition against lesbianism, for instance, is not the same kind of equal, essential, basic fact, nor is lesbianism an obvious or sure road to freedom. Lesbianism is a transgression of rules, an affront; but its prohibition is not a basic constituent part of sex oppression and its expression does not substantively breach or transform sex oppression. There is no state of being or act of will, including lesbianism, that changes the circle: there is no state of being or act of will that protects a woman from

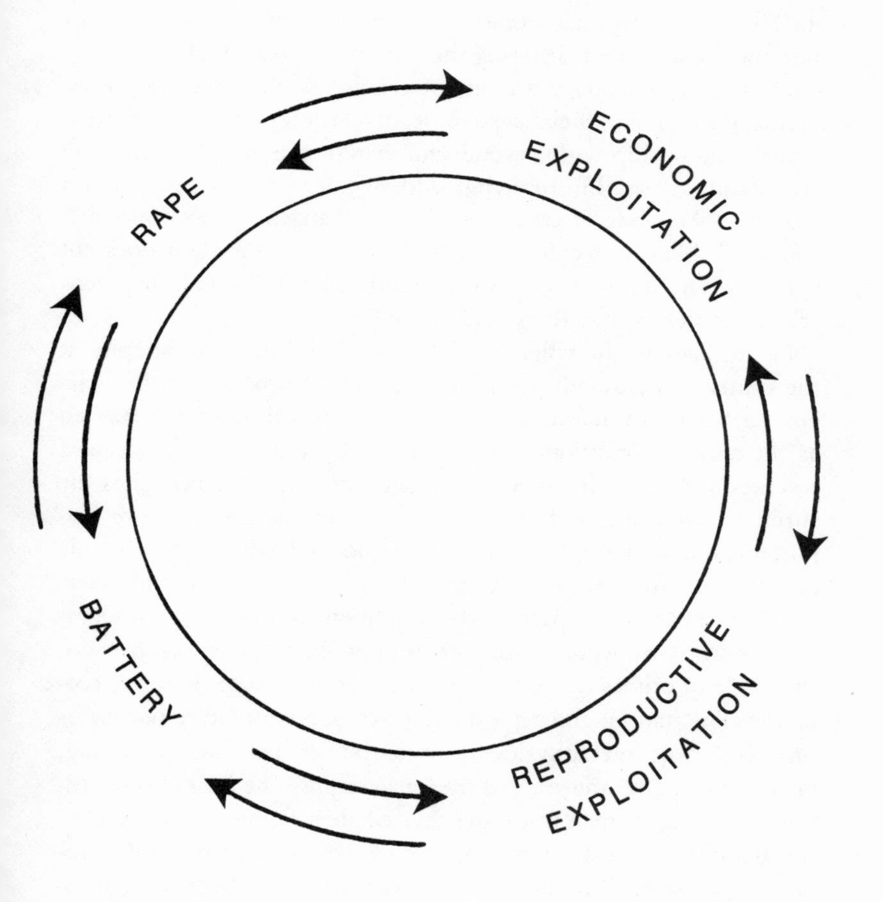

DRAWING 2. THE CIRCLE OF CRIMES AGAINST WOMEN

the basic crimes against women as women or puts any woman outside the possibility of suffering these crimes. Great wealth does not put a woman outside the circle of crimes; neither does racial supremacy in a racist social system or a good job or a terrific heterosexual relationship with a wonderful man or the most liberated (by any standard) sex life or living with women in a commune in a pasture. The circle of crimes is also not changed by how one feels about it. One can decide to ignore it or one can decide it does not apply for any number of reasons, emotional, intellectual, or practical: nevertheless it is there and it applies.

Going back to the whole model—the circle, the pornography at the center of it, the all-encompassing wall of prostitution that circumscribes it—it does not matter whether prostitution is perceived as the surface condition, with pornography hidden in the deepest recesses of the psyche; or whether pornography is perceived as the surface condition, with prostitution being its wider, more important, hidden base, the largely unacknowledged sexual-economic necessity of women. (See drawings 3 and 4.) Each has to be understood as intrinsically part of the condition of women—pornography being what women are, prostitution being what women do, the circle of crimes being what women are for. Rape, battery, economic exploitation, and reproductive exploitation require pornography as female metaphysics so as to be virtually self-justifying, virtually invisible abuses; and they also require the wall of prostitution confining women (meaning that whatever women do is within the bounds of prostitution) so that women are always and absolutely accessible. The heart of pornography and the wall of prostitution mirror each other in that both are meant to mean—and concretely do mean in the male system—that women deserve the crimes that define their condition, that those crimes are responses to what women are and what women do, that the crimes committed against women define the condition of women correctly—in accordance with what women are and what women do.

The meaning of this description of what women's subordination is, how women are kept subordinate, how that subordination is acted out on women systematically, is simple for feminists: breaking the circle up, breaking down the wall, annihilating the system's heart, are what we must do. The meaning for antifeminists is also simple: whatever strengthens or vitalizes any aspect of the model is of great practical value in keeping women subordinate. Antifeminists can disagree strategically (for instance, on whether pornography should be public or private) without disagreeing in principle on what is necessary to keep women encapsulated in subjection (the use of pornography, its cultural and psychic centrality whether it is public or private, the use of women as pornography in public and in private). But one cannot be a feminist and support any element in this model: there are no exceptions—not civil liberties lawyers or liberals or sympathetic men or so-called feminists who indulge in using the label but evading the substance. Antifeminist politics come in many guises, but a vivid memory of what the condition of women is—what crimes articulate it, what is at its heart, what is the impenetrable boundary beyond which women do not pass—provides a standard for discerning antifeminism in any political stance. No one can defend or give aid and comfort to that which keeps women subordinate and at the same time claim to be acting in behalf of women's liberation: feminism is not a lifestyle or an attitude or a feeling of vague sympathy with women or an assertion of modernity. Antifeminism saturates the political spectrum from Right to Left, liberal to conservative, reactionary to progressive. Antifeminism is resistance to the liberation of women from the sex-class system, that resistance expressed in constructing political defenses of the constituent parts of sex oppression. This antifeminism is a vital part of programs, values, ideologies, philosophies, arguments, actions, economic, sexual, and social manipulations that are the substance of most political discourse and organizing. Antifeminism is a potent expression of reaction, backlash, and suppression;

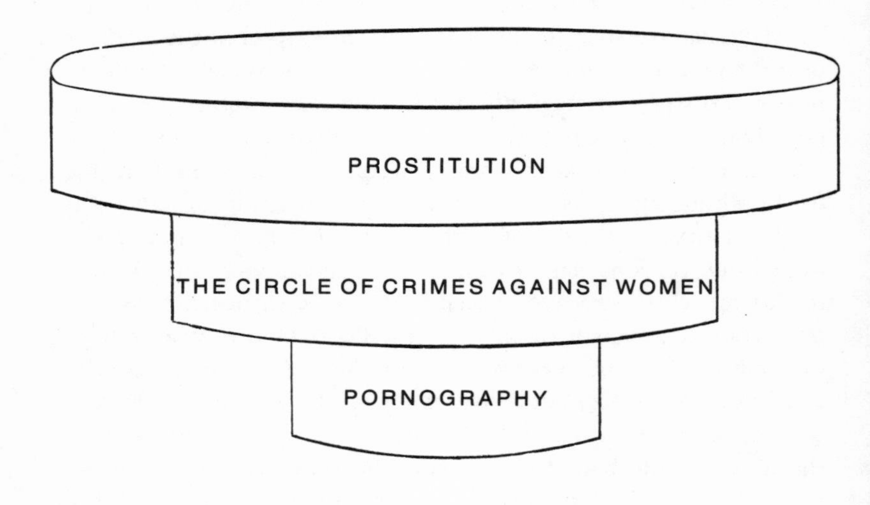

DRAWING 3. PROSTITUTION AS
THE MATERIAL REALITY;
PORNOGRAPHY AS
THE UNDERLYING IDEOLOGY

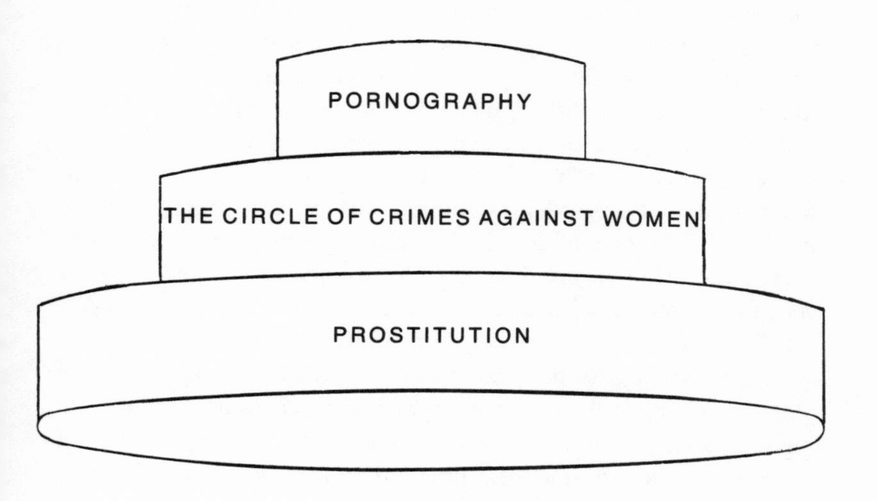

DRAWING 4. PORNOGRAPHY AS
THE SURFACE PHENOMENON:
PROSTITUTION AS
THE UNDERLYING SYSTEM

it is protean; it is easy, popular, and always fashionable in one form or another.

Antifeminism is also operating whenever any political group is ready to sacrifice one group of women, one faction, some women, some kinds of women, to any element of sex-class oppression: to pornography, to rape, to battery, to economic exploitation, to reproductive exploitation, to prostitution. There are women all along the male-defined political spectrum, including on both extreme ends of it, ready to sacrifice some women, usually not themselves, to the brothels or to the farms. The sacrifice is profoundly antifeminist; it is also profoundly immoral. Men mostly accept the disposition of women under the sex-class system and they mostly accept the crimes committed against women: but sometimes the status of women is addressed, those crimes are addressed, in political discourse. Whenever some women are doctrinally delivered to sex exploitation, the political stance is corrupt. Virtually all ideologies are implicitly antifeminist in that women are sacrificed to higher goals: the higher goal of reproduction; the higher goal of pleasure; the higher goal of a freedom antipathetic to the freedom of women; the higher goal of better conditions for workers not women; the higher goal of a new order that keeps the sex exploitation of women essentially intact; the higher goal of an old order that considers the sex exploitation of women a sign of social stability (woman's in her place, all's right with the world). Some women are sacrificed to a function—fucking, reproducing, housecleaning, and so on. A political promise is made, and kept, that some women will do some things so that all women must not do all things. Women accept the sacrifice of other women to that which they find repugnant: a seduction of antifeminism that outdoes worship of female good in getting female adherents because it is more practical. Men all along the political spectrum manipulate this seduction with great skill. Some women are sacrificed by race or class: kept doing some kinds of work that other women will then not have to do. Supporting the use of *some* women in any area of sex exploitation is the willful sacrifice of women on an altar of sex abuse and it is a political repudiation of the sex-class consciousness basic to feminism: it is—whoever does it—antifeminism. And then there is the psychological use of the same reactionary strategy: *some* women, of course, like being . . . (beaten, raped, exploited, bought and sold, forced to have sex, forced to have children). Antifeminism is also a form of psychological warfare, and of course *some* women do like . . . Women intend to save themselves when sacrificing *some* women, but only the freedom of all women protects any woman. This is practical and true because of the nature of sex oppression. Men, who use power against women in sex exploitation, know that it is practical and true: which is why it is a fundamental strategy of antifeminism to encourage the sacrifice of *some* women by *all* women.

Now look at the world as right-wing women see it. They live in the same world as all women: a world of sex segregation and sex hierarchy; a world defined by the crimes of rape, battery, economic and reproductive exploitation; a world circumscribed by prostitution; a world in which they too are pornography. They see the system of sex oppression—about which they are not stupid—as closed and unalterable. It is unchangeable to them, whether they take as their authority God or man. If sex oppression is real, absolute, unchanging, inevitable, then the views of right-wing women are more logical than not. Marriage is supposed to protect them from rape; being kept at home is supposed to protect them from the castelike economic exploitation of the marketplace; reproduction gives them what value and respect they have and so they must increase the value of reproduction even if it means increasing their own vulnerability to reproductive exploitation (especially forced pregnancy); religious marriage—traditional, correct, law-abiding marriage—is supposed to protect against battery, since the wife is supposed to be cherished and respected. The flaws in the logic are simple: the home is the most dangerous place for a woman to be, the place she is most likely to be murdered, raped, beaten, certainly the place where she is robbed of the value of her labor. What right-wing women do to survive the sex-class system does not mean that they will survive it: if they get killed, it will most likely be at the hands of their husbands; if they get raped, the rapists will most likely be their husbands or men who are friends or acquaintances; if they get beaten, the batterer will most likely be their husbands—perhaps 25 percent of those who are beaten will be beaten during pregnancy; if they do not have any money of their own, they are more vulnerable to abuse from their husbands, less able to escape, less able to protect their children from incestuous assault; if abortion becomes illegal, they will still have abortions and they are likely to die or be maimed in great numbers;* if they get addicted to drugs, it will most likely be to prescription drugs prescribed by the family doctor to keep the family intact; if they get poor—through being abandoned by their husbands or through old age—they are likely to be discarded, their usefulness being over. And right-wing women are still pornography (as Marabel

*Before 1973, both abortion and contraception were mostly illegal. Perhaps two thirds of women aborting were married (in one good study 75 percent were married) and most had children, as far as can be discerned from the scanty evidence. With legal abortion and legal contraception, about three quarters of the women seem to be single. As many people suggest, women no longer feel compelled to marry on becoming pregnant, which accounts in part for the demographic change. But I think that the availability of contraceptives in conjunction with abortion is mainly responsible for the lower percentage of married women among those aborting. I suspect that married women use contraceptives with more precision

Morgan recognized in *The Total Woman*) just like other women whom they despise; and what they do—just like other women—is barter. They too live inside the wall of prostitution no matter how they see themselves.

More than anything else, it is antifeminism that convinces right-wing women that the system of sex segregation and sex hierarchy is immovable, unbreachable, and inevitable—and therefore that the logic of their world view is more substantive and compelling than any analysis, however accurate, of its flaws. It is not the antifeminism of the Right specifically that keeps the allegiance of these women: it is the antifeminism that saturates political discourse all along the political spectrum, the antifeminism that permeates virtually all political philosophies, programs, and parties. Antifeminism is not a form of political reaction and suppression confined to the far Right. If it were, women would have compelling reason for moving away from the far Right toward philosophies, programs, and parties not fundamentally antifeminist; women would also have good reason to see sex-class oppression as transformable, not absolute and eternal. It is the pervasiveness of antifeminism, its ubiquity, that establishes for women that they have no way out of the sex-class system. The antifeminism of Left, Right, and center fixes the power of the Right over women—gives the huge majority of women over to the Right—over to social conservatism, eco-

---

and consistency than do single women—certainly than do the teenagers who characteristically do not use contraceptives at all and who skew the percentages toward single women. If the Human Life Amendment or Statute passes, or any similar legislation, both the intrauterine device and the low-dosage birth control pill will become illegal. They will be considered abortifacients because they are known to stop the fertilized egg from implanting in the uterine wall, thereby "killing" it. If effective contraception is once again unavailable—so that both contraception and abortion are inaccessible—I suspect the percentage of married women having abortions will once again skyrocket.

nomic conservatism, religious conservatism, over to conforming to the dictates of authority and power, over to sexual compliance, over to obedience—because as long as the sex-class system is intact, huge numbers of women will believe that the Right offers them the best deal: the highest reproductive value; the best protection against sexual aggression; the best economic security as the economic dependents of men who must provide; the most reliable protection against battery; the most respect. Left and centrist philosophies, programs, and parties tend to vicious condescension with respect to women's rights; they lie, and right-wing women are quite brilliant at discerning the hypocrisy of liberal support for women's rights. Right-wing women do not buy the partial truths and cynical lies that constitute the positions of various liberal and so-called radical groups on women's rights. They see antifeminism, though they call it simple hypocrisy. They are outraged by it.

What is it that right-wing women see, then, when they look at feminists? The Right, Left, and center have firm bases of power in that they all come out of and serve and are led by the top class in the sex-class system: men. They are all profoundly opposed to the destruction of the sex-class system. Feminists want to destroy the sex-class system but feminists come out of and serve and are led by the bottom class in the sex-class system: women. The feminism of women cannot match the power, the resources, the potency of the antifeminism of the whole male political spectrum. Looking for a way out of the sex-class system, a way beyond the boundary of prostitution, a way around the crimes of rape, battery, economic exploitation, and reproductive exploitation, a way out of being pornography, right-wing women look at feminists and they see *women:* inside the same boundary, victims of the same crimes, women who are pornography. Their response to what they see is not a sense of sisterhood or solidarity—it is a self-protective sense of repulsion. The powerless are not quick to put their faith in the powerless. The powerless need the powerful, especially in sex oppression because it is inescapable, everywhere: there are no free zones, free countries, underground railways away from it. Because feminism is a movement for liberation of the powerless by the powerless in a closed system based on their powerlessness, right-wing women judge it a futile movement. Frequently they also judge it a malicious movement in that it jeopardizes the bargains with power that they can make; feminism calls into question for the men confronted by it the *sincerity* of women who conform without political resistance. Since antifeminism is based in power (the sex-class power of men along the whole political spectrum) and feminism is based in powerlessness, antifeminism effectively turns feminism into a political dead end. It is the antifeminism of Right, Left, center, and all variations thereof, that makes the situation of women hopeless: there is no hope of escape, no hope of freedom, no hope for an end to sex oppression, because all power-based political parties, programs, and philosophies abhor the liberation of women as a basis of action, as a real goal, even as an idea. Being doomed by a reactionary political stance to social subordination is not the same as being doomed by God or nature to metaphysical inferiority—a crucial point—but it is still real rough. The defenses of sex exploitation are simply too consistent, too strong, too intensely felt, all along the political spectrum of power-based discourse and organizing to be ignored by women who recognize that they are women, not persons, as right-wing women do. Simply put, the Right will continue to have the allegiance of most women who see how real the sex-class system is, how intransigent it is, as long as antifeminism is the heartfelt stance of those with other political views, whatever the views. Those optimistic women who think the antifeminism of the Left or center is somehow more humane than the antifeminism of the Right will ally themselves as persons with whatever groups or ideologies best reflect their own social or human ideals. They will find without exception that the antifeminism they ignore is a trenchant political defense of the woman hating they are victimized by. Right-wing women, who are less queasy in facing the absolute nature of male power over women, will not be swayed by the politics of women who practice selective blindness with regard to male power. Right-wing women are sure that the selective blindness of liberals and leftists especially contributes to more violence, more humiliation, more exploitation for women, often in the name of humanism and freedom (which is why both words are dirty words to them).

Facing the true nature of the sex-class system means ultimately that one must destroy that system or accommodate to it. Facing the true nature of male power over women also means that one must destroy that power or accommodate to it. Feminists, from a base of powerlessness, want to destroy that power; right-wing women, from a base of powerlessness, the same base, accommodate to that power because quite simply they see no way out from under. Those with power will not help; those who are powerless like themselves arguably cannot. Feminists, after the defeat of previous movements throughout history and facing some kind of disintegration again (with the defeat of the Equal Rights Amendment in the United States, the possible enactment of the Family Protection Act, the Human Life Amendment or Statute, and other social, political, and legal initiatives promoting female subordination*), have to face the real questions. Can a political movement rooted in a closed system of subordination—with no political support among power-based political movements—break that closed system apart? Or will the antifeminism of those whose politics are rooted in sex-class power and privilege always destroy movements for the liberation of women? Is there a way to subvert the antifeminism of power-based political programs or parties—or is the pleasure and profit in the subordination of women simply too overwhelming,

*Feminists all over the world report similar backlash.

too great, too marvelous, to allow for anything but the political defense of that subordination (antifeminism)? Will it take a hundred fists, a thousand fists, a million fists, pushed through that circle of crime to destroy it, or are right-wing women essentially right that it is indestructible? Can the wall of prostitution be scaled? Can what is at the heart of sex oppression—the use of women as pornography, pornography as what women *are*—be stopped? If antifeminism triumphs over the liberation movement of women—now, again, always—whoever has political power or represents social order or exercises authoritarian rule—whatever they are called, whatever they call their political line—has women for good; the Right, broadly construed, has women for good. Stasis and cruelty will have triumphed over freedom. The freedom of women from sex oppression either matters or it does not; it is either essential or it is not. Decide one more time.

Notes

1. The Promise of the Ultra-Right

1. Marilyn Monroe, in a dressing-room notebook, cited by Norman Mailer, *Marilyn: A Biography* (New York: Grosset & Dunlap, 1973), p. 17.
2. Terrence Des Pres, *The Survivor: An Anatomy of Life in the Death Camps* (New York: Pocket Books, 1977), p. vi.
3. Leah Fritz, *Thinking Like a Woman* (Rifton, N.Y.: Win Books, 1975), p. 130.
4. Anita Bryant, *Bless This House* (New York: Bantam Books, 1976), p. 26.
5. Marabel Morgan, *The Total Woman* (New York: Pocket Books, 1975), p. 57.
6. Ruth Carter Stapleton, *The Gift of Inner Healing* (Waco, Tex.: Word Books, Publisher, 1976), p. 32.
7. Ibid., p. 18.
8. Morgan, *Total Woman*, p. 8.
9. Ibid., p. 96.
10. Ibid., p. 60.
11. Ibid., p. 161.
12. Ibid., pp. 140–41.
13. Anita Bryant, *Mine Eyes Have Seen the Glory* (Old Tappan, N.J.: Fleming H. Revell Company, 1970), pp. 26–27.
14. Ibid., p. 84.
15. Bryant, *Bless This House*, p. 42.
16. Bryant, *Mine Eyes*, p. 83.
17. Bryant, *Bless This House*, pp. 51–52.

18. "Battle Over Gay Rights," *Newsweek*, June 6, 1977, p. 20.
19. Phyllis Schlafly, *The Power of the Positive Woman* (New Rochelle, N.Y.: Arlington House Publishers, 1977), p. 89.

2. The Politics of Intelligence

1. Norman Mailer, *Advertisements for Myself* (New York: G. P. Putnam's Sons, Perigee Books, 1981), p. 433.
2. Edith Wharton, "The Touchstone," in *Madame de Treymes and Others* (New York: Charles Scribner's Sons, 1970), p. 12.
3. Carolina Maria de Jesus, *Child of the Dark: The Diary of Carolina Maria de Jesus*, trans. David St. Clair (New York: New American Library, 1962), p. 47.
4. Catharine A. MacKinnon, "Feminism, Marxism, Method and the State: An Agenda for Theory," *Signs: A Journal of Women in Culture and Society*, Vol. 7, No. 3, Spring 1982.
5. De Jesus, *Child of the Dark*, p. 29.
6. Florence Nightingale, *Cassandra* (Old Westbury, N.Y.: The Feminist Press, 1979), p. 49.
7. Virginia Woolf, *The Pargiters: The Novel-Essay Portion of "The Years,"* ed. Mitchell A. Leaska (New York: The New York Public Library & Readex Books, 1977), pp. 164–65.
8. Abby Kelley, in a speech, cited by Blanche Glassman Hersh in *The Slavery of Sex* (Urbana, Ill.: University of Illinois Press, 1978), p. 33.
9. Alice James, *The Diary of Alice James*, ed. Leon Edel (New York: Dodd, Mead & Company, 1964), p. 66.
10. Woolf, *Pargiters*, pp. xxxix–xxxx [sic] (speech given January 21, 1931).
11. Olive Schreiner, *The Story of an African Farm* (New York: Penguin Books, 1979), p. 148.
12. Nightingale, *Cassandra*, p. 25.
13. Victoria Woodhull, "Tried As By Fire; or, The True and The False, Socially," 1874, *The Victoria Woodhull Reader*, ed. Madeleine B. Stern (Weston, Mass.: M&S Press, 1974), p. 19.
14. Ibid., p. 8.
15. Victoria Woodhull, cited by Johanna Johnston, *Mrs. Satan* (New York: G. P. Putnam's Sons, 1967), p. 205.

16. Woodhull, "The Principles of Social Freedom," 1871, *Victoria Woodhull Reader*, p. 36.
17. Woodhull, "Tried As By Fire . . . ," *Victoria Woodhull Reader*, p. 39.
18. Ibid.
19. Robin Morgan, "Theory and Practice: Pornography and Rape," 1974, pp. 163–69; *Going Too Far* (New York: Random House, 1977), p. 165.
20. William Makepeace Thackeray, *Vanity Fair* (New York: New American Library, 1962), p. 168.
21. De Jesus, *Child of the Dark*, p. 50.
22. Kate Millett, *The Prostitution Papers* (New York: Avon, 1973), pp. 78–79.
23. Linda Lovelace and Mike McGrady, *Ordeal* (Secaucus, N.J.: Citadel Press, 1980), p. 66.
24. Maryse Holder, *Give Sorrow Words* (New York: Avon, 1980), p. 3.
25. Millett, *Prostitution Papers*, p. 95.
26. Jenny P. D'Hericourt, *A Woman's Philosophy of Woman; or Woman Affranchised* (New York: Carleton, Publisher, 1864), p. 41.
27. Joseph Proudhon, in D'Hericourt, *Woman's Philosophy*, p. 36.
28. Woolf, *Pargiters*, p. 120.
29. Ellen Glasgow, *The Woman Within* (New York: Hill and Wang, 1980), p. 108.

3. Abortion

1. Jerome E. Bates and Edward S. Zawadzki, *Criminal Abortion* (Springfield, Ill.: Charles C. Thomas, 1964), p. 4.
2. Jesse L. Jackson, "How We Respect Life Is Over-riding Moral Issue," *National Right to Life News*, January 1977. Reprint.
3. R. D. Laing, *The Facts of Life* (New York: Pantheon Books, 1976), p. 27.
4. Colette, *My Apprenticeships*, trans. Helen Beauclerk (New York: Farrar, Straus & Giroux, 1978), p. 23.
5. Marge Piercy, "The Grand Coolie Damn," pp. 421–38, *Sis-*

terhood Is Powerful, ed. Robin Morgan (New York: Random House, 1970), p. 430.
6. Robin Morgan, "Goodbye to All That," 1970, pp. 121–30, *Going Too Far* (New York: Random House, 1977), p. 122.
7. Ibid., p. 128.
8. Robin Morgan, "Take a Memo, Mr. Smith," pp. 68–70, *Going Too Far*, p. 69.
9. Morgan, ed., *Sisterhood Is Powerful*, p. 559.
10. Jim Douglass, "Patriarchy and the Pentagon Make Abortion Inevitable," *Sojourners*, November 1980, p. 8.

4. Jews and Homosexuals

1. Maimonides, "Book of Holiness," fifth book of the Code of Law, in *Sex Ethics of Maimonides*, ed. Fred Rosner (New York: Bloch Publishing Company, 1974), p. 101.
2. Utah Delegation, "Utah Delegation Challenges the IWY, Resents Smear Tactics," press release, no date (but issued at conference November 18–21, 1977), mimeographed.
3. From the public law mandating the conference, cited by National Commission on the Observance of International Women's Year, Press Release 103, September 1977, mimeographed, pp. 1–2.
4. IWY Press Release 103, p. 3.
5. Ibid., p. 2.
6. Jean-Paul Sartre, *Anti-Semite and Jew*, trans. George J. Becker. (New York: Schocken Books, 1970), p. 10.
7. Ibid., p. 13.
8. Adolf Hitler, *Mein Kampf*, trans. Ralph Manheim (Boston: Houghton Mifflin Company, 1962), p. 325.
9. Frederick Douglass, *The Life and Writings of Frederick Douglass*, vol. 4, ed. Philip S. Foner (New York: International Publishers, 1975), p. 194.
10. Ibid., p. 195.
11. Ibid., p. 492.
12. Ibid., p. 493.
13. Maimonides, *Sex Ethics of Maimonides*, pp. 97–98.

14. Charlotte Perkins Gilman, undated ms., Schlesinger Library, cited by Linda Gordon, *Woman's Body, Woman's Right* (New York: Grossman Publishers, 1976), p. 145.
15. Phyllis Schlafly, *The Power of the Positive Woman* (New Rochelle, N.Y.: Arlington House Publishers, 1977), p. 47.

5. The Coming Gynocide

1. John Langdon Davies, *A Short History of Women*, cited by Virginia Woolf, *A Room of One's Own* (New York: Harcourt, Brace & World, 1957), p. 116.
2. Adolf Hitler, 1934, cited by Clifford Kirkpatrick, *Nazi Germany: Its Women and Family Life* (Indianapolis: The Bobbs-Merrill Company, 1938), pp. 111–12.
3. W. Andrew Achenbaum, *Old Age in the New Land* (Baltimore: The Johns Hopkins University Press, 1979), p. 94.
4. Bruce C. Vladeck, *Unloving Care: The Nursing Home Tragedy* (New York: Basic Books, 1980), p. 3.
5. Ibid., p. 4.
6. Muriel Nellis, *The Female Fix* (New York: Penguin Books, 1981), p. 68.
7. Ibid., pp. 1–2.
8. Frances Fox Piven and Richard A. Cloward, *Regulating the Poor: The Functions of Public Welfare* (New York: Vintage Books, 1972), p. 138.
9. Roland A. Chilton, *Consequences of a State Suitable Home Law for ADC Families in Florida* (Tallahassee: Florida State University/Institute for Social Research, 1968), p. 65, cited in Piven and Cloward, *Regulating the Poor*, p. 140.
10. Linda Gordon, *Woman's Body, Woman's Right* (New York: Grossman Publishers, 1976), p. 311.
11. William Acton, *Prostitution* (New York: Frederick A. Praeger, Publishers, 1969), p. 26.
12. Josephine Butler, cited by Kathleen Barry, *Female Sexual Slavery* (Englewood Cliffs, N.J.: Prentice-Hall, 1979), p. 25.
13. Elizabeth Cady Stanton, "The Solitude of Self," in *History of Woman Suffrage*, vol. IV, ed. Susan B. Anthony and Ida Husted Harper (New York: Source Book Press, 1970), p. 189.

14. Abram Tertz, *The Trial Begins*, cited by Richard Lourie, *Letters to the Future: An Approach to Sinyavsky-Tertz* (Ithaca, N.Y.: Cornell University Press, 1975), p. 91.
15. Hipponax of Ephesus, cited by Mary R. Lefkowitz and Maureen B. Fant, ed., *Women in Greece and Rome* (Toronto: Samuel-Stevens, 1977), p. 18.

6. ANTIFEMINISM

1. Phyllis Schlafly, *The Power of the Positive Woman* (New Rochelle, N.Y.: Arlington House Publishers, 1977), p. 166.
2. Frederick Douglass, *Frederick Douglass' Paper*, October 30, 1851, *Frederick Douglass on Women's Rights*, ed. Philip S. Foner (Westport, Conn.: Greenwood Press, 1976), p. 55.

Index

WOMEN'S STUDIES/POLITICS

"GROUNDBREAKING!

THE MOST IMPORTANT BOOK OF THE DECADE."

—Bella Abzug

WHAT does the Right offer to women?

HOW does the Right mobilize women?

WHY is the Right succeeding in opposing women's rights?

With the stark precision and forceful passion that characterize all of her work, Andrea Dworkin answers these timely questions. And by providing the first clear analysis of the impact on women of the Right's position on abortion, homosexuality, anti-Semitism, female poverty, and antifeminism, she demonstrates how the Right attempts both to exploit and to quiet women's deepest fears.

After first discussing how such right-wing advocates as Phyllis Schlafly, Marabel Morgan, and Anita Bryant have accommodated themselves to the world in male terms, she moves to the heart of her analysis: how male violence against women contributes to the need of so many women for a fixed, predetermined social order—a conservative and reactionary social order—and how antifeminism along the whole political spectrum fosters resignation among women to the traditional modes of female inferiority.

Following the defeat of the Equal Rights Amendment, *Right-Wing Women* raises provocative questions that affect every woman living today, for, as Dworkin sees it, this book is "an emergency attempt to articulate the centrality of feminism and women's rights to the search for human freedom."

PERIGEE BOOKS
are published by
The Putnam Publishing Group

ISBN 0-399-50671-3